# ECLIPSE OF A STAR

Two explosions burst through the clatter and rumble of the city dusk. Maggie said doubtfully, "Backfire?"

"Maybe." They looked at each other a second, then turned and ran back to the corner where they had left Ramona. A woman was standing there screaming. As they ran toward her, a woman in a miniskirt began soothing her.

"What happened?" Nick asked them.

"Don't know," said the miniskirted woman. "There were shots, and I heard Carlotta screaming. She was running away from that building."

A scaffold covered the sidewalk in front of the building she indicated and plywood blocked most of the facade. Maggie had disappeared into the shadows under the scaffold. "Nick," she called. "Get an ambulance!"

Sprawled on her back on the dirty cement floor, Ramona Ricci lay very still, a dark stain spreading across the pale fur of the cape rumpled beneath her.

Bantam Books offers the finest in classic and modern American murder mysteries. Ask your bookseller for the books you have missed.

# REHEARSAL

*for*

# MURDER

*(Maggie Ryan, 1973)*

## P. M. CARLSON

**BANTAM BOOKS**

TORONTO • NEW YORK • LONDON • SYDNEY • AUCKLAND

REHEARSAL FOR MURDER

*A Bantam Book / August 1988*

Lyrics from *Victoria R* by P. M. and M. A. Carlson used by permission of authors.

ISBN 0-553-27234-9

*Published simultaneously in the United States and Canada*

*Bantam Books are published by Bantam Books, a division of Bantam Doubleday Dell Publishing Group, Inc. Its trademark, consisting of the words "Bantam Books" and the portrayal of a rooster, is Registered in U.S. Patent and Trademark Office and in other countries. Marca Registrada. Bantam Books, 666 Fifth Avenue, New York, New York 10103.*

PRINTED IN THE UNITED STATES OF AMERICA

O      0 9 8 7 6 5 4 3 2 1

*To the Yankee and the Rebel*
*with love and thanks*
*for everything*

# *Acknowledgments*

Special thanks for sharing their expertise go to Dana Mills and Barbara Dean, who against all odds succeed in being fine actors and fine parents simultaneously; and to Robert Bruyr, Senior Business Representative of Actors' Equity.

# *Contents*

I hold the world but as the world, Gratiano;
A stage, where every man must play a part,
And mine a sad one.

—*The Merchant of Venice*,
act I, scene i

*part one*

# LOVE AND DUTY

*(Tuesday and Wednesday,
March 6–7, 1973)*

# I

*Tuesday afternoon*
*March 6, 1973*

"Damn!" yelped Ramona Ricci, catching at a nearby elbow to keep from falling. "I'm supposed to be giving birth to a prince. Not an elephant. Not a goddamn woolly mammoth!"

"Sorry." Sprawled inelegantly between her feet, the ancient dust of the rehearsal loft gritty in his mouth, Nick O'Connor apologized to her leg warmers. "I tried to make myself tiny and embryonic. But Stanislavsky can only take you so far."

"The Prince of Whales," murmured Larry Palmer, who owned the lean and handsome elbow Ramona was clutching.

"Har-har." Ramona jerked her rehearsal skirt clear of Nick's ears. "Think it's funny, do you? You'll think so when we close after three days. You unemployed, and me in debtor's prison. Hilarious!"

Ramona was small, vibrant, and still famous at forty. Nick liked her in her better moods. A little body with a mighty heart. But just now she was whirling furiously on the slender black choreographer, eyes ablaze. "Daphne, sweetie, observe! I'm five four. Nick down there is about seven feet tall and weighs hundreds of pounds. How can you expect him to somersault between my legs?" Her angry gaze flicked to the black teenage girl dressed in jeans and a vibrant orange and black dashiki who was sitting quietly against the back wall. "Plus we're running a goddamn baby-sitting service for you!"

"Hey, wait a minute, you skunky bitch!" roared the girl, jumping to her feet. Her hair was puffed into an Afro twice as big as Daphne's, and scowling, she reminded Nick of an enraged dark dandelion.

Daphne pointed an imperious finger at her. "Hush your mouth, Calypso Weaver!"

The girl sat again, lips still curled and eyes fiery with indignation. Ramona said regretfully to Daphne, "Guess I'd better retract all those glowing references I wrote you. Parents need a touch of intelligence."

Propped now in a sitting position, Nick could see the sudden angry tears in Daphne's eyes. Damn Ramona. What was eating her today? Though always opinionated, she had never been vicious. He said briskly, "Daphne, do you think it might work with a slide instead of a somersault? So I could keep my butt down until I was clear?"

"Maybe. Though the somersaults look good, more surprising." Daphne was professional again, running lean fingers through her Afro as she squinted thoughtfully at the unpromising configuration of platform, dusty floor, and sweaty bodies in the SoHo loft and somehow visualized a rollicking moment in the theatre. "Maybe we could use the platform, gain eight inches that way."

Nick brushed the dust from his balding head, glad that his dumb question had helped. Though he was not quite as large as Ramona claimed and was in fact quite nimble, he was feeling huge and clumsy at the moment. Brontosaurus Nick. He hoped that disabling the star was not to be added to his other fiascos today.

It had not been a good day, despite its promising start. Nick had awakened to a visual feast of long legs, warm breasts, sleepy blue eyes smiling into his. Five-thirty A.M. They should have an hour. Groggy but enthusiastic, he had set himself to rousing his friendly partner to share the delights. *So conjunctive to my life and soul.* Maggie was more than compliant. For a few moments it seemed like the old days.

Then came the noise.

"*Merde!*" she swore, suddenly still in his arms.

"Ditto," said Nick, pausing with her.

But it came again, and swiftly she was gone.

Nick lay, angry and detumescent, in the abandoned milky bed. His head told him she had no choice; but the rest of him screamed betrayal. "There's *Casablanca*," he called after her. "There's *Cyrano*. There's even *Spiderman*. A million stories about the conflict between love and duty. Doesn't love ever win?"

"How about *Romeo and Juliet*?" Maggie—baby Sarah in her arms—was giving the question due consideration. "Or *Carmen*? But I think they're saying if it wins, you lose."

"You lose both ways," grumped Nick, and got up to shower. The disposable lover, O'Connor Interruptus. And all because—

"Let's try it from the platform," Daphne's voice broke into his thoughts. Poor Daphne, trying to choreograph a steamroller and getting chewed out for her pains. But, plucky creature, she was disguising her rage, saying almost eagerly, "Dive down to the roll on this level, then line up in front of Victoria and Albert instead of behind them."

"In front of us?" asked Ramona suspiciously.

"We'll be on the platform, Victoria dear. Very regal," said Larry, striking an appropriate pose. A gold chain winked against his manly chest. Nick, thick and far from handsome, envied Larry's flair for looking romantic even in rehearsal sweats. A very riband in the cap of youth. Love probably won over duty in Larry's life.

Not with Ramona. Not today. Ignoring Larry's virile charms, she stalked away to slump into a folding chair and light a cigarette. "Well, let's have a look at this great idea. Jaymie, hop to!"

Her understudy hurried from the chorus. Jaymie Price, the daughter of a well-to-do Chicago divorcée, was one of the few chorus members who didn't have to scramble for table-waiting or typing work between jobs. She was as dimpled and dark-haired as Ramona. But she was taller, quieter, and her voice, while lovely, lacked the emotion and power that had lifted Ramona, fifteen years ago, to stardom. On stage Ramona flamed; Jaymie merely glittered. Ramona stopped her now wearily. "No, no, sweeties, from the end of the assassination scene. We have to get up on the platform somehow."

"Right, mates." Derek Morris wiped back his pale hair and shifted to an earlier melody. His piano sat at the side of the big industrial loft, behind one of the peeling steel support columns that marched inconveniently through the battered former factory. The actors scrambled to a different configuration, picking up top hats and canes that were incongruous with their shabby rehearsal outfits of old shirts, tights, and sweats. Looped and windowed raggedness. Well, acting was a good way to avoid getting rich. Nick stationed himself at the rear of the scruffy group.

"Bang!" The young actor who played the assassin aimed a plastic rehearsal water pistol at Jaymie and the others gasped dutifully. "Bang!" A second pistol pointed at her. Then Nick and the others swarmed over him, imprisoning him behind the vertical bars of their walking sticks. He peered out of the sudden cage with mournful eyes.

"The would-be assassin was jailed immediately," intoned Cab Collins, the hearty Chairman, from his podium across the stage. "Fortunately he had forgotten to load his pistols." The others cheered. "Queen Victoria's popularity soared!" The cheers grew louder. Larry and Jaymie were slipping away from the group to the center of the raised platform, while the others, under Daphne's direction, lined up at the rear. "And soon there was reason for more popularity still. Because, back in the royal bedchamber . . ."

"Ooh! Albert!" giggled Jaymie.

"Ooh! Victoria!" Larry pulled Jaymie into a cliché clinch. They both leered happily at the row of folding chairs as Derek launched into the introductory bars of the next music-hall melody.

"But Albert, will we always be so happy? What does the future hold?"

Daphne was calling over the music, "Same steps here, Larry, but stay up on the platform. Right, that's it."

"The future?" sang Larry. "The future holds nine children!"

"Nine?" Jaymie looked dismayed.

"You'll love 'em!" Larry twirled her to the front edge of the platform and stood aside while she planted herself, legs apart, rehearsal skirt ready to hoist. "We'll have, first, a girl!"

Thickset Edith Bigelow plunged off the platform between Jaymie's feet, rolled forward, then rose to a kneel, grinned at Ramona and the folding chairs, and shuffled on her knees to the side.

"Next, a boy!" sang Larry. Nick repeated Edith's feat without toppling Jaymie. Thank God, he thought, it'll work this way. He heard Daphne murmur, "Terrific!"

"Then a girl, then a boy!" Actors dove through to join Nick and Edith until nine knelt in a row. "A dynasty!" exulted Larry. "Vicky, future Empress of Germany! And Bertie, Prince of Wales, future King of England!" He continued the roll call of the grand duchesses, princes, and dukes that Victoria and Albert had spawned. Hopping on his knees in the kick line with the other royal children, Nick had to sympathize with Victoria's dismay. Even one child could disrupt a life. Could lock into a person's emotions even while destroying sleep, career, sex life. Nine would be appalling.

The song ended. Ramona jetted a last fierce stream of smoke at them and ferociously ground out her cigarette with the toe of her laced dancing boot. "Possible," she admitted. "Let's give it a try this way. It looks a little dead, of course. But thanks to dearest Daphne, I've never missed a performance in my life, and I won't start now."

Daphne's glance at Ramona crackled with black-eyed fury. Jaymie herself turned away from Ramona with seeming calm and retrieved her can of Sprite. But Nick saw that her hands were shaking.

Ramona bounded into her place. "Okay, Derek, let's go!"

"Right." Derek was British, a compact, pale-eyed young man in jeans and a fraying Aran sweater. He was composer, rehearsal pianist, and nominal director of *Victoria R*. "Take it from 'Bang, bang!' mates!"

They worked through "Nine Children" again on their bruised knees, then on to the act-final "Death of Albert—Widow of Windsor" sequence. Derek talked them through it. " 'Death of Albert' is a poem, Victorian music-hall style, a few chords under the spoken lines. The poem ends with Albert's death."

"Same business as the old king's death at the beginning?" asked Larry.

"Right. You pull on the black gloves and step back into the shadows. Albert and Victoria will do a series of heartrending tableaus while Edith recites, and—"

"I don't say anything?" exclaimed Ramona.

"Not till you sing 'Widow of Windsor' at the end."

"Ramona, really, tableaus look better when the mouths don't move," said Larry.

The watching girl giggled.

Ramona didn't speak for a moment. She bent over the prop box, pulled out the black gloves Larry would use, and then hurled them at his feet like gauntlets. Their eyes met for an ugly instant before Ramona said mildly, "Okay, Derek, Edith recites. But I've decided the second act is too long. Let's drop the Disraeli solo."

Nick tensed. In the second act he and Larry played Victoria's two prime ministers, Gladstone and Disraeli; and Larry's solo as Disraeli was vital to both plot and character.

Derek exclaimed, "Ramona, that won't do!"

Larry, rage contained except for the bunching of muscles in his jaw, said, "It's my only solo, Ramona. If I offer abject apologies and promise to keep my mouth shut for the rest of the day, can we keep it? Pretty please?"

"We don't want to bore people."

Derek said desperately, "Ramona, we'd better talk this over. We need the information in that song."

With her dark head flung back, hands on hips, Ramona set the air quivering with unspoken demands. Yet her voice, except for the huskiness, seemed reasonable. "Come, Derek, no need to be totally faithful to your ideals! Besides, we could just add a verse to another song!"

Nick could see that they were pushing her into a stance she'd regret in a sunnier mood. Time to attempt a daring rescue. Enter Bozo O'Connor, superhero of petty squabbles. Or superklutz? Nick leaped to stage center and exclaimed, "Hey, great idea! We could add the whole second act to 'Nine Children!' 'First a girl, then a boy, then an empire, then a death!' " His mimicry of Larry's voice was exact as he flipped a prop crown onto his bald head only to cover it in turn with the pair of black gloves. They drooped rakishly over his eyebrows.

For a quaking instant Ramona stared at him. Then she guffawed, slapping her knee. The tension in the room dissolved into chuckles.

"All right, you clowns, let's get on with this rehearsal!" Still smirking, she abandoned the fight and moved on. "What's the first tableau?"

Nick watched from the sidelines as Derek and Daphne worked with Ramona and Larry to set the first pose. A handsome pair: Ramona's riveting intensity set off by Larry's languid virility. Surely the critics and the public would be enchanted too. Nick allowed himself the luxury of a little hope. He could use a long run about now. Even a medium run. His fortieth year could be glimpsed on the horizon. And although he had a solid reputation among casting directors and producers, he was not famous, not bankable. He still had to make the rounds, had to attend dozens of auditions for every job he landed. And there were new responsibilities. A smidgen of security would taste very good just now.

Derek and Daphne were still adjusting the pose when Ramona's expression darkened again. Following her gaze to the door, Nick saw a man in a pinstripe suit, jowly and regal as a Great Dane, reminiscent of President Nixon himself.

"Well, Simon! Slumming?" asked Ramona, breaking the pose.

"I want to know what you're doing." The big man sounded sad.

"None of your business."

"It's my money."

She laughed. "Sorry, honey. Not a penny is yours."

"Prove it!" Sadness turned to anger; gray brows bunched. A shiver of unease ran through the company.

Ramona lifted her big Italian shoulder bag from a rickety chair, rummaged in it, and pulled out a desk-size maroon leather appointment book. "I will, Simon, at—let's see, eleven-thirty tomorrow. I'm seeing Martin about the property division. He's got all the proof you'll need." She smiled again, but Nick was aware that she was trembling a little. "Don't worry. It's watertight. The money belongs to the production company, free and clear. Nobody can get it back now."

Ramona waggled the embossed leather book right under the man's nose, and he turned and strode out. "Sorry, sweeties," she said to the actors as she slid the appointment book back into her bag. "Ex-husbands can be difficult. Especially when they aren't quite ex. Come on, Derek, let's get on with it."

They got on with it.

Steve Bradford paced the damp streets of SoHo. It wasn't raining, though it was humid as the jungle. Cooler, of course. Couldn't mistake the Hudson for the Orinoco. Self-portrait of Steve: thirty-five, a handsome man with blue-gray eyes, a first touch of gray in his hair, a solid job that made use of both his ready smile and his logical mind. Logical. Yes, thought Steve, but passionate too. Adventurous. *A ruddy fire-eater*, as Hemingway would describe it. Ready to take on great lions or jaguars. He stepped around a pile of drizzle-soaked lumber on the sidewalk. SoHo was booming now. Seemed like every third building was being renovated. That was all right with him. His firm had its share of investments here.

He turned the corner and stopped abruptly. A pair of female ankles hovered just above his startled eyes. Lean ankles in neat business-height heels. A lanky young woman, dark hair and red scarf stirring in the misty breeze, was balanced on the bar of a builder's scaffold, fingering the pattern in the cast-iron facade.

"Note the acanthus leaves," said Steve.

Blue eyes, quick and intelligent, glanced down at his cashmere scarf and Burberry and classified him as harmless. "I was noting the floral swag, actually. I wanted to see how it turned the corner above the door."

"Yes, interesting design. Do you need a hand getting down?"

"Nope. But thanks." She turned a little and for the first time Steve noticed that a carrier holding a small baby was strapped half under her coat. But she grasped the bar and sprang down easily to the sidewalk before he could protest, her black curls and red scarf blowing, bright as toucans.

Steve was enchanted. Sometimes the gods were kind. He said, "Haven't I seen you around here the last few days?"

"Possibly," she acknowledged.

"Do you live here?"

"No."

Coolness in the syllable. He was going too fast. He shifted to a better subject. "Your little one seems to like architecture too."

"Yeah. A great kid." Beaming down at the baby snugged against her breast, the young woman's smile was as radiant as Susan's. "She's helping me in my research."

"Are you an architect?" Her clothes and the briefcase she was now retrieving from the scaffold looked professional.

"No. But we've got an old brownstone we're fixing up. They were kind enough to put up this scaffold, so I thought I'd take a look at the decoration up there. Reminds me of our mantel."

"Yeah, it's interesting, isn't it? Some friends of mine up in the Village have been working on their place for years. Love it. And I may be in for the same thing. I've just rented a pied-à-terre in an old factory they're converting around the corner here."

"Good for you. A cast-iron building?"

"Yes. Not as fancy as this one, though, and the apartments are pretty straightforward. But it's what I need. Your baby's so cute! A girl, you said?"

"Yes."

"Mine too. My little Muffin. She's two and a half."

"Sarah's five months."

"Well, she's the cutest! Except for Muffin, of course. Listen, good luck with your brownstone, Miss—um, Mrs. . . ."

"Maggie."

He approved of her caution; friendly yet reserved, no last names broadcast to strangers. He said, "My friends call me Buzz. Nice to meet you, Maggie. See you around, maybe."

"Maybe." She smiled that vivid smile again and left him standing by the scaffold.

The gloom was lifting, he was sure.

"Last stanza, Edith, Larry's death, right?" said Derek.

As Edith pulled her thick little body up to its full five foot two and began the verse for the last tableau, Nick saw a young woman slip into the rehearsal loft. A liquid fall of blond hair, strategically tight flare-leg jeans, leather jacket. She glanced at the scrawny teenager and eased into a folding chair next to her by the flaking side wall, listening to Edith's words and watching as Larry rose gracefully, pulled on the black gloves, clicked his heels and bowed as he had on first meeting Victoria, and backed slowly into the area that would be in darkness when the final lighting was in place. A pause; a choked sob from the crumpled Ramona; and then the pounding dirge from chorus and piano.

Ramona straightened slowly, as though lifting a crushing weight, and pulled a black shawl about her. The chorus moved back with measured steps, leaving her solitary in the center of the stage. The music modulated, and very quietly she began to sing "The Widow of Windsor." For the first time that day she did not have to worry about new dance steps or new movements, and she invested the words with a powerful emotional energy. "Alone," she sang, "in the crowds, still alone; among the princes, alone; forever alone." Nick, standing in the silent chorus, felt his throat tightening. The small isolated figure, the husky beauty of the voice that shimmered on the edge of tears, communicated a human truth that transcended history, geography, wealth, gender. She bound them all into Victoria's grief.

The last chords faded.

Then the stage manager cleared his throat and said, "Blackout," in his flat twang.

The spell was shattered. Derek exclaimed, "Super! But you know that, Ramona. On to act two?"

"Let's stop a minute early today, Derek. It's been a long afternoon." Ramona, drooping, pulled the shawl from her shoulders, then noticed the blond onlooker for the first time and stiffened. "Well! So Larry's evening revels have begun already. Though the brunette that came for him yesterday was prettier. Treat him well, sweetie." She winked at the young woman. "Your competition is formidable."

The few words reawakened the sizzle of rage in all of them. Derek dropped the piano lid too hard, and Nick repressed an appealing image of his own fist connecting with Ramona's famous chin. Larry himself, jaw set, tossed the gloves to the sideline and scooped up his own jacket and street clothes. He swept the lithe blonde from the room, murmuring reassurances. Ramona lit a cigarette and watched them go, her expression unreadable. Behind her back the teenager stuck out her tongue at her, but at a curt, almost terrified gesture from Daphne she again put on a polite face. The other actors were preparing to leave, but Ramona walked over to talk to Edith and Jaymie, who were handing the stage manager their rehearsal props. All three tensed as she approached.

Nick, in no hurry, stripped off his soaked sweats to don jeans and turtleneck. The other actors had scrambled into their street clothes quickly, but Ramona had removed only her rehearsal skirt and was still in her dark tights and pink leg warmers. She left Jaymie and, appointment book in hand, walked over to Derek at the piano. A trim figure for forty, thought Nick. Very trim. He sat down on the edge of the platform to wait.

Most of the actors left in a subdued clump. Daphne

joined Derek, however, and they bent over the book at the piano as Ramona approached Nick.

"Still hanging around?" she asked.

"Waiting for Maggie," he said cautiously, hoping he wouldn't inadvertently reignite her rage.

"As usual." She stood looking down at him a moment, then sat beside him, laid her cigarette carefully on a used Pepsi can next to her Italian bag, and began to pull the leg warmers from her elegant ankles. She smelled of jasmine and smoke. She said, "Don't know what you see in a bony kid like her, Nick, when you could have a sexy little tiger like me."

"Guess I'm kinky."

She laughed and rolled up the leg warmers carefully. Derek and Daphne, their consultation finished, put on their coats. Daphne waved good-bye, said, "C'mon, Callie," to the teenager, and hurried out with her. Their clog shoes rang on the old stairs. Derek paused at the door.

"How about a drink right now, Ramona?"

"I'm having one in half an hour. It's in my book." She tapped the appointment book that lay on her bag and picked up her cigarette again.

"And the book is sacred. I know! Well, we'll talk soon. See you later, then. Bye, Nick!" Nick could see that he was still upset, though he went out bravely humming "Nine Children."

They were alone now in the cavernous loft. Ramona turned to Nick again. "I wasn't kidding, Nick. I like you."

"Of course. Us big, bald woolly mammoths are irresistible. Best-sellers from Fisher-Price." He stood up, wondering uneasily if he should wait downstairs and hoping the faint noises he heard were footsteps coming up the stairs.

But Ramona was laughing. "Nick, you're never serious! Pay attention!" She bounced up, locked her arms around him, snuggled her dark, jasmine-scented head against his chest. She felt good. Hot blood begets hot thoughts. Unfortunately Nick had other commitments. Gently he put his hands on her shoulders.

"Look, Ramona—" he murmured, coaxing.

The door banged.

"Jesus, Nick!" It was Maggie, the baby strapped in the carrier, the briefcase clutched in her hand, the blue eyes darkening as she took in the scene.

Ramona jumped back guiltily. "God! Your wife!" She wasn't quite able to keep the satisfaction from her voice, though, and Nick realized without surprise that she'd deliberately set up this awkwardness.

But he was more interested in Maggie's urgent words. "Nick, I got your test result from Dr. Rank today!" She sounded alarmed, too alarmed to have noticed Ramona.

Dr. Rank? Of course. Nick's tone echoed hers. "My test result? Was it . . . favorable?"

A slow shake of her head. "Still positive! Certainty!"

"Absolute certainty?" groaned Nick.

"Yes. Oh, Nick, sleep well!"

Ramona was bewildered. "Test? Certainty?"

Maggie's eyes, blue pools of anxiety, turned to her for the first time. "Hepatitis," she explained in a tragic tone.

"Hepatitis!" Ramona sprang back in dismay.

Maggie nodded. "Infectious," she added helpfully.

Ramona wasted no sympathy on Nick. "Hepatitis! Damn, Nick, you've exposed us all! How could you be so goddamn selfish?" She was still backing away from him.

"Oh, it hasn't been all that bad for him," soothed Maggie.

"Not bad! Are you kidding? Hepatitis lays you flat! I had a friend who was in bed six months! And her skin turned *yellow*! My God, Nick, why didn't you say something? That's about the lowest . . . You've been rehearsing with us a week! And God, why didn't you make me stop horsing around just now? Why didn't—" She stopped abruptly, back against the wall, staring at him, then added slowly, "You're not yellow. And you've been bouncing around . . ." Her big eyes switched to Maggie. They revealed a war of disbelief and rage and laughter. "You knew?"

"Oh, shucks," said Maggie, grinning at her. "She's found us out, Nick."

"My God!" Laughter won and Ramona hooted in giddy relief. "Hepatitis! God! I'll have to remember that if I ever meet Simon's tart! Nick, you clown, I ought to can you! Lucky for you you're a damn good Gladstone and Prince of Wales. And you make me laugh. And so does your goddamn wife." Still giggling, she turned to Maggie. "Hey, are we even now?"

"All even. You gave me a bad moment too." Maggie had expertly unbuckled the baby carrier and was helping Nick strap it on. Nick the kangaroo. Best-seller from Fisher-Price. His tiny daughter opened drowsy dark eyes, noted his presence and Maggie's, and crumpled again into sleep against his chest. Balm of my age, most best, most dearest. Effortlessly she had seized control of his life.

Maggie turned back to Ramona. "Did Nick do something bad today?"

Under the friendly searching gaze, Ramona grew abruptly serious. "You mean, to deserve such a mean joke?"

"Sure, I deserved it," said Nick. "I was pretending to be a woolly mammoth and almost knocked her down."

But Ramona's mood had shifted. "No, she's right, Nick. I've been doing the great bitch-star routine today. I always thought I was too grown-up for that game. Haven't been this childish since I was sixteen! It's just that everything— No, you didn't deserve it. Nobody deserved it. It's nothing to do with the show, nothing to do with you. It's just Simon."

"Is there some way we can help?" asked Maggie.

"You? Mr. and Mrs. Happy Wedlock? Salt in the wound," said Ramona bitterly. "Still goddamn soul mates, aren't you? I'd forgotten what it's like."

So had I, thought Nick, till Dr. Rank. No time these days for souls. Or bodies, for that matter.

Maggie was hugging Ramona. "God, it must hurt!"

Ramona let herself relax in the lanky arms a moment. Maggie could have that effect on people, Nick knew. Her vitality and lively compassion had often in the past been a source of strength to him too. But in a moment Ramona drew a deep breath and objected, "You can't know, kid. You've never been divorced, right?"

"Not in a law court, no. Even so, I've been totaled a couple of times."

"But you're not forty."

"Not yet."

"Well, that makes it worse when your marriage is disintegrating. If yours lasts that long, you'll see. Oh, some days I'm almost glad it's ending. Glad to get out and conquer the world before it slips by. Other days I feel worthless. Old. Jealous of people like you. Wondering where all our magic went. What I did wrong."

Maggie patted her shoulder. "Nothing, probably."

"I know that with my *head*. He's crazy. But inside, you know, you're suffering and you think, 'I must have done something to deserve this.' " She moved away, started pulling on her flame-red pantsuit and stylish Italian stack-soled boots. "When I was young and dumb and about to throw my life away, my best friend shoved me into a room and locked the door. I yelled and screamed. In the morning she came in and told me I was a good kid, but she'd had to slap me on the wrist because I'd forgotten. And then she gave me cocoa and everything was okay."

"You're a good kid," said Nick, "but I'm afraid we forgot to bring the cocoa."

Ramona looked at him in surprise. "God! You're right! It's the same stupid game I'm playing, isn't it?"

"We play all kinds of games when we hurt."

"Mm." She adjusted the flared pant legs over her boots before glancing back at him. "Someone said Maggie was your second wife."

"Yes."

"You must know what it's like, then, Nick. Divorce."

"Not exactly. My first wife died."

"Oh, I'm sorry! That's different."

"Yeah, maybe. But anytime you're rooted psychologically in another person, any kind of end has to hurt."

"You don't say."

"Sigmund F. O'Connor, part-time shrink, at your service," said Nick cheerfully in a thick Viennese accent. "In your case, madam, I prescribe cocoa."

She was laughing again. "Clown!"

"Insight of the day. Free introductory sample."

"But you're right, you know. I've got to stop taking it out on you people. This business of ours is hard enough on the ego. One day you're applauded, the next you're on welfare. All your self-doubts thriving like leeches. And then this thing of Simon's." She shook her head fretfully.

"You won't have to worry about welfare, Ramona. You're still famous."

She stubbed out the cigarette, lips thin. "Still famous. Yes, indeed. Let's get out of here."

Nick held her wrap for her, a cape lined with blond fur. "Where's your date?"

"Not far. We're meeting at L'Etoile on Spring Street."

"Mind if we come along partway? We're going to Canal."

Ramona locked up and they descended the metal stairs of the old factory building and walked out into the dusk. It had stopped drizzling but was still damply unpleasant. Nick adjusted the flap around his sleeping daughter's head. Maggie, curious as always, asked Ramona, "What did you mean in there? About still famous?"

In the dim light Ramona looked downy, her dark eyes and dimples youthful in the frill of pale fur. After a moment she said, "Well, kid, Nick might remember. You're too young. But in 'fifty-five everyone loved me. A new Garland, they said. An elfin Merman. Et cetera. I was famous. Turned down lots of great parts because *Devil* ran two and a half years. After that there were TV specials, and one film. It would have done better but the cutesy photography didn't work. Hell, I could have done better with a Brownie! Anyway, on to more TV, a splashy tour for the GI's in Saigon, a couple of nightclub spots. And somewhere along the line I slipped from 'famous' to 'still famous.' The next step isn't hard to see."

The truth of her analysis was too obvious to debate. Maggie said, "So you bought yourself this show."

"Right. All that's left of the film money. I was very

prudent, you see, investing it for my favorite charity or
for retirement, in case Simon had a reversal or something. But then my agent brought me an offer for a
frozen-food commercial. My God, that's what I was doing
in 'fifty-four!" She gave a short harsh laugh. "And here
I am, parading around like the great bitch-goddess. What
kind of goddess sells frozen peas?"

"The Jolly Green Midget?" offered Nick.

"Yeah, laugh if you want. But I decided if I was ever
going to have decent parts again, I'd better get to work
and create my own luck. This is it. Ramona's big gamble.
I'm betting it all."

"Scary. But necessary," said Maggie, impressed.

"It's a great part," said Nick.

"Yeah, Victoria from birth to death. It'll prove I'm
not just a decaying ingenue. I can play a wider range."

"Good idea."

"Derek's idea of doing it music-hall style is cute, I
think. But of course everything seems to be rock these
days."

"*The Fantasticks* is still going strong."

"Well, if I win, we'll all be set for a while. And if it
flops, I suppose we'll meet again in the unemployment
lines."

"The true New York Actor's Club."

"Right. Well, that's show biz. Here's my corner."
Ramona indicated the lighted restaurant sign at the end
of the block.

"We'll walk you down."

"Absolutely not! You've done enough. Slapped me
on the wrist and listened to me."

"Next time we'll bring the cocoa too."

"No next time. I'll reform. Last thing I want to do is
hurt this show!" She shook her head soberly. "God, I've
got a lot of fences to mend."

Nick remembered the pulsing rage in the atmosphere
and had to agree. "We all love the show. People won't
be difficult."

"Hope not. Well, see you tomorrow, Nick." She grinned
suddenly. "And congratulations!"

"On what?"

"On your quick recovery from hepatitis."

They laughed and parted. Maggie peered at her daughter, nestled against Nick's chest. "How're you doing, *chouchoute*?"

Nick looked down at the baby and observed proudly, "She's sleeping."

"Amazing child! What will she think of next?"

"A prodigy, all right." He put an arm around Maggie's shoulders. "Risky, that hepatitis bit."

"So was everything else. Ignoring it would have insulted her, right? As for acting hurt and jealous—well, that might be what she wanted tonight, but she would've hated herself tomorrow."

"That's true. Up until today she's been pretty reasonable. Put the show first. I haven't seen this cruel streak before."

"Yeah, you always said she was a good sport. So I decided to risk it. Hey, we're pretty good, aren't we? The old improvisation team."

"You've missed it too?"

She walked a few steps in uneasy silence. "I guess I haven't had time to notice it was gone."

*A lot of things you haven't had time to notice, love.* Nick quelled his resentment and said, "Sarah takes a lot of energy. But it's been weeks since we've talked about anything besides who does dinner or who takes her to the pediatrician."

"Well, things are still shaking down."

"It's been five months!"

"But she changes every day! And you're working now, and—"

Two explosions burst through the clatter and rumble of the city dusk. Little Sarah stirred and whimpered. Maggie said doubtfully, "Backfire?"

"Maybe." They looked at each other a second, then turned and ran back to the corner where they had left Ramona. A few people had paused on the sidewalks to peer toward the middle of the block. A woman, not Ramona, was standing there in the light of the streetlamp, screaming. As they ran toward her, a coatless woman in a miniskirt began to soothe her.

"What happened?" Nick asked them.

"Don't know," said the miniskirted woman. "There were shots, and I heard Carlotta screaming, so I came out. She was running away from that building. But she's not hurt, I can see that."

A scaffold covered the sidewalk in front of the building she indicated, and plywood blocked most of the facade. Maggie had disappeared into the black shadows under the scaffold. "Nick!" she called. "Get an ambulance!"

There was no arguing with the urgency in her voice. Nick sprinted the half-block to the restaurant, despite Sarah's complaints about the jouncing, and grabbed the phone by the register. The headwaiter stopped protesting when he heard Nick's request for the police and an ambulance.

Nick ran back to the scaffold, murmuring distracted explanations to the indignant Sarah. One of the plywood sheets was split, and the blackness of the gutted building loomed beyond. When he shielded his eyes from the glare of the streetlight, he could see Maggie in the shadows, kneeling. And more.

Sprawled on her back on the dirty cement floor, Ramona Ricci lay very still, a dark stain spreading across the pale fur of the cape rumpled beneath her.

# II

## Tuesday night
## March 6, 1973

"How bad is it?" he asked.

"Bad." Maggie was kneeling beside her, pressing her red scarf against Ramona's side. "She's in shock. Blinked a couple of times when I yelled for you, but her eyes haven't opened since."

"The ambulance is on its way." Nick knelt to feel the fluttery pulse, but Sarah began to wail. "I'd better remove the distraction," he said, straightening.

"Okay. Do you see her bag anywhere?"

"Not out there. I'll look."

It wasn't near Ramona. He moved a couple of steps into the shadowed building and paused. Shafts of twilight broke through the clumsy wall of plywood and spattered the heaps of rubble, twisted stumps of utility conduits, trash cans. There was no movement. The assailant, he reasoned, would be gone; he could see a clear route through the gutted building to the next street, where the door in its plywood barrier was cracked open. No hiding places; a staircase zigzagged up the side wall to future upper stories that now were bare girders, but the stair was blocked by a solid, soundly padlocked metal door where it started down to the basement. No one could hide in this bare cavern. Still, he picked up Maggie's briefcase and shielded Sarah with it as he moved cautiously toward the other end of the building. "Hush," he murmured soothingly to the fretful infant. "How are we going to become world-famous secret agents if we can't sneak up on people? You think James Bond whimpers on the job? You think Sherlock Holmes fusses?"

She whimpered on. Easy to see why the great detectives were not family men. Well, at least there was no danger of panicking someone by a too-stealthy approach.

Ramona's bag gaped open, on its side, in a splash of light a few yards farther on. Nick knelt, still shielding Sarah with the briefcase, to inspect the spilled items— makeup, a pack of tissues, cigarettes, lighter, pens, checkbook. One of her long gloves was crumpled, the other lay full length, palm up, as though in grotesque supplication. There was no sign of a billfold. He went on a cautious tour of the space, exploring the loose plywood barrier along the next street. It would have been easy for the attacker to slip out this way; someone had broken the hasp of the padlock on the jerry-built plywood door. A few people moved calmly along the sidewalks of the next street.

Sarah's opinion of their expedition was still decidedly negative. He returned to Maggie.

"Her bag has been dumped over there. I think her billfold is gone. How is she doing?"

"Still breathing. Is that the ambulance?" The sound of sirens was becoming louder. Nick hurried to the street to meet the squad car.

"Gunshot victim," he explained, and pointed. "Back there. My wife is giving first aid." The two officers ran through the broken panel, and he heard one of them starting to question Maggie as the ambulance turned into the block. Nick saw Carlotta, no longer screaming, retreating with her friend toward a narrow doorway across the street. He hurried across to them.

"Excuse me, please, but you should probably tell them what you saw."

Carlotta was still snuffling. Her coatless friend, arms crossed against the damp chill, or against Nick's questions, said, "We don't want trouble. She says it was just a black kid anyway. Addict, probably."

"But why was the woman in the building?"

The friend shrugged. Carlotta didn't answer because she and Sarah had noticed each other and were smiling and cooing. Nick let the mutual therapy proceed for a moment, then asked gently, "Do you remember why she went into that gutted building?"

Carlotta glanced at him quickly, then back at Sarah. "I was walking a little behind her. She stopped where the boards were broken, sort of surprised, and then said something. Maybe, 'Are you hurt?' She went a step closer, then the black kid grabbed her and pulled her into the darkness. I ran away."

"What did he look like?"

"I didn't see his face. Just a shadow in the shadows. She went closer and his arm came out and pulled her into the dark. I was running away when I heard the shots, and I thought he'd come for me next." Her lips were trembling again and she looked fearfully at the scaffolding.

Nick said, "He's gone. I went all the way through the building to check. Hey, my baby sure likes you."

She turned back to Sarah gratefully. "She's a wonderful baby!"

"Yes," said the friend firmly. "But I still think you need coffee. Besides, I'm cold." She took Carlotta's elbow and led her into the door. Nick noted the number and crossed back to the other side of the street.

The paramedics had Ramona on a stretcher and were hurrying her into the vehicle. In a moment the siren yowled and it roared away. More police had arrived, plainclothes and technicians. Nick saw Maggie under the streetlight talking to what was probably a detective. He joined them. She was nearing the end of her account.

"I asked Nick to call an ambulance. She seemed bloodiest around her left waist so I felt for the wound and jammed my scarf and a diaper on it. I just pressed it there. Hope it was the right thing to do." She was cleaning blood from her hands with Sarah's baby wipes.

"Yes, ma'am." The detective was stocky with a thick neck and receding curly hair. He seemed deeply weary, alert out of habit rather than interest. "What next?"

"I just held the scarf in place until you came. Pulled her cape around her to keep her warm. She was in shock, but I couldn't think of anything else to do. I knew we shouldn't move her. Nick came back and I asked him to look for her bag."

"Nick?"

"Me. Nick O'Connor. I was the one who called you. When I got back here, I walked through the alley to the next street. Her bag was halfway along, emptied out. I didn't really search because I didn't want to touch anything."

"Good. We're checking it out." The gutted building was lively with flashlights now. The detective added, "I'm Detective Sergeant Perez. Did you see anyone in the building when you arrived?"

"No. But I didn't really look until after I'd called you. You'll want to talk to a woman, Carlotta something, across the street at number fifty-two. She says she saw someone pull Ramona into the building just before the shots were fired. She's very upset, of course. A friend is trying to calm her."

"I see. Now, Miz Ryan here said you worked with Miz Ricci?"

"Yes. We're doing a musical. I'm one of the actors."

"An actor?" Perez glanced at him with no recognition. Not surprising; Nick was one of those actors who dissolve into their parts, and few recognized him even if they had seen his Elson Beer commercial a dozen times. Of course in the Elson Beer thing he hadn't been wearing a fussy baby.

Perez asked, "Is Miz Ricci one of the actresses?"

"She's the star. Also the producer."

"Producer? Puts up the money?"

"Yes."

"Rich lady, then. Wait a minute. Not Ramona Ricci? *The Devil's to Pay?*"

"Yes."

"Jesus." Like Nick, Sergeant Perez was old enough to remember 'fifty-five. He made a note, then returned to his question. "So she'd probably have money on her."

"Some."

"And wearing that fur. Can you tell me anything else? What she was doing here?"

"She was going to meet someone at L'Etoile."

"Yes, Miz Ryan said that. Do you know who?"

"No. Ramona didn't say."

"Is she married?"

"Well, she's about to get a divorce, I think. Her husband is named Simon Jenkins. Banker, she said."

"I see. Children?"

"I don't know. She never mentioned any."

"Boyfriends?"

"We've only been rehearsing about a week. I don't know her very well."

"We'll check. Now, Miz Ryan said you were walking together?"

"To the corner there. We were on our way to the subway."

"I see." Perez looked at Sarah, who was beginning to fuss again. "Well, let's get your statements so you can go. Wait here a minute."

It took more than a minute. Perez conferred with his colleagues, toured the gutted building, and fetched Carlotta and her unwilling friend from their apartment before escorting them all to the precinct house.

"Where did they take Ramona?" asked Nick as they climbed the steps.

"Bellevue E.R. Of course, someone like that, they may move her when she's stabilized."

There was another weary time of waiting while Perez organized the machinery of investigation. No wonder the detective looked permanently tired. Nick tried to soothe Sarah while Maggie phoned her partner to explain why she would not be on time for the second half of her noon-to-nine working day. "Hey, Dan, sorry I'll be late. There was a shooting and I'm sort of a witness. . . . Yeah, I did that this afternoon while you were cursing the computer. . . . No, no, Sarah was entertained, and anyway she hears worse from me in French. . . . Basically I'm waiting on the new program now. . . . Well, I hope you get it figured out. Leave me a note and I'll be there as soon as I can."

At last Perez sent for them and they went over the grim story again and he sent them on their way.

They started slowly back toward the subway. Nick said, "Hell." Maggie didn't answer, just put an arm around his waist. But there was no time for comforting each other on their current schedule. Maggie still had to go back to her job farther uptown to complete the day's work, while Nick and Sarah headed for the subway and Brooklyn. The train, inside and out, was mantled in meandering curls of spooling graffiti, as though snagged in the unraveling fabric of the disintegrating city. Sarah, jaded city child, was mysteriously soothed by the screeching, crowded, swaying car and dropped into sleep. Nick, gym bag between his legs, one hand gripping a strap and the other sheltering Sarah from the press of their fellow travelers, was left alone to worry about Ramona and about his job and about his marriage.

"Look, Steve! She's dancing!"

Elaine was in her element as mother. Steve looked over his shoulder from where he stood mixing Bloody Marys at the tiled counter. Little Muffin was making repeated flat-footed jumps on the kilim carpet, not quite in time with the Glenn Miller music that Elaine and Rachel had on the stereo.

Rachel said, "Nah. She's just practicing her karate stance. Wants to terrify the other kids at Montessori." She was roundly pregnant, a pleasant woman of definite features: wide smile, strong nose, long dark hair caught in a clasp at the nape of her neck. She had become good friends with Elaine last fall when she and Bob had moved in next door.

Steve tended to agree with her about Muffin's "dance." But Elaine only laughed, still delighted with her daughter. Portrait of Elaine: a proud carriage, a warm smile, a cultured voice. Shiny caramel-blond hair. Hazel eyes, the first laugh lines at the corners. Long supple body in cashmere and silk. And total conviction that her daugh-

ter was precocious. Steve delivered a tomato juice to
Rachel and a Bloody Mary to Elaine. "Time to sign her
up with Martha Graham," he teased.

"Well, eventually, don't you think?" said Elaine, not
backing down. She loved to dance herself, still took lessons in the Village. "She enjoys music so much."

"I know she does. C'mon, Muffin, may I have the
next?" Steve dropped to his knees and took his daughter's rather sticky fingers. He moved their linked hands
up and down as she jumped. Muffin gave him a smile
that pierced his heart, and Elaine laughed.

"Steve, you're crazy!"

"Wait'll you see us tango!" He swooped Muffin up,
laid his cheek on hers, and circled the room with sweep-
ing Valentino strides.

"Crazy!" Elaine was clapping her hands. Muffin was
squealing with delight.

Steve released his daughter and retrieved his own
Bloody Mary. "Don't let Lainey kid you," he warned
Rachel. "She knew I was crazy when she married me."

"No false pretenses, huh?" Rachel's dark eyes smiled
at them.

"None at all," admitted Elaine, still amused. "But
of course Muffin makes him worse."

"Yeah, I can hardly wait to see Bob with ours. He's
so obsessive anyway. He'll probably mortgage the boat
to buy teething rings."

"We're all a bit crazy, I guess," said Steve. He was
astonished, these days, at the extent of his own craziness.
Here, in this house on Long Island, was the American
dream come true. His blessings, counted: Oriental car-
pets, stereo, Woodmode kitchen, a Porsche and an Olds
in the garage, a sailboat at the private dock. Vietnam
winding down, the business poised to do better than ever.
A long-awaited daughter, sticky-fingered but beloved. A
wife of beauty, wealth, connections. Good family, good
house, good job. And yet—

And yet, he found himself dreaming of South America, of jaguars and bougainvillea, of an untamed woman
somewhere in Caracas, of work that required steely nerve

instead of his pleasant smile, of rafts on jungle rivers instead of Porsches on the expressway. Crazy.

"Oh, baby, I'm going to miss you!" Elaine's voice brought him out of his reverie. She was giving Muffin a big kiss before placing her in her chair by the kitchen counter.

"It's only for a few hours, Lainey," said Steve sharply. "You'll be back before midnight. And my secretary already reserved your tickets."

"Don't I know it! Myra called and talked to me half an hour about it. Did I want an aisle seat, who was watching the baby, and so forth. But it's Muffin I'm thinking of. It's the first time I won't be there to pick her up after playschool. The very first time!"

"I imagine she'll survive it," said Rachel drily. "But I'm not sure you will."

"Well, you'll understand when you have one," declared Elaine, pouring a glass of milk for Muffin. "It was hard even leaving her with Mitzi, and Mitzi's been my buddy since junior high."

"I know," sighed Rachel. "I'm totally unqualified. Boorish even to express an opinion. I'll just shut up till the nine months are up."

"And then, abracadabra, you'll be an instant expert!" Steve teased. But he doubted that Rachel would ever know the feverish devotion that Elaine felt for Muffin. Rachel hadn't suffered those anxious years of not conceiving, those heartbreaking miscarriages.

"Yes, and then you'd better watch out! If you think I meddle too much now, just wait till I'm a pro too!" said Rachel. "But you do owe your parents something too, Elaine."

"Yeah," Steve agreed, "you'd want Muffin to come see you if you were having the operation, wouldn't you, Lainey?"

"Oh, I know. I'm going," said Elaine, dutiful daughter to Avery Busby as well as loving mother to Muffin. "But I'll still miss her." She handed a carrot stick to Muffin, who chewed on it single-mindedly, oblivious to the passions she aroused in the adults.

"I'm surprised you aren't taking her along," said Rachel.

"Oh, she makes Dad nervous," explained Elaine regretfully. "And Muffin's doing so well at Montessori, I hate to have her miss it. And Steve can pick her up."

"That's right," said Steve.

"Sure you don't want me to get her?" asked Rachel. "I'm just hanging around here, waiting for my water to break, and that won't be for weeks."

"No, no, I can get her. The playschool is only a few blocks from work."

"Well, phone me if you need anything, okay? How's your dad taking it, Elaine?"

Elaine shrugged. "He's furious. Says he was healthy all those years he was working, so why does his system kick out now that he's trying to retire? But in him I think it's a healthy reaction to be angry."

"True," agreed Steve. "I'd only worry if he was meek about it."

Elaine wafted a smile at him. "Anyway, he won't stay out of action long. Mom says he's planning another African hunt next month. Can't decide if he wants to go after rhinos or zebras."

Steve had a sudden vision of Elaine's tanned, balding father on his hospital bed, wearing a white gown and a pith helmet, being rolled across the veld by a combination of native bearers and nurses in white, his big-game rifle booming to bring down herds of charging rhinos in the best Hemingway fashion. No mere operation would stop Avery Busby. A spirit as free as Susan's.

Rachel seemed to agree. She said, "Boy, you've got quite a dad. Well, listen, I'd better get my casserole out of the oven before it fuses together. Your plane is at noon Thursday, right?"

"Yes. I'll drop Muffin at Mitzi's, then drive to the airport. Dad should be coming out of the anesthesia about the time I arrive in Palm Beach."

"Not a complicated operation, then?"

"Just a typical male complaint. But he's not pleased."

"He doesn't think he's a typical male," said Steve.

"But he'll be pleased enough to see you."

"Oh, I know. But he'll bluster around and send Mom and me on lots of pointless errands and won't admit he hurts." Elaine sighed in resignation. Avery Busby liked his men rugged and his women refined, and had seen to it that his daughter spent her summers at a Swiss finishing school, her college years at Mount Holyoke. Steve appreciated the results. Convincing Elaine and her formidable father that he would be the best choice among her suitors was one of the great victories of Steve's life. His elation had lasted months, even years. He felt a nibble of melancholy now; did all joys in life become flat eventually? He had been happy then. He'd thought it would last. And in a way it had; he loved Elaine deeply, loved his enchanting daughter, appreciated the good life they lived here. But somehow joy had succumbed to time, worn away by little daily frustrations, and by big ones. Catalog of the decline of joy: A bleak night at the hospital, the doctor's professional sympathy: "I'm sorry, Steve, we couldn't save the baby. Your wife needs your support now." At the office: "I'm sure you'll understand, Steve, Bill's in a better position to take the assignment in Japan. No family to worry about. We all thought it would be better just now to send him." At his own doctor's office: "You're in great shape, Steve, but we'd better keep an eye on that blood pressure. We middle-aged types can't be quite as carefree as teenagers, you know." At the target range, his father-in-law's genial reiterated confidences: "I always told Elaine she and her family would make their own way. Advice, sure. Recommendations, sure. But no handouts. That's how I was raised. It makes a man sharper, hungrier, ready for a little adventure." And Steve, the Japan adventure so recently snatched from his grasp because he was married to this man's daughter, could only nod soberly and blast away at a cardboard target. And yet—

And yet, he knew the value of what he had. Count blessings: security, status, health, love, the beginnings of wealth.

Rachel was letting herself out the kitchen door, saying

something about dinner. He waved good-bye and wondered if love and wealth could survive in South America.


Sarah's waving fist smacked against the spoon in Nick's
hand and sent a dollop of oatmeal splattering onto the
refrigerator door.

"Thou clay-brained guts!" complained Nick.

She stared in fascination at his face and breathed
reverently, "Ah-yah!"

His annoyance dissolved into addle-brained rapture.
Nick the besotted. Gazing into her delightful brown eyes,
he murmured, "Fond of Shakespeare, are you? How
about, 'thou nott-pated fool?' "

"Ah-yah!"

"Obscene, greasy tallow-keech!"

Sarah chortled and slapped the tray of the high chair.

"All right, now, enough of this idle banter." Nick
succeeded in getting most of the last spoonful into her
mouth, then mopped her chin, dropped the unspeakable
bib into the pile of souring laundry in the corner, called
the dog to lap up the spills on the floor, and got out her
bathtub.

She had just dropped off to sleep and Nick was swab-
bing down the refrigerator when Maggie returned from
work. "Hi, love," she said. "How's it going?"

"The usual. Gracious surroundings, scintillating conversation, impeccable linen."

"You're right. Time for the laundry." She dropped
her briefcase and coat in the butler's pantry and picked
up the armload of soiled bibs and blankets. "Any word
about Ramona?"

"No. I called Derek to tell him. He said he'd go to
the hospital and ring me back when he heard something.
But he hasn't called."

"I'm worried, Nick."

"So am I, love."

"And I can't figure it out." She was stuffing things
into the washer.

"What?"

"Why did she go into that building? Why was she
shot? Why there?"

"Carlotta said Ramona seemed to think someone was hurt in there."

"Okay. So her soft heart overcame her street smarts. But someone grabbed her, right? Made contact? Carlotta saw that?"

"Yes."

"Grabbed her, threatened her with the gun, got the bag. Okay, I'm with it so far. But next?"

"Shoot her and run."

"Shoot her where?"

Nick nodded. "You're right. The guy is close enough to grab her. He'd probably have the gun against her head. Maybe her heart."

"Couldn't miss."

"You're sure the only wound was the one at her waist?"

"Yeah. I kept checking for trouble somewhere else because there'd been two shots. But that was it. Entrance and exit wounds."

"Couldn't have been two different shots?"

She shrugged unhappily. "Then why both at her waist? Why a powder burn on the front of that light cape and none on the back? It was close range, Nick."

"Maybe she was struggling."

"You don't struggle if the other guy has a gun!"

"Ramona's feisty."

"Okay. Here's another problem then. Why that street? Lots of other places are more deserted."

He rinsed his dishcloth and tossed it to her to add to the laundry. "Maybe he didn't want to wait too long for a victim to happen by. And maybe with construction scaffolds on both streets he thought it was a good setup to escape. Somebody pried off that hasp, after all, and broke down the plywood, and I doubt if it was the building's legal owner."

"Maybe."

"There's something else, though," Nick admitted reluctantly.

"What?"

"Well, you remember the mood she was in. How we kidded her out of it? She had us all fuming."

Maggie considered. "But even supposing it was one

of you people, that doesn't explain any of the problems we've been talking about."

"I know. And besides, no matter how nasty she might be, every one of us wants her to be wildly successful in this play. We're part of the show. We aren't going anywhere without her."

"Yeah. And none of you are black kids, either."

"Well—"

"What?"

"There's Callie. Daphne's niece. Expelled from school for the day, just visiting. She watched very politely, but Ramona lit into her too."

"A kid?"

"This particular kid has a tongue as rough as Ramona's. But she shut up when Daphne told her to."

"Daphne seemed to have control?"

"I thought so."

"Well—hell, it's just that nothing quite fits. Guess I'll let the police worry about it." Maggie added the soap and started the washer. "Is Sarah sleeping?"

"Like a baby." Nick followed her upstairs to the bedroom floor. Sarah's nursery and the kitchen were the only two finished rooms in the house. If Ramona recovered and he got his promised pay, they might get two more painted this year. Damn, this was not the profession for home and family. Ninety-five percent unemployment, and that was among actors good enough to belong to Equity. He'd been lucky so far, a couple of jobs a year, waiting tables or janitoring in between. This risky, up-and-down life had seemed full of freedom and joy when shared with an eagerly adventurous companion like Maggie. But his choice of profession felt rash and irresponsible now as he looked down into the crib at Sarah, tiny and defenseless.

Maggie adjusted the cotton blanket over her, smiling, then met Nick's eyes and grew serious again. "You're worried about Ramona," she said.

"Yeah. Not just because she's a friend. Goddamn it, Maggie, in most businesses if the boss has an accident, you don't lose your job!"

"There are two of us, Nick." Her blue eyes were troubled. He threw an arm around her shoulder.

"Hell, Maggie, maybe it'll all work out. But somehow, now that Sarah's here, the future counts. I'm not quite as carefree and liberated as I thought I was."

He half expected her to argue that she could provide for them all, that his own career was surprisingly dependable, that their successes to date were more than freak good luck—all true observations. But instead she burrowed her nose into his neck and murmured, "Neither am I, Nick. Neither am I," and somehow he was more comforted than if she had said all those other true things.

# III

## Wednesday
## March 7, 1973

By the time Nick arrived at the loft on the drizzly Wednesday, Derek was mounting the platform to call the rehearsal to order. Nick was struck at the alteration in the mild little Englishman. Today the pale twinkling eyes were feverish and worried, the genial optimism converted to anxiety. The subdued actors quieted instantly. Most had not heard what had happened until their arrival minutes ago.

"We've got a problem, mates," Derek announced. "To be brief, Ramona was badly hurt last night during a robbery. She is in hospital and in quite serious condition. Still unconscious."

Edith stroked the blond wig she wore as young Victoria's German nurse. "Was it a mugging? A knife? What?"

"The hospital blokes were not very forthcoming, but I gather the problem is internal bleeding from a bullet that nicked her liver. They assured me that she has been attached to all the appropriate machines. I can't give you a firsthand report because only relatives can visit."

"God!" said Edith with an indignant heave of her ample bosom. "That bastard Simon? He won't visit. She'll be alone!" Alone. The words echoed in Nick's mind: *in the crowds, still alone, forever alone.*

Derek shrugged. "It's regulations. And she's unconscious at the moment."

Daphne asked anxiously, "Is her life in danger?"

Derek licked his lips. "They made no predictions. Just repeated that it was serious. My own feeling is, if there's any sort of a chance, she'll rally round. She's a fighter."

"That's true," said Edith, slightly consoled.

"How did it happen?" Larry, who had been quietly inspecting his shoes, looked up.

"She was on her way to a restaurant, and—but here, Nick, you tell it. You were there."

"You were there?" exclaimed Jaymie.

"Not quite. Half a block away," said Nick. Poky O'Connor, dull and muddy-mettled. The big man who wasn't there. "We—Maggie and I—walked with her most of the way to the subway, but she turned off before we reached Canal. She was meeting someone at L'Etoile. We went on a few steps, then heard shots and ran back. We found her in a gutted building, already unconscious. Maggie gave what first aid she could while I called the ambulance."

Larry's hard glare burned across the room at him. "Why the hell didn't you stay with her?"

"Guess I forgot to consult Madame Astra yesterday," snapped Nick. Larry's words rankled. It was not the first time that he had found himself standing by, helpless to prevent tragedy. Last night had brought back old nightmares of his first wife limp and cold in a dressing room, of a teenager machine-gunned by the Berlin wall.

"Hey, he did what he could," Edith was saying. Short, bosomy, thick-waisted, she viewed herself as peacemaker. "None of the rest of us would have gone anywhere near her, the mood she was in yesterday."

"Did you say it was a robbery?" Daphne's fingers jabbed at her Afro, mushrooming it away from her slender neck.

Nick said, "A witness told us she was pulled into the building. I saw that the things in her bag had been dumped out, but there was no sign of her billfold."

"But God, why not just snatch the bag? Why shoot her?" asked Daphne.

"I know. We wondered about that too. We thought maybe she was struggling."

"She wouldn't have resisted if there was a gun!" Edith objected. "We were talking about it just last week. Remember, Jaymie? When we all left together? She'd gotten herself a little pistol and was telling us we should get one too. She said she was ready for anybody now. And I said, what if a mugger already had his gun out? And she said of course she'd be sensible then. She wasn't pretending to be the fastest draw in the West."

"Did she keep this gun in her bag?" asked Nick.

"That's where it was when she showed it to us. Why?"

"Well, there was no gun in the stuff he'd dumped."

"You think he took it too?"

"I think you should tell the police it might have been there. If there's a record of it somewhere, it might help trace the guy eventually." He didn't add the grim corollary: when it was used on another victim.

"You mentioned a witness," said Larry.

"Yes, did someone see it?" asked Jaymie. She tapped her cigarette into the battered brown wastebasket by the piano.

"A woman walking a short distance behind her. She said she saw Ramona pause, then step closer to the gutted building. There's a temporary plywood wall with a missing piece. She said a black kid pulled Ramona into the shadows. The woman panicked and was running away even before the shots were fired."

"So maybe she can identify him!" exclaimed Edith.

"She claims she didn't see much. But maybe in a lineup . . ." Nick shrugged.

"What happened next?" asked Daphne.

"Maggie and I came blundering back, and the police and ambulance got there soon and took over. We told the officers what we knew and they sent us away. I called Derek, and he found out the rest."

"God, why couldn't you have walked her just that one block farther?" demanded Larry.

Derek cut off Nick's angry response. "Steady, mates, no use now playing what-if."

"Right," agreed Daphne hastily. She stretched and added, "Well, Derek, what do we do now?"

"I got through to Ken Martin this morning. Ramona's partner in the production company. He's a lawyer and said he'd check into the contract. His first response was to let you people go immediately, and . . ."

A din of objections drowned him out. Derek nodded and raised his palms for silence. "I know, I know. I suggested we continue working for a few days until we know more certainly how long she'll be recuperating. He said to go ahead till the weekend and he'd let us know."

"Anyway, he can't fire us!" exclaimed Jaymie. "Ramona told her husband there was no backing out! Or—do you mean the contract is tied to her being able to perform? I mean, she'll be back!"

"Martin's checking on the legal bits. And of course he agreed that if she was going to be back soon, it would be silly to disband the cast even if he legally could. And you know Ramona will tell him the same thing when she wakes up."

"Still," said Edith, "it'll be hard to work without her. She's in most of the numbers."

"We've got Jaymie," said Daphne. Jaymie flashed her a trembly smile.

"Ramona will never agree to do things Jaymie's way," said Larry.

"Well, we can at least do the rough blocking," insisted Daphne. "Work on the choruses. And if you think about it, she usually doesn't object to the concepts. She just adjusts details sometimes."

"Yeah. Details like cutting a whole solo," griped Larry.

Nick said, "I don't think we should take her complaints yesterday too seriously."

"You didn't have a number cut!"

"Look, Larry, she had other problems. She told me she'd been taking it out on us and said she'd try to be better about it."

Edith, dubious, shook her head. "After everything she said yesterday? I don't know."

"She meant those things," agreed Jaymie. Even Derek looked skeptical.

Nick felt he had to defend her. "You all know she's not usually as difficult as yesterday. She's got personal problems right now. Under a lot of strain. And she's opinionated, and around here she gets her way. She should! We've all worked in star vehicles before, and that's the way things are. But Ramona's been pretty decent. Doesn't usually hurt people. I think she'll be reasonable. She even apologized yesterday."

"Whether we believe all that or not, Nick, it doesn't solve our problem now."

"Well, we can't just quit!" said Jaymie. "She'll probably be better soon. Doctors fall all over themselves for famous people. Not like most . . ." She bit her lip, bowed her head.

Daphne reached over to pat her hand and said, "What do you think, Derek?"

"I think we should try. Believe me, mates, as soon as I have any real answers, I'll let you know. But for now it seems best to assume that she'll be back in a couple of weeks and rehearse without her as best we can. We'll lose less time in the long run."

Larry shrugged. "Well, then, let's start."

Everyone nodded, willing to go along with this least unsatisfactory plan. Derek plunked himself onto the piano bench, announcing act two, and Daphne explained, "Kick line comes on from stage left, everyone except the Disraelis and Gladstones. And Victoria of course." She demonstrated the steps quickly, her lithe dark body flitting impudently through the comic music hall routines. It was basically a repetition of the show opener, called "Sixty-four Years," the length of Queen Victoria's reign. The verses were different, but the choreography echoed the opener.

"And at 'running an Empire alone—all alone' you all pull back into a vee. Lights up on Victoria's throne at the apex. Okay, Jaymie?"

"Okay."

"And then when the Chairman says 'Two!' Nick and

Larry leap out, one through each side of the vee. Land center stage, maybe five feet apart. Strike a pose, mirror images."

"Waving top hats," suggested Larry.

"Yes, something like that. We'll work out the details later. And we go straight into 'Dizzy and the Grand Old Man.' "

Rehearsing was hard work. Twenty actor/dancers, years of sacrifice and training behind them, more years of sacrifice and training ahead of them, followed the complex instructions with intense concentration. There were few actual missteps even this first time, but hours of rehearsal would still be required to get knees at precisely the same level, fingers and canes at the correct angles, transitions timed. From behind the line, Nick— who shared their folly—wondered again at the foolish passion that led otherwise normal adults to sacrifice and sweat, beg and lie, for the opportunity to— What? Not make money; they'd all do better driving cabs. Not become famous; Ramona was the only one with a part that might bring fame, and she had it already. He and Larry had a chance of being noticed, especially Larry, if he could keep his solo. But the others were basically chorus members, their brief turns in the spotlight too ephemeral for lasting attention. He watched Jaymie: slim, serious, dark wavy hair pulled into a ponytail, bouncing through the kick-line steps, then hurrying to Ramona's place on Victoria's throne and shifting to a stately queen. Once, during a five-minute break, he teased her, "Don't you think you're working too hard for scale?"

"Oh, it's not the money," she said earnestly between gulps of Sprite. "You know that, Nick. Hell, my mom made me promise I'd never think of the money. She did and regretted it ever since. Married Dad, and he made her quit. And then ran off with someone younger, and by then Mom was in her thirties—Anyway, she must be right. Look at Ramona. How old she is, and people still love her!"

"Not her husband, babe," observed Daphne cheerfully.

"Yeah, but that's not what I mean. It's the energy, Mom said. You give it, you get it back from the audience. She said no amount of money could buy that."

True. They would all slave in exhausting anonymity, poorly paid, briefly appreciated by an audience that would promptly forget them and leave the theatre discussing Ramona. And when the show closed, even if it had a good run, there would be only an extra line in their resumes to help get the next job with similarly ridiculous working conditions. If there even was a next job.

And yet they considered themselves lucky. Those instants of communication with the audience, that sense of being an instrument that revealed the spark of divinity in ordinary humanity—even chorus lines had those moments. Jaymie's mom was right; money couldn't buy it. And as Ramona had admitted, that was even the reason for wanting success. Fame itself was only a means to that end.

But was it enough? Nick wondered. Was he sacrificing Sarah's future to the whimsical god of show biz?

"Running an empire alone—all alone," the chorus was singing.

"Not quite alone," amended Cab, as Chairman. "Queen Victoria had the help of her prime minister. And not just one prime minister. Two!"

Nick leaped through the wall of the kick line and landed together with Larry, their upstage hands raised with the hats, twin smiles directed at the nonexistent audience.

"Fine," said Daphne, and showed them the routines for their duet, an almost vaudevillian soft shoe involving lots of high-spirited prancing and spinning together, bent elbows linked. "Okay, give it a try. Let's just honk through it."

Nick and Larry waved their hats, gave a preliminary prance to the piano's rollicking phrases, and began.

"Oh, Gladstone and Disraeli, Victoria's glorious pair! There's fame enough for Dizzy and the Grand Old Man to share!"

The Chairman waved a hand from his podium at the

side and announced, "Mr. Gladstone, the Grand Old Man!"

Nick stepped forward. Even in his bedraggled rehearsal sweats he radiated the energy and righteous zeal of the famous orator. "I'm William Ewart Gladstone," he sang. "My talent's heaven-sent. I try to work God's purpose in the halls of Parliament! I work for fallen women, for the Irish, for the crowds! My heart is with the people!"

"His head is in the clouds!" sneered Larry, elbowing Nick aside to claim center stage. He exuded a languid cleverness, the perfect foil for Nick's pompous enthusiasm, as he sang, "I'm Benjamin Disraeli, a Tory with a twist. I'm known as wit, as Jew, as Brit, as great imperialist! I work to find what's useful in Gladstone's woolly dreams. I work for Queen and Empire!"

"For selfish Dizzy schemes!" Nick, scornful too, shouldered him aside in turn and began the argumentative refrain: "Extend the vote!"

"The Empire!"

"God's will!"

"And glory bright!"

"There's fights enough for Dizzy and the Grand Old Man to fight!" they chorused together, spontaneously flashing their canes in mock swordplay as they skipped around. The other actors were chuckling.

"Both happily married!" announced the Chairman, and Edith and the actress playing Mrs. Disraeli joined them from the chorus.

Nick and Edith held hands in an affectionate but thoroughly proper manner. "A ragamuffin husband and a rantipoling wife, we'll fiddle it and scrape it through the ups and downs of life!" They two-stepped neatly around the stage; but Disraeli and his wife high-kicked. The contentious prime ministers quarreled on through three more stanzas. Then as Jaymie stepped regally down from the rickety chair that was standing in for a throne, Nick launched the final chorus. "There's land reform!"

"There's India!"

"Peace!"

"War!"

"And jubilee!" Jaymie broke in. The prime ministers looked at her, astonished. Increasingly assured, she went on, "And majestee! And dynastee! There's work enough for Dizzy and the Grand Old Man—and me!"

The three linked elbows and skipped around the stage to the closing chords.

"Super!" Derek enthused. "Funnier than I thought! I'm rather taken with that sword fight with the canes, aren't you, Daphne?"

"Love it. We'll keep that. Larry, I like that scarecrow quality you're giving Disraeli. But tone it down just a little in your choruses with Nick, so it looks like the same dance."

"Okay. Nick isn't exactly a scarecrow."

"Yeah, everybody tells me. Woolly mammoth. Prince of Whales," grumbled Nick.

"It's going to be cute. Nice job, Jaymie," Daphne said, and Jaymie glowed. Then Daphne added almost casually, "Okay, Derek, what's next?"

A little pulse of tension ran around the room. Everyone knew what was supposed to be next. But Derek, as casually as Daphne, said, " 'Top of the Greasy Pole.' Disraeli's solo."

"Oh, can that," said Larry vehemently. "What's the point in rehearsing it?"

"We'll save it," said Derek. "It's important to the show."

"Ramona wants the show to be perfect," Nick said. "She'll see reason."

"Ah, yes," said Larry bitingly. "Quite the expert on her state of mind, aren't you? Especially when she's in a coma."

"Yeah, in my spare time I practice telepathy." Nick and Larry glared at each other.

"Let's go, Larry!" Derek broke in briskly. Obediently Larry and Daphne began working on the number, a philosophical reflection on the joys and pains of leading a great empire, salted with bits of Disraeli's wit. But some of the zest had gone out of Larry's performance, and worry about Ramona gloomed over them all.

* * *

"And what was your favorite?" asked Edith.

"Hamlet, of course," said Larry.

"Oh, God, the biggie! Where did you play him?" Edith stretched an arm past Nick and across the scarred table of the booth to tap cigarette ashes into the dented metal ashtray in front of Jaymie. Mike's Place, read the ashtrays before they were filled with butts. This was not Mike's Place. The sign painted on the window said Guarneri's Coffee Shop, but for all Nick knew that might have been recycled too, like the Mike's Place ashtrays and the Gimbels bags that enclosed the take-out sandwiches and coffee. Anna Maria, the plump owner, was not a spend-thrift.

"In the Oregon boonies," Larry answered curtly.

But Edith, who had just confessed over a cottage cheese and pineapple salad that her own favorite role had been Fraulein Schneider in a road company of *Cabaret*, seemed determined to keep the conversation away from their worries. "What's so great about that part?" she demanded. "I mean, from an actor's point of view. Not a professor's."

"Lots of solos," said Larry bitterly, then thought better of it and gave her a quick grin to pretend that it was only a quip. In a more civilized tone he went on, "Actually the complexity is what's fascinating. This Oregon thing was a summer festival. A good experience because I had time to work with the part and with the director. Not your usual stock situation, where you've got maybe a week to plumb the depths of a character and figure out how to get it across. And Hamlet is so human—frail, frightened, full of passionate love and passionate hate."

"And passionate wit," said Nick.

"That too. Black humor. And when you come right down to it, can any motive be more powerful than revenge? A father killed, a mother stained—that complicates a guy's life, even without that ghostly cheering section. Anyway, I'd hate to try the role with a New York rehearsal schedule. This cartoon version of Dizzy is about the deepest you can go in the short time you get here."

"What about you, Nick?" asked Cab.

"Oddly enough, no one ever thought to cast me as Hamlet," Nick confessed, running a hand self-consciously across his bald head. "But one brave fellow cast me as Cyrano once in summer stock. I loved it. It was a great change from the businessmen or evil kings or clowns that I usually get. Wildly romantic."

"Not that you got the girl," Larry said.

"Sure I did, spiritually!"

Larry snorted but Edith the peacemaker headed off the incipient quarrel. "Jaymie! What was your favorite role?"

Jaymie had been sitting pensively, listening quietly to the others and sipping on a Sprite. She raised her eyes now and said, "Hedvig. In *The Wild Duck*."

"Hedvig?" Edith frowned.

"That's the little girl, isn't it?" asked Nick. "The one who shoots herself to prove she loves her father?"

"Yes, that's right. I was twelve when I played her. A rep company in a Chicago suburb jobbed me in."

"What was fun about it, honey?" asked Edith, mystified.

Jaymie pushed the can away and frowned. "Not fun, exactly. Just—a revelation."

"That's funny. You've done a lot of musicals, haven't you? I think they're more fun. Did you like it just because it was different?"

"Yes, partly. I'd always done these little-girl things. Song-and-dance, like showing off for Daddy before he— Or you know, baton twirling, tap dancing. So Hedvig was the first time I'd really acted. Got out of myself into someone else's skin. Before, I was always little Jaymie the trained dog, you know? Good at jumping through hoops. But in that show I learned there was much more to acting than that."

"Yeah, that's a heady moment," Nick agreed. "When you find you can be anything. You're not limited to your own boring self. Suddenly you have a ticket to infinity."

"Yes. And after that the other stuff seemed different too," Jaymie said. "I might be doing Queen Victoria or

Annie Oakley, but I wasn't just going through the motions anymore. I could really *be* Annie Oakley, even though she has these silly songs."

Anna Maria appeared by their booth, teetering on thick-stacked clogs, a pad in the too-tight band of her black apron. Frugal with personnel as well as ashtrays, she ran the place with a part-time waitress and a part-time cook to assist her, filling in all the gaps personally. She peered at them through heavily mascaraed eyelashes and inquired, "Anything more, you guys?"

"No, we better get back upstairs," said Edith.

Anna Maria pulled a pencil from the dense frizz of her hair and began to calculate. Larry, suddenly jovial, said, "Anna Maria, you've been onstage!"

She smirked, glancing at him over the edge of the pad. "Only in high school, you know that!"

He gave her the full dazzling benefit of the Palmer smile. "And what was your favorite role?"

She pursed her mouth and drew down her brows in fierce thought for a moment. "It'd have to be Hedda Gabler," she said.

Nick managed to swallow the guffaw inspired by the thought of plump Anna Maria as the athletic, tragic Norwegian, but an unseemly snorting escaped Larry. Anna Maria stiffened indignantly. "Well, I know it's a gloomy play and all," she argued, "but she was trapped, you know? After that play I told myself, Anna Maria, you're going to get a good job and hang on to it, or you'll be at the mercy of some nerd just like Hedda Gabler was. So you needn't laugh, chum," she flung at Larry.

Edith said hastily, "It's a wonderful play, Anna Maria. You're right."

"Well, I own this place, right?" She ripped the bill from the pad and smacked it onto the table. "And I daresay it's more than you guys will ever get out of the theatre!"

"Ouch!" said Larry, fixing her with contrite dark eyes, all humor erased from them now. "Anna Maria, you are the most cruel woman alive. And the most honest."

"Well—didn't mean to hurt your feelings." She gave

a flirty little simper to acknowledge Larry's apology and clogged her way back behind the counter to help another customer.

Reflecting on the unhappy raw truth that Anna Maria had presented to them, they settled the bill and dodged through the rain to the loft entrance next door. Upstairs, Derek was looking idly through the prop box, the stage manager was studying the prompt book morosely, and a few actors were warming up already. But they had to wait because Daphne was late. At last she banged through the door, tossing her damp raincoat into a corner and kicking off her clogs in the same general direction. "Fucking Human Services!" she fumed. "You get an appointment, tell them you have to get back to work, does it make any difference? They made me sit there twenty minutes while they drank coffee! And then they wonder why their clients can't keep jobs!"

"You ought to just walk out on them," suggested Cab.

"Hey, man, you've been on unemployment! This is worse! This is the third appointment I've had this week. Every other time I did walk out, but that doesn't count in my favor, you can bet. Besides, the hearing is Friday afternoon." She was stripping to her burnt-orange leotards. "And then they pop in with a home visit during working hours, and they pretend to be shocked to find a fifteen-year-old baby-sitting her little sister. Want me to get someone to baby-sit the baby-sitter. Christ!"

Nick asked, "What right do they have to meddle?"

"None! No right, man. Power is what they have. Raw power." She was hanging her dashiki-pattern dress carefully on a hook. "See, they aren't my kids. They're my cousin's kids. She OD'd two years ago, okay? And I took in her kids because we'd always been like sisters and because those kids need me. I mean, who else is going to be a mother to a fifteen-year-old black kid who's been expelled twice?" She began to do a few warm-up stretches. "But the agency says no, I've been on unemployment too often, I've got a bad background, I'm not a fit mother."

Her words clanged in Nick's mind. How often had he been on unemployment? How would he score on the fit parent test? He asked, "What do they want to do with the kids?"

Daphne shrugged an eloquent burnt-orange shoulder. "Oh, there's another cousin, a tight-ass school-teacher, they think would set a better example. Kids hate her. Sort of a black Phyllis Schlafly, you know? I mean, the only reason Callie was expelled was that she talks back when her teachers put her down. You heard her mouthing off at Ramona, little idiot."

"Ramona mouthed off at her," said Nick.

"Hey, that's the way this old world works. We had a heart-to-heart on the way home, about choosing battles. But hell, she's a kid yet."

Jaymie asked anxiously, "They won't really take them away, will they?"

"Not while I live, baby! I'm ahead now because I've got good references and because the kids themselves vote for me. But those old bitches look at me and they see Angela Davis Junior. And they think I'll raise the kid to be Angela Davis the Third. God!" Still propelled by anger, she bounded onto the platform. "I swear, that kid can be anything she wants as long as it's not a social worker! Hey, let's get busy. Where are we, Derek? 'The Highland Fling'?"

"Right."

They got busy.

# IV

## Wednesday evening
## March 7, 1973

"See you tomorrow, Myra."

"Okay, Mr. Bradford. And listen, get some rest, okay?"

"Sure. I'll try, Myra." Steve smiled benevolently at his secretary. Myra Goodwin was competent and grandmotherly. Her own beloved son had unfortunately become a gambler and had left New York for the headier atmosphere of Las Vegas. Steve had inherited Myra's motherly concern.

"Yes, do try. You're looking tired these days." Myra ground out her cigarette in the big amber glass ashtray, them tapped an envelope that sat on the edge of her desk. "And here, don't forget your wife's plane tickets. I do hope Mr. Busby will be all right."

"Thanks. I'm sure he will, Myra."

He was lucky enough to find a seat on the commuter train, and glanced out the streaked window as they emerged from the tunnel. Gloomy and rainy; but warmer, at least, than yesterday.

He'd seen Maggie again from a distance today, soaring through the drizzle toward her mysterious destination, a scarlet umbrella shielding her and the baby from the drops. Her smile had been so bright. And she moved with such grace. Those long legs—he let himself daydream a moment. Did he dare hope?

Women came to the white hunter in his tent at night.

The train slowed and Steve sat upright in alarm. Where was he? Only Douglaston. He sagged back into the seat with a sigh.

He wasn't there.

Not yet.

Derek hung up the phone in the stair hall and came back into the rehearsal loft. "Oh, Nick. You're still here."

"Maggie's late tonight. Do you want me to wait outside so you can lock up?"

"No hurry." Derek sank onto a folding chair. He looked desperately tired.

"Was that the hospital you just called?"

"Yes. I waited till the actors were gone so they wouldn't come crowding around. But there isn't any news. They say there's no change."

"Twenty-four hours." That was bad. Nick looked out the big window that opened on a grimy view of the wet roof of Anna Maria's kitchen. He shook his head grimly.

"You saw her, Nick. Was it terrible?"

Remembering, Nick nodded. "You know how lively she always seems, even just sitting still? All that energy was gone." Once he had seen Maggie unconscious, and the shock had been similar: the limp emptiness doubly distressing because her radiant vitality was such an essential part of her presence.

"It's hard to imagine." Derek stroked back his faded hair, and Nick noticed that there were streaks of gray among the blond. "I just can't believe anything could quench that spirit of hers."

"Well, as you said, if she's got any chance at all she'll make it."

"God, I wish they'd let me see her!"

"They have to do their job as they think best, I suppose."

"Yes, but—oh, you're right, of course." Derek lapsed into glumness. After a moment there was a quick beat of steps on the stairs and the door opened.

"Sorry I'm late." Maggie breezed in, shaking out a damp umbrella. "Sarah took her time finishing dinner. Hi, Derek!"

"Hi." He rallied and stood up. "How's the little one?"

"Fine, just slow today." She had put down her briefcase and was unsnapping flaps preparatory to lifting Sarah out.

"May I hold her?" asked Derek.

"Sure. I'll help Nick saddle up."

Derek told Sarah she was a super baby and allowed his nose to be squeezed by a small, inquisitive hand, then helped return her to the carrier, now strapped to Nick. "I wondered," he said very casually, "if you three would like to come along to my place for a bite of steak. I've got a couple of questions about Ramona."

"I'd love to compare notes," said Maggie. "But I've got to help Dan with the Department of Corrections program at work. And Nick has to take care of Sarah."

Derek gave her a wry smile. "Dirty nappies no longer shock me, if that's your worry. I've got three kids of my own back in England."

"That's great!"

"And a dog."

"Yeah, that's another thing. The dog," said Maggie.

Nick could see that she was curious about Derek's proposition and eager to accept despite the obstacles. So was he. He said, "I'll phone Julia." Their downstairs neighbor had their key. "If she can let the dog out, I'll take Sarah over to Derek's and you can meet us there at nine."

"We'll hold the steaks until you arrive," Derek promised. "And we'll pick up anything Sarah needs on our way over. She'll have two expert dads waiting on her."

Derek's apartment was in the Village, two big rooms and a kitchenette. "Belongs to a friend of Ramona's," he explained as he hung their rain-spattered things next to the door. "I've got it for three months. The mess is my fault. The wall things aren't." Ramona's friend went in for metal sculpture, and massive assemblies of straps and chunks of weathered steel, copper, and brass hung on every wall. "Bit like a boiler room, I think."

"Or the inside of a coffee grinder," agreed Nick, touching a jagged edge gingerly.

"Are steaks okay?" asked Derek. "Last week I finally mastered the grill here."

"Sounds great."

"Just pop the infant onto the rug by the sofa there while you fix her dinner. Tidied up there today. Practically the only place I did."

"It won't be tidy when she finishes her cereal," Nick warned.

"Right. We'll lay down something waterproof." Derek pulled out a plastic tablecloth. While Nick fed and changed Sarah, Derek picked up hastily, readied the steaks for the broiler, and prepared a salad. "I wish I had the nerve to call her husband," he said suddenly. "Maybe he's seen her. But I don't want to muddy those waters. She's got problems enough."

"He didn't know she was doing the show?" asked Nick curiously.

"I don't know. She did tell me that if I met him, I shouldn't mention that she's an investor. Maybe he thought she was merely acting in it."

"That would fit," said Nick. "And that little interchange at the rehearsal yesterday meant he'd found out."

"That would be my guess. I wonder how he heard of it? None of us are chums with him. I wondered if it might be Ken Martin. He's the family legal adviser as well as her partner."

"But surely he would know if Simon shouldn't be told!"

"It might be difficult for Martin, though, if he owes allegiance to both of them. You know, I can't help wondering if Simon might have hired—I mean, if he couldn't legally gain control of the production money?" He cocked an eyebrow at Nick.

"Surely not," said Nick. "But I have to admit he was angry." Could Derek be right? Could things have been that ugly between Ramona and her husband?

The intercom sounded and they let Maggie in. She checked Sarah first, who was on the rug again, kicking sturdily and cooing at the lamp. The steaks were ready in a few minutes.

"Well, mates," said Derek as he passed the salad around for the second time, "I wanted to ask you something."

"Fire away," said Maggie, attacking her steak and salad with her usual gusto.

"Nick said she was—what was it? Contrite? Apologetic? About yesterday?"

"Yes," said Nick. "She said she was upset about Simon and had been taking it out on us. Claimed she'd reform."

"She didn't apologize for anything specific?"

"Not really. You're thinking about Larry's solo? I'm afraid not."

"But I think it was included in the general apology," said Maggie.

"I see," said Derek. "Well, it was just a hope."

Sarah was kicking too energetically now, and her cooing had given way to occasional whimpers. Maggie, chewing the last of her steak, excused herself and settled with the baby into a chrome rocking chair. Derek poured Nick the last of the wine and asked, "I was wondering, too, why she suddenly decided to confide in you."

"Instead of you, you mean?" asked Nick, stalling for time. He didn't want to spread stories about the pretended seduction. But his question seemed to upset Derek.

"No, I didn't mean that!" he exclaimed. "Not exactly. Though I am the composer, and so forth."

Nick studied his wine glass a moment, then said, "You know the two of us were the last to leave."

"Yes."

"She was still in a truculent mood and was trying to embarrass me when Maggie walked in," he continued carefully. "So Maggie asked her why, and she admitted being upset over the divorce. The first thing I knew they were hugging and crying and confiding in each other like sisters."

"I see," said Derek, glancing down at his plate. Nick thought his account had been cautious enough, but Derek suddenly slammed his fist against the tabletop and cried,

"Trying to embarrass you! Damn her!" Then he stood hastily and took his plates to the sink. He stood there stiffly a moment, looking at the faucet, then added, "Sorry, mates. I'm just upset about everything," and began scraping the plates vigorously.

"We're all upset," said Nick. "It's not just the work, though God knows that's important to all of us. But also, you can't help getting attached to people when you're working on a show. She's like a member of the family."

"Right." Derek came back for more plates. Nick helped him clear the table.

Maggie was still rocking serenely with the baby. She asked, "How old are your kids, Derek?"

"Eight, six, and the little one is three."

"A lively household."

"Yes." He continued scraping plates.

"Does your wife have a job?"

"Yes, in an office."

"Will she come see the show?"

"No. Look, do we have to talk about my bloody wife?"

" 'Scuse me," Maggie apologized, but Nick, knowing her so well, could see that her interest had quickened. "I'm too curious, as usual. Just wondered what it was like, being a composer in London."

Derek plunked a plate into the sink with unnecessary emphasis and swung around to face her. "It's bloody awful, if you must know. We all live on Elizabeth's earnings. That means a council flat and a pair of new shoes a year, right? Her mum lives a few streets away. A mixed blessing. She minds the children and complains about the rotter Elizabeth married."

"The artist's usual fate," observed Nick.

"Right. I pick up a bit giving music lessons or helping in my friend Ron's pub, and Ron lets me organize little shows in his upstairs room. A few people come to see them. My kids adore them. But they don't make money, of course. Elizabeth's mum complains."

"And Elizabeth?"

"She liked them at first," said Derek shortly.

Nick could imagine the situation: the young wife, ex-

cited about her man's talent and dreams, slowly worn
down as years passed, babies arrived, and neither money
nor fame materialized. At least Maggie loved her work,
was not a hired hand in someone else's office, he reminded himself. But his empathy for Derek had a chilling
personal edge.

"How did Ramona find out about you?" Maggie shifted
subjects, and Derek relaxed visibly.

"Well, I'd put on an early version of *Victoria R* upstairs at Ron's." He opened the dishwasher and added
the scraped plates. "One of the people who saw it there
was a friend of a friend of Ramona's. About a year later
Ramona was looking for a musical piece with a strong
female part, and the friend remembered hearing about
*Victoria R*. Ramona called, I mailed off a tape, and that
was it." His pale eyes were soft with remembered wonder.
"It was amazing, don't you know, after twelve years of
trying to be noticed. Well, I'd sold some songs and had
some good notices for the pub theatre pieces. But it was
a great leap to meet a New York star, offering a New
York production."

"She also asked you to direct."

"Yes, that was amazing too. At first she said she'd
want me for technical advice, history and vocal coaching,
that sort of thing. She flew me here. And then after we'd
talked, she said, let's direct it together."

"And found you an apartment," said Maggie.

"Yes. And even a salary. Most of it goes for the apartment, but still . . ." He grinned, boyish in his pleasure.

Nick forced himself to be a little more temperate in
his enthusiasm; he'd had plenty of friends who had been
convinced that their big break had finally arrived, only
to have the show die in preview, or their part disintegrate
in the rewrites. It was a hard business, with higher highs
and longer lows than most people had to cope with. And
yet Derek's dreams were necessary, almost reasonable.
Nick, too, hoped desperately for good reviews, for splashy
publicity, for a small piece of the glory. "It's a cute
show," he said, "and Ramona's a great performer. We're
all excited about being part of it."

Maggie stood and asked apologetically, "All right if

Sarah and I use your bathroom? She needs a wash and a change."

"Nappie time," said Derek. "Of course. Here, let me get you a clean towel." He bustled into the bathroom and emerged a moment later with a bundle of clothes and towels. "The housekeeping in this place is dreadful. I'd fire the chap who does it if I weren't the chap myself. But go right ahead now, and then come have dessert."

While Derek got out ice cream and raspberries, Nick asked, "Was there anything else you wanted to ask us?"

"A couple of things."

"Okay."

"Did she tell you whom she was meeting?"

"No." Nick was surprised at the urgency of Derek's interest. "We could ask at L'Etoile, I suppose."

"Well, actually I did," Derek confessed. "When I spoke to the police they asked me about it. And this morning I inquired there myself. They were rather cross with me because the police had already been there. But it seems that there was a table for two booked in Ramona's name, but no one had claimed it. Not Ramona, of course, but no one else either."

"That's odd." Like Derek, Nick found this new information troubling. "I wish she'd said something. But she only mentioned the restaurant in passing."

"We were in the midst of a deep conversation," Maggie explained, returning to the table with a fresh-diapered Sarah. "All about divorce and growing old and her hopes for the show. We didn't discuss cocktail plans."

"Hopes for the show?" repeated Derek eagerly.

"She loves her part," explained Nick, "and likes the music-hall approach."

"Yes, she hopes it will sell even if it's not rock."

"It's fun. I like our prime minister duet."

"You were hilarious today!" Derek grinned. "Exactly what Gladstone would be in a warm-up suit! Did you know that the verse you and Edith sing is something he actually sang with his wife?"

"Really? The 'ragamuffin husband' and the 'ranti-poling wife'?"

"Yes. Different tune, I imagine."

"What's 'rantipoling'?" asked Maggie, removing Sarah's fist from her raspberries.

"Rude, noisy, rowdy," said Derek.

"Did Gladstone really have a rantipoling wife?"

"Of course not," said Nick. "She was a member of the highborn Glyn family, a jolly group. They did joke a lot, even invented their own secret language. If they wanted to say someone was worthless, they'd call him a grasshopper's uncle. That sort of thing."

"You've been doing your research!" Derek exclaimed. "But these people are fascinating, aren't they? I mean Victoria and her crew. Marvelous contradictory personalities. Terribly moral and proper but with such unsuitable attachments. Disraeli's young platonic mistress. Victoria's Scotsman. Gladstone's pet prostitutes—you must have read of them?"

"Oh, yes. He'd pick one up, bring her home, and lecture her in the kitchen about how she ought to reform."

"The great orator," said Derek, playing with the salt shaker. "And afterward he'd flog himself because he'd got himself, shall we say, excited."

"Even so," said Nick, "he really believed God wanted him to reform those women, whatever his hidden motives might have been."

"Did the rantipoling wife know about this?" asked Maggie.

"Oh, yes, he was quite open about it," Derek explained. "She helped reform them. They founded a shelter for the repentant. She understood some of his conflicts, I think. He didn't really like politics, would have preferred the clergy. But God had given him the talents of a statesman, and he had to support his family, so he stayed in government and wrote theology in his spare time."

"Any artist would recognize that conflict," murmured Nick, glancing at Sarah. Was Gladstone right? Should he forget his hopeless profession, use his talents for ordinary human things such as money, a solid job, a family?

"Whichever choice you make, the other keeps nagging for attention," agreed Derek soberly. "Do you betray your family or betray yourself?" He glanced at Maggie, suddenly confused. "No, I mean—that's not what I meant!"

But Maggie's eyes were fixed on Nick. She said, "I think the rantipoling wife might have understood, whichever he chose. Women smack into the same dilemma. It's hard to manage to have both." She shifted Sarah to the crook of her arm and smiled at Derek. "Was there anything else you wanted to ask us?"

"Oh. Well, I just wondered if you could tell me a bit more about her injuries. They said internal bleeding."

"Yes." Maggie's deep blue eyes were serious. "She was bleeding in front here, on the left. And from the exit wound in the back. I gave first aid as best I could, but she slid right into shock anyway. I knew there were problems I couldn't see. She'd lost some blood, but not enough to knock her out like that, I thought. So internal bleeding sounds right."

"Can you show me where she was wounded?"

Maggie handed Sarah to Nick and stood up. She rucked up her shirt and pointed to a spot by her lower rib cage. "Right there," she said, then turned around. "And the exit wound was back here, a little closer to her spine. But I don't think the bullet touched bone."

Derek stared at her exposed waist a moment, then leaned his face miserably into his hands. "Oh, bloody hell!"

"I'm sorry, Derek." Maggie's hand dropped to his shoulder.

"I didn't see her, you see." He cleared his throat to get his voice under control. "Up to this very minute it didn't seem real."

"I know. It makes me hurt too."

"At least you were there to help! The police told me if you hadn't been there, there wouldn't have been any chance for her."

"I hope it's a big enough chance."

"She's a fighter," said Derek with little conviction.

"Yes, she is." Maggie patted his shoulder before taking the dessert plates to the dishwasher. Then she looked at Nick and Sarah. "We'd better get our little one home, Derek."

"Yes, I'm sorry to be so silly."

"Will you be all right? We can stay a little while if that's better."

"No, no. I'll manage better alone, I think. It's just that I need time to absorb it. I—well, it just didn't seem real until now." He tried to smile. "It makes one feel such a grasshopper's uncle."

"Well—thanks for the yummy steak."

"I'll see you tomorrow," said Nick.

Derek walked them to the door, his despondence almost palpable.

On the subway, Maggie pulled something from her bag. "Don't know if I should have stolen this," she said. "But I had the feeling he'd be embarrassed if he saw he'd missed it when he cleaned the bathroom."

It was a little purse-size bottle of cologne. Maggie opened it, sniffed, and held it to Nick's nose.

"Damn," he said.

"What?"

"Jasmine," said Nick. "Ramona's."

Sarah did not interrupt that night. She was slumbering soundly before she'd finished nursing. And when Maggie joined Nick in bed, she didn't collapse into instant sleep as usual. She gave his ear an affectionate nibble. Nick's lot in life, despite the exhaustion and uncertainty, had a full share of delights. Grateful and drowsy, he nuzzled her in return, but soon had to give up. He slid into sleep with his hand on her breast.

Nick the dud.

*part two*

# GOD IS WEIRD

*(Thursday, March 8, 1973)*

# V

## *Thursday Afternoon*
## *March 8, 1973*

"My God, Buzz! What happened to you?"

"Maggie! Thank God! You won't believe the day I've had!" His leg bandaged from calf to instep, Steve turned awkwardly on his crutch to face her as she crossed the street to him.

"I'll believe it's been a bad one," she said, the lively eyes sympathetic. She stood patting the baby in the carrier while she looked him over with interest. The afternoon was clearing and she wore her trench coat open over her bright-but-businesslike blue plaid. This year's short skirts showed off her athletic legginess. A springlike breeze ruffled her dark curls. He felt his spirits rising.

"It's not just my leg," he explained. "You see, my wife is out of town today, so I'm in charge of Muffin. And then at lunchtime I took a spill down the stairs at the office."

"Oh, dear."

"Nothing serious, but the ankle's out of commission. And it took hours at the doctor's. And now I'm behind in everything. But the big problem is, Muffin's playschool gets out in fifteen minutes and I have to pick her up. I've got to finish some urgent business that I couldn't do while I was at the doctor's. A lot of big people to apologize to. So I called a sitter to my pied-à-terre around the corner so

I could leave Muffin there and then go back to my office for a couple more hours."

"Sounds like you're solving the problem, more or less. How did you fall down?"

"Just a stupid misstep. I use the stairs for exercise. For my health, ha-ha."

She grinned. "Exercise has that effect on me too. I've taken my share of tumbles from the beam and bars."

"A gymnast?"

"Amateur."

"So you weren't really risking young Sarah's life up on that scaffolding." He felt better about that.

"No, I won't let her do the really tricky stuff with me. The scaffold was a piece of cake. But hadn't you better hurry to pick up Muffin?"

He held up his free hand in hesitant supplication. "Look, Maggie, could I ask a huge favor?"

"Anything I can do in twenty minutes," she said cautiously. "I have to drop off Sarah and get back to work too."

He realized that she feared being asked to baby-sit and hastened to reassure her. "That's all it should take, really, unless you sprain your ankle like me. The sitter's at the apartment already. But you see, they don't have the elevators installed, and I just don't have the hang of this crutch yet. It's three flights up."

"With a two-year-old." She understood the problem instantly. "Hard to carry and harder to lead. How do you want me to help?"

"Well, if you could pick her up at the playschool and take her up to the sitter, it would be a lifesaver."

"How far is the playschool?"

"Four or five blocks. I'll call Mitzi and tell her you're coming. Just ask for Muffin. Please?"

"The sitter couldn't pick her up?"

"I'm sorry. The Carstairs people said the only one available on such short notice was an elderly woman."

She looked at his crutch again and back to his imploring face. "Okay, it shouldn't take long. What are the addresses?"

He found a company memo pad and tore off the

bottom half of a sheet to scribble the numbers. "Here's the key to the apartment," he added. "It's right up this street. Just leave the key with the sitter."

"Okay. And this second address is the playschool?"

"Right. Ground floor. And this is for the sitter." He pressed an envelope into her hand. "Tell her I'll call. And thanks a million, Maggie."

"Sure. Take care of yourself."

He said apologetically, "I wouldn't impose on you but this is really a big project I'm working on at the office. Life or death."

"Well, run along and get it done, then. And don't worry about Muffin." She hurried off.

Steve hobbled to the edge of the sidewalk to watch her winging around the corner, trench coat flaring in the breeze. Then he made his way to a bar and its phone booth. Muffin was safely taken care of. Now he'd ring Mitzi. And he'd give Rachel a call too. Take her up on her offer to help in case of need.

This was need.

God, what a day!

Victoria was screaming.

"Hush, Liebling! Don't be frightened!" Her flaxen wig arranged in frizzy side curls that reminded Nick of extravagant blond earmuffs, Victoria's German governess patted the royal head. "It's naptime. Come!"

Derek commenced a slow waltz-time melody. Jaymie, child-height on her knees, big eyes fearful under the shadow of her dark bangs, stopped screaming and gazed up at Edith, who adjusted the princess's bonnet, coaxed Jaymie's head onto her lap, and sang the lullaby. "Vickelchen, nap in your wee elfin cap, sleeping happy with never a tear." She was projecting the character well, reflected Nick, just a trace of a German accent in the warm voice. "I know a charm that will keep you from harm, and disarm all the demons you fear."

If only something really could disarm demons. Nick's own fears increased with every hour Ramona spent in the hospital. It was Thursday now; she'd been shot Tuesday night. If her coma had been caused by loss of blood alone, the hospital should have had her improving by now, shouldn't it? Derek and Daphne were doggedly referring to Ramona's return as a sure thing, but Nick knew that Derek at least was far from confident. Her condition was still so serious that none of them had been allowed to see her.

Her husband, though, had apparently been visiting her regularly, despite Edith's fears. Derek had met him twice in the hall, he said, but Simon Jenkins looked haunted and had apparently not recognized Derek.

But there was nothing they could do. Except to throw themselves into the rehearsals with professional dedication and with hope.

Jaymie was snuggling up to Edith's ample lap, soothed by the lilting words and the friendly arms.

"Life, like our stories, has goblins and glories. It's gentle and hard as a stone. But I'll be beside you to keep you and guide you. You won't have to face it alone!"

"Won't have to face it alone," echoed the princess drowsily.

"Won't have to—"

"Excuse me, Mr. Morris." A heavy masculine voice broke in.

Derek froze, hands poised above the keys, and twisted his head to look at the intruders. Two policemen stood by the door. Nick recognized the thickset detective who had interviewed him when Ramona was shot.

"Sorry to interrupt, Mr. Morris. But Sergeant Dwyer and I need to ask some questions."

"Certainly, Detective Perez," said Derek, hiding his annoyance in his mild tones. "How many of us do you need?"

"Everyone, I'm afraid, one at a time," said Perez. "The rest of you can continue."

Edith stepped forward, her hands gripping each other nervously. "Does this mean there's news about Ramona?"

"Miss Ricci's condition is unchanged. Our questions are in connection with the mugging and robbery."

"Might I be first?" asked Derek. "Then I could continue with the rehearsal."

"Fine. Pete, talk to him now while I get all the other names."

Derek followed Dwyer out into the stair hall but was back within minutes, and the rehearsal got underway again. It was difficult with people coming and going irregularly, and Daphne finally gave up on the dance and told them to stand still and concentrate on the vocal interpretation. Finally it was Nick's turn, and he joined the detectives in the stair hall while behind him in the rehearsal loft people continued to sing exuberantly about Victoria's sixty-four years on the throne.

In the gray daylight that seeped into the stairwell from the unwashed skylight, the bull-thick Perez still seemed tired, his olive skin lined, curly hair thinning and flecked with gray. He could use a vacation, Nick decided, on a beach somewhere for a week. But the brown eyes were no less intelligent for being weary. "Mr. O'Connor, right?" he asked.

"That's right."

"I know we already have your statement about Tuesday night. Could you just go over it again? Starting with leaving here."

Nick told the story again; he'd gone over it often in his own mind, puzzling over what he might have done.

When he'd finished, Perez asked, "You heard two shots?"

"Yes. But Maggie said she thought there was only one wound."

"Right. Now, did you see a gun in the building when you looked?"

"No. And I wondered about that later, because Edith mentioned that Ramona carried one. But I looked over what had spilled from her bag pretty carefully, and I don't remember a gun."

"Did you personally see Miss Ricci's guns at any time?"

"No, she never showed them to me. I didn't even know she carried one until Edith said so. There were more than one?"

Perez didn't answer, but brought out a plastic bag containing a little ivory-handled derringer and showed it to Nick. "Did you ever see this before?"

Nick shook his head. "Never. Is that what shot her?"

"So you can't identify it."

"No. If it's Ramona's, Edith must recognize it. And Jaymie saw it too, I think, and maybe some others."

"Yes, we've checked with Edith Bigelow." Perez held the bag containing the little pistol in his palm a moment and shook his head. "Pete, did Garcia tell you about that nut in Queens yesterday?"

"No."

"Druggist. Arrives at his store in the morning, sees it's been burglarized, calls the cops. Good citizen, right? Then he takes his gun and goes into the basement himself. Cops get there, hear someone, yell, 'Police, drop your gun!' So the citizen jumps behind a pillar and shoots."

"Christ! What happened?" asked Dwyer.

"They took him out. Serious-but-stable condition. Probably lying in his bed planning his police brutality suit."

"Beats the drugstore business," said Nick.

"Jesus, this town is crawling with make-believe John Waynes who don't realize that thing in their hand shoots real bullets." He replaced the little pistol. "And when they get in trouble, they blame the cops." Perez sighed wearily and turned back to Nick, resigned, not a bull but a curly-polled ox hauling the massive machinery of police investigation to its useful conclusion despite a maverick citizenry. "Now, when you arrived at the building, did you see anyone?"

With an inward sigh he said it again. "No. The only person I know who saw anyone was the young woman. Carlotta something."

"You didn't hear footsteps or anything?"

"We were all the way around the corner. And even Carlotta didn't see much, she said. The shadows were already pretty dark. We couldn't see Ramona until we stepped right in next to her."

Perez brought out a set of police photographs: young black men with Afros, so alike in the baleful boredom with which they regarded the camera that Nick had to focus consciously on the difference in features. "Recognize any of these people?"

Nick looked closely, but shook his head. "Sorry, Detective Perez. Guess I'm not much help today."

"Well, thank you, Mr. O'Connor. Let me know if you remember anything more. Would you please ask Miss . . . let's see, Miss Jaymie Price to come in next?"

Nick returned to the rehearsal, whispered to Jaymie that it was her turn, and took his place in the line. "Sixty-four years!" he sang exuberantly, years of technique and training hauling up an enthusiasm, an emotional memory, that he certainly did not feel today. He prayed that Ramona would have her sixty-four years.

After rehearsal Daphne leaped off the platform and strode angrily toward the door. "All right, Callie, I told you two to wait at Anna Maria's!"

Nick saw the two girls then, pert Callie and a smaller child, skulking next to the door. Callie said impudently, "Hey, Aunt Daph, we saw all those cops coming out! Wanted to see if you'd been collared!"

"I'll tell you who's gonna get collared!" Laughing, Daphne cuffed Callie affectionately on the shoulder, then hugged the younger girl. "How're you doing, Mellie?"

"Fine," said the small one.

Larry, pausing at the door with his jacket slung over his shoulder, asked, "Callie and Mellie? How do you keep them straight, Daphne?"

"It's tough, yeah. My cousin thought she was so musical. Calypso and Melody, she named them. But I don't complain, chum. Gonna make them into dancers yet." She sprang suddenly into a jumping jack, fingers splayed, and capered through a quick little tap step. The girls, grinning, mimicked her.

"Way to go!" Larry clapped enthusiastically. Nick found himself smiling too. Someday maybe he could teach Sarah to dance. Nick Balanchine.

"I'll be dressed in a minute," said Daphne to the girls, and loped away to gather her street clothes.

Callie was looking Larry up and down with frank interest. "Hey," she said, "I know something about you."

"Oh, dear. Hope it's not one of my dirty secrets." He grinned down at her.

She giggled and covered little Mellie's ears. "And about that bitchy Ramona. And also about—"

"Calypso Weaver!" Daphne shouted from across the room. "Hush up!"

"How come?" Callie demanded indignantly. "Just cause she's hurt doesn't make it a lie."

"Nope." Daphne, sliding into her dashiki and clogs, tossed her other things into a tote bag and strode noisily back to the girls. "What makes it a lie is, she's not bitchy. One bad day doesn't make a monster. Else you two would both be bogeymen, right? Now, out!" She shepherded them through the door.

Edith, dressed now, bounced over to Nick. "Who were those fellows in the police photos?" she demanded.

"No idea," said Nick. "I imagine they've connected the gun to one of the men."

"But that was Ramona's gun!"

"I thought it must be. Did she have more than one?"

"She only showed me one."

Derek and Jaymie and some of the others had crowded around. Larry, instead of following Daphne out, joined the group too. "Did anyone recognize any of those photos?" Nick asked generally.

"No," said Derek, "but I noticed that none of them looked particularly young. Do you suppose the witness was mistaken? That it was a teenager, I mean?"

Jaymie said slowly, "I might have seen one of them."

"Really?" They all turned to her eagerly.

She shook her dark head, uncertain. "It might have been someone else. I'm really not sure. But I was walking toward Canal Street right after rehearsal, as usual. I saw someone across the street who might have been one of them."

"Across the street? Are you sure?" Larry sounded dubious.

"No, that's just it. I'm not sure. But there was a guy, and I remember because he looked so tense. But of course I never connected him with what happened to Ramona."

"Still, if you're right, it puts one of them in the area." Nick found himself fired with eagerness to identify the criminal who had hurt Ramona and through her all of them, their families, even little Sarah. "Did the police tell you anything about him?" he added hopefully.

"No. They were pretty secretive."

"Did anyone else see him?" asked Derek.

They all shook their heads. Cab said, "A lot of us went that direction, toward Canal. But I wasn't paying a lot of attention."

"Well, I wasn't looking very carefully either," Jaymie admitted. "But they're going to ask me to look at a lineup tomorrow. Maybe I'll know him."

"Which way did Daphne go that night?" Nick wondered.

"I think she took Callie to Anna Maria's." Jaymie adjusted her paisley scarf.

"Is there a real chance she'll lose the kids?" Nick asked.

"Well, the social workers favor the other relative. That schoolteacher. But she's ahead, she thinks, because the girls prefer her, and because she's got good character references from the head of her dance school and even from Ramona."

"That's good. She's really good with them."

"Yes. I don't know what they've got against her!" declared Jaymie vehemently. "She's a little unconventional, but she's a wonderful mother! Sort of adopted me when I first came to New York." Her voice was warm with gratitude. "She reminds me so much of Loreen. My nursemaid when I was little. And Daphne's a terrific dance teacher of course. That's why my mother signed me up at that school. But she's also willing to hold your hand when you need it."

"She backed you for this job, too," Derek said.

"Yes, she's loyal to her students. It seemed so lucky, because Ramona liked her, and I thought maybe this time . . ."

She trailed off, glancing at the floor, her eyes shadowed by her thick bangs. But most of her listeners could complete the thought. They too had had hopes for this time and had had to suspend hope and ambition for the moment, waiting for Ramona to wake up.

# VI

*Thursday evening
March 8, 1973*

Susan in bed was a wild woman, small and tawny and enthusiastic about every inch of Steve's anatomy. Even a bandaged foot. Just now she was mouthing his toes, affording him a glorious view of rump and thigh. He could wait no longer and hauled her close to wrap his arms around her. "God, Susan, you're the most fantastic thing that ever happened to me!"

She was giggling. "Shut up, lover, and get down to business!"

To see her in the outside world you might not guess her appeal. First impression of Susan: short, pleasant, businesslike except for hair that was always a little mussed. Six months ago she had taken the seat next to his at the bar of a Boston convention hotel to order a beer. Steve, representing Avery Busby at a three-day conference, had looked her over surreptitiously. Not his type, but he'd seen worse. Then she'd asked, without preamble, "Do you think I ought to go to Caracas?"

"Not a question of 'ought,' " Steve had answered. "Some people should, some shouldn't. It's a question of who you are."

She had looked at him squarely then, blue eyes surprised, and something in him had stirred to their promise. "You're right!" she'd exclaimed. "I've been trying to be logical about it. But logic is beside the point, isn't it? I'm going!"

She was Susan Norwood, it turned out, a junior manager for a New Jersey oil company. The position in Venezuela, overseeing employee facilities, could make or break her career. Steve, who had so recently wrestled with a similar decision in his thwarted attempt to go to Japan, knew exactly what she was feeling. The sympathetic discussion in the bar had progressed naturally to a pleasant night, and early morning, in her room. Nothing serious, Steve had told himself as he flew back to New York the next day. Just another one-nighter, like a couple of others back during Elaine's difficult pregnancies. He prepared for this one to join them in the realm of pleasant but unimportant memories. He loved Elaine. He loved Muffin. His life was just about perfect. And anyway, Susan, though pleasant, really wasn't his type.

This happy delusion had lasted four days. But at lunchtime Tuesday he had suddenly realized that he was standing in the checkout line of a bookstore, holding a stack of illustrated books on Venezuela. A hundred dollars' worth. Ridiculous, he'd thought, replacing the books firmly. He already had everything he'd ever wanted. Susan was just a pleasant adventure on the road. Nice, but next to Elaine's beauty, a bit frowzy. Dumpy, almost. Still, he thought as he reshelved the last book, he was mooning over her like a teenager. Better see her here on home territory. Cold light of day. Get her out of his system. From a booth he'd called her office, got her extension, coolly set up a date for a drink after work.

She'd been as tousled as before. As untamed. Twice as fascinating. Steve, dazed, found himself arranging to see her for lunch Friday at her place. Heard himself claiming to be in the process of getting a divorce. And over these last six months, watched himself grow from a typical serious suburban executive on the verge of middle age, into a passionate, adventurous, complete man. Young at heart. And yet—

And yet, he loved Elaine. Truly. They'd been through so much together to achieve their home, their child, their comfortable intimacy. He was an adult, with a reasoned adult love. And he kept an adult grip on reality. He knew the difference between love and mere infatuation.

Therefore, said logic, his feeling for Susan had to be far more than infatuation.

Far, far more. Anything that would lead him to consider leaving a beloved wife, inflicting tragedy on the family he loved deeply, truly, maturely, had to be a passion of fateful proportions.

Susan felt it too. Just last month she had snuggled up to him one lunch hour and confessed, "Steve, you bastard, it's because of you I'm going to Venezuela. And now because of you I don't want to leave."

"God, Susan, then stay!" He pulled the sheets up around them, her green-and-yellow jungle-print sheets.

"What you told me in that bar in Boston was right, though."

"I retract it, then! On sober reflection."

"Sober!" She laughed. "We're a couple of giddy kids, Steve!"

"Well, I love it. I don't want you to go away. I want things to be like this forever."

"Well, I don't!" She'd swung around to sit on the edge of the bed, the short sensuous curve of her back to him. "You know why I'm divorced, Steve? Basically because Bill wouldn't let me grow. Wouldn't let me find out what I can do. It was stifling." She looked at him, unexpected shrewdness in the silvery blue eyes. "You know what I mean, Steve. You're stifled too."

"No, I just like the way things are."

"No, you don't. Otherwise why tell me you're getting a divorce?"

God, she could walk in and out of his mind as though she lived there. He remembered stammering, "Well—"

"Oh, you don't have to lie again, Steve. I never believed that anyway. Any guy who only sees me at lunchtime and maybe an hour after work is not trying to get rid of a wife. I ain't that dumb, honey. I know you don't want to leave her. You just want to play around. Well, fine, that's all I wanted too."

He'd seized hungrily on the past tense. "Wanted? What do you want now?"

"Caracas. Money. Power. Adventure."

"This is adventure! It's not playing around, Susan. It's love."

"Maybe." The remembered sadness in her eyes still gave him a pang. "We know each other pretty well, Steve. Not all the surface details maybe. I don't really want to hear about your wife and all that. But we know each other deep down. You knew from the minute you saw me that this move was right for me. You cut right through the tangle and said it was a question of who I was. I'll always be grateful for that."

Dismayed, Steve had swung around to sit beside her. "But we can't give each other up! This is so right!"

"Maybe." She'd kissed him briskly on the forehead and stood to dress. "But I'm not about to give up my future to stay around and have a lunchtime affair. And I don't hear you saying that you're coming to Venezuela."

"To Venezuela? But my job . . ." He trailed off and hid his confusion in buttoning his shirt.

"Yeah, your job. Your wife. Your whole life. Right." She held up a palm to stay his protest. "It's okay, I don't expect anything more than this, Steve-o. I never did. We'll go on playing around, okay?"

He'd said uncertainly, "Maybe I could fly down sometime, Susan."

"Shhh!" She smiled a sad smile. "Lunch hour's over, Steve. Time for the giddy kids to get back to real life. Like you said, it's a question of who you are."

She was right of course. His own words; he'd been right. That had been a month ago; and though they hadn't talked of it since, Steve had pondered it. And now he had to take the question seriously. Who was he? Was he a man who could accept the challenge of change, of passion, of Venezuela? Who could look death in the eye and emerge a man? Or was he doomed to mere dreams of Kilimanjaro, just a stolid soul playing at being a giddy kid?

Of course he had thought of simply leaving Elaine,

but that was a kid's solution. Hopping a freighter to Venezuela, living off the jungle. And things were so complicated. Muffin, sweet baby, might be too young to be much affected; but a lump came to his throat at the mere thought of leaving Elaine, so good, so loving, so deserving. It couldn't be true that she had been marked for tragedy; that he, who loved her so deeply, had been chosen by fate to hurt her! He wished that things could stay as they were. But Susan couldn't stay, she was right; it would stifle her glorious spirit. Her destiny was in Venezuela, in adventure. But Steve felt sundered: how could he love both these women so deeply?

He thrust the worry away. Susan was leaving; he mustn't fret away these last minutes together. He gave her a squeeze.

"So this is the last time? You can't see me off tomorrow?" Susan asked wistfully.

"God, I wish I could! But there's no way to get away tomorrow. But I swear, Susan, I'll see you somehow in Caracas. This isn't the last time."

"I wish I could believe you! But thanks for understanding anyway. You know you're the only guy I know who understands?"

"Everyone else thinks you're crazy to go?"

"Well, not Wilson." Wilson was her boss. "He sees it as a shrewd career move. But even he thinks it's a wild country for a woman alone."

"Not for you, Susan. You'll tame it. Easy."

"Mmm." She returned his squeeze. "That's for saying all those nice things I wish I could believe. But anyway, don't worry. I'll be fine."

"I know. I just wish—" He stopped himself, kissed her, and reached for his jacket. There wasn't time to say all the things he wished. They hugged each other good-bye, and he caught a cab for the airport.

After rehearsal Nick had to wait for Maggie a few moments. She and Sarah hurried in at last. "Had to run an errand for someone," Maggie explained. "And then Sarah needed changing, at an inopportune time. As usual."

Nick made a fierce face at his daughter. "Were you inopportune?" he demanded.

Like Nick, Sarah had brown eyes and almost no hair. She produced a huge gummy smile that lit up the universe. "Jesus Christ," muttered Nick.

Maggie was amused at his susceptibility. "Amazing, isn't she?"

"Lethal." He ticked off a list as he strapped on the carrier. "Also useless, demanding, expensive, time-consuming. She has repulsive personal habits. She monopolizes our house with her junk and our time with her mewling and puking. All that's on one side. On the other side, there's that stupid grin."

"And?" Maggie was grinning too as they started down the stairs.

"No contest," Nick admitted.

"Yeah. Lethal," Maggie agreed. She leaned over to kiss Sarah, who cheerily drooled onto her scarf.

Nick helped her wipe it off. "Listen. They probably won't tell us anything, but I'd sort of like to stop by the hospital. Want to come along?"

"Yeah. I was thinking of doing that myself. Things are slow at the office anyway. Dan's hit a glitch in the computer program we're using for the Corrections project, so I can't do much anyway till it's straightened out. Actually I was just going to work on the taxes."

"And you with a Ph.D. in theoretical statistics."

"Listen, tax consultant ain't so bad. I'm also washerwoman and wet nurse, and Sarah here pays less than minimum wage."

"I've noticed. Hope Actors' Equity doesn't find out I've been moonlighting for her. Has she—"

"Nick? Nick O'Connor?" A new voice halted them.

"Yeah?" He looked back.

It was the blonde who had visited the rehearsal two nights ago. Tonight she was in a skinny purple sweater, suede miniskirt, stylish clogs that made those splendid legs look even longer. She fell into step beside them. "I'm Didi," she said, fidgeting with her purple beads, wrapping them around her finger one way, then the other. "Friend of Larry's."

"Yeah, I saw you the other night. If you're looking for Larry, he left about fifteen minutes ago."

"I know."

"Oh. Um, this is Maggie, and this is my daughter, Sarah."

"Hi." Didi wasted only a glance on them before turning back to Nick. "Look, is Larry in trouble? About this Ramona Ricci thing?"

"We're all worried about her. About the show."

"No, I mean the cops."

"Not that I know of. Maybe you should ask him."

A pretty shrug. That purple sweater was a very effective garment. "Yeah, but we had sort of a fight the other night. But I noticed today the pigs were here."

"They talked to all of us."

"But the paper said it was a mugging. If they're looking for a mugger, why are they talking to you?"

"Good question. I think they may have found the gun that shot her. Wanted to know if any of us recognized it or the guy who had the gun."

She spiraled the beads around her finger again. "Why should you guys recognize it?"

"It belonged to Ramona, they tell me."

Maggie mused, "So the idea is that the mugger got Ramona's own gun away from her and shot her with it?"

"Why not? Happens all the time," said Nick. "But they were there to ask questions, not answer them. I'm just guessing from what they asked about."

Didi said, "Ramona's not dead, is she?"

"No. We hope she'll be okay."

"That song she sang about being alone blew my mind. But afterward she seemed a real bitch."

"Not really. She was having a bad day when you saw her."

"Larry says she's after him. He can't shake her."

Nick started to answer, but Maggie was ahead of him. "Must be annoying to him," she interjected sympathetically. "Do you know Larry pretty well?"

Didi shrugged again. "That's just it. Not very well. My girlfriend Linda dated him a couple of times and

brought him over to the apartment. I liked him. Then
he dropped her and split for a couple of months. Then
I bumped into him at a dance class, and he called me
that night. But he's hard to get close to. The other night
was only the third time I'd seen him and we had that
fight. Linda said she hadn't learned anything about him
either, except he splits if you get too serious. Some kind
of ego trip, she said. I should have paid attention."

"He was getting ready to split, you think?" The full
power of Maggie's sympathy was directed at Didi. I've
got two lethal women, Nick realized.

"I was trying not to let it get heavy. But Ramona
made some crack as we were leaving, about a brunette.
Nick, was there really a brunette?"

Sometimes cruel truth was kindest. Nick said, "There's
been someone or other, a couple of nights a week. Not
that we've been rehearsing that long."

"Yeah." She was not surprised, just morose. She
dropped the strand of beads. "I should have known.
Half a dozen decent guys I could have, and I fall for the
prick."

"God, that hurts." Maggie had known a prick or two
in her day. "He lied to you?"

Didi squared her shoulders, tossed back the blond
fall of hair. "Okay, I don't want to knock him. Larry
told me he was one hundred percent for his career. Told
me he couldn't get committed, you know, just wanted
everyone to have fun. Big deal. Say that and then—well,
shit, a guy says you're gorgeous, and you're having a
good time, really tripping on each other—well, you sort
of hope it'll go on awhile."

"I know. It's happened to me. Before Nick."

"Yeah, and all those complaints about Ramona chasing him, maybe that was just a warning for me. Damn."

Maggie had stopped at the corner. "You think you
can drop him? I mean, if his idea of just having fun isn't
enough for you."

"Why do I always think they'll reform?" Didi, hands
thrust into her miniskirt pockets, shoulders hunched,
had found a stray sheet of newspaper in the gutter and

was industriously trying to maneuver it into the storm sewer grating with the toe of her clog. "Anyway, I suppose I can tell the pigs he was with me that night."

Maggie's eyes narrowed a fraction. "But not long, because you had a fight about Ramona, right?"

"Look, don't tell them that, okay? No sense in screwing him up. See, we were supposed to be together all night, so he couldn't have planned to shoot her, no matter how pissed off he was!"

"I'm sure he didn't," soothed Nick, jiggling Sarah, who didn't approve of standing still. "He's got a terrific part in this show. Two terrific parts, Albert and Disraeli. No matter how much he hated Ramona, he wouldn't endanger that."

"One hundred percent for his career," agreed Didi bitterly.

"Right. No need to lie to the police, they'll figure that out."

"Maybe. Maybe they won't even ask me. Anyway, it doesn't make any freaking difference to me anymore, does it?" With a toss of the golden hair she abandoned the sewer grating and strode back down the street. Nick's eyes lingered on the unconscious grace, the swing of trim hips. Larry must be crazy.

Maggie turned toward the hospital but gave Nick an uneasy glance. "He sounds like the original Playboy."

"Mm-hmm."

"Do you feel tied down, Nick?"

"Of course. But I had a turn at Larry's kind of life. Depressed me."

"But this gets depressing too." There was an odd raw note in her voice. Fear? Was she worried too?

"Occasionally," admitted Nick. Not eager to explore the question, he reassured her with another truth. "But you see, my taste in women has changed. Voluptuous blondes are all very well, but nowadays the ones that really make me melt are bald and toothless."

Maggie laughed, the shadow between them diminished. "Yeah, those are my favorites too. Sorry I was late tonight."

"You said you had an errand. Not just Sarah, then?"

"No, can't blame it all on her." She frowned. "It was odd. I'd like your reaction."

"Sure."

"Okay. A day or two ago I met a guy named Buzz. Well dressed, thirties, some sort of banker or executive maybe. Seemed pleasant. He has a little two-year-old daughter. We just talked a minute and went our ways. Then today I saw him again. He had problems. Battalions of them. Most notably, he'd fallen down the stairs and sprained an ankle. They'd bandaged him up, but he had some sort of big deal going and wanted to finish today, though it meant working late. But his wife was out of town and he was in charge of his kid."

"Well, he's got my sympathy!" said Nick fervently.

"Yeah, mine too. He was coping fairly well. He'd arranged for a sitter to meet him at his little pied-à-terre, he called it. It's a fourth-floor studio in an old cast-iron building they're renovating, not far from here. The building doesn't have elevators yet."

"And him with a bad ankle."

"Yes. He seemed desperate, Nick. How was he going to get her from the playschool and up to the sitter?"

"The trials of papahood. Two-year-olds are supposed to be even harder to manage than Sarah." Nick too had been reading Spock. He inspected his daughter's drowsy head uneasily.

"And they're a lot heavier than Sarah," Maggie agreed. "Anyway, he asked me to do it, and he was so desperate and so rushed I said yes. Neither place was far away. He also gave me the money for the sitter, in an envelope."

Nick frowned. "Trusting soul."

"Maybe Sarah gave him confidence in me. Anyway, there weren't any problems. I went to the school, a Montessori school not far from your old stomping grounds, the Sullivan Street Playhouse." Nick nodded. That had been a good part, back when he'd had some hair. Life had been very different then. Maggie went on, "I asked for Muffin. They said her dad had called, and they handed her right over. Cute little girl. Very solemn about me, but she got interested in Sarah and didn't complain. So I took her to the apartment. Only one section of them is finished. The rest of the building is all stacks of two-by-fours and Sheetrock."

"Sounds like home."

"Yes. The sitter was there in the hall of the finished section. Complaining about her arthritis and how lucky I was to be young. Her name was Mrs. Golden. Working-class grandmother. Smoked a lot and talked more. I gave her the key and Muffin and asked if I could change Sarah there."

"So what's your worry?" Nick adjusted the strap of Sarah's carrier on his shoulder. "Sounds as though he'd solved his problems."

Maggie scowled at the DON'T WALK sign. "It's a bunch of little things I got to thinking about on my way over. For one, Mrs. Golden wasn't quite what I think Buzz would hire. I'd expect a nanny or maybe a motherly Jamaican or a college-bound high-schooler. Of course he had to arrange it all in a rush, but I'd think he'd have people he could call on."

"Well, it was an unexpected problem."

"Yeah. But also, the apartment was odd. It's tiny, all newly furnished, and just doesn't look like Buzz's place."

"How do you know what his place should look like?"

"He's doing well, okay? Burberry, nice watch, shoes, briefcase. But the apartment was small and dark. Opens onto an airshaft. From the hall you can see that some others in the finished section have much better views. Even if there's a price difference, he seems like the kind of guy who'd want the better one."

"Maybe he puts all his money into clothes."

"Maybe. But the furniture was odd too. New but cheap. I mean, somebody with a Burberry, who uses words like 'pied-à-terre,' doesn't get his furniture at Woolworth's."

"I see what you mean. Still, it's obviously not his main home."

"Yeah. It just seemed fishy. Like walking into a stage set. Or as though he'd got it for someone else."

"Well, as long as the little girl was all right, it's not your job to worry about his private life."

"You know, that would explain why he didn't get his regular sitter. Maybe he doesn't want anyone he knows to know about the apartment."

"You're sure she's not his regular sitter?"

"She said it was the first time she'd worked for Mr. Hartford. She chattered on about her own family. Her daughters and her nephew. Jerry something. Abelson? Anyway, she did point out that the lock was lousy. She was right. I wouldn't have needed the key he gave me."

Nick grinned at his dexterous and not always law-abiding wife. "Not everyone has your talents."

"Some bad guys do. And Nick, this was his daughter!"

"Yes." Nick glanced down at his own and was flooded with protective feelings as they turned up the walk to the hospital entrance. "I sure wouldn't have done it that way. I would have called someone I knew. Do you think Mrs. Golden is okay?"

"I guess so." She remained dubious. "She may talk poor little Muffin's head off, but except for that, she seemed competent and kind."

"Well, you did the favor as requested," said Nick reasonably. "What more could he expect?"

She shrugged and nodded. He pushed open the doors, and they turned their worries to Ramona.

# VII

*Thursday night*
*March 8, 1973*

The hospital desk was besieged by a milling crowd of worried people—a gaunt man in a frayed parka who was head of a chattering Hispanic family, a black woman carrying a wide-eyed little boy, a pale and very pregnant Northern European woman, a stocky nun holding the hand of an olive-skinned girl, a florid man in a moving-company jacket. Nick and Maggie finally worked their way to the desk and asked about Ramona.

"No change," said the receptionist crisply. She probably didn't lack compassion, Nick decided; but she wouldn't be able to do her job if she became involved with every sad case. Her light eyes focused on the observant Sarah an instant and she asked, "Are you immediate family?"

"No. Friends."

"I'm sorry. Only family is allowed to visit until her condition improves."

"Thank you." Maggie glanced at Nick, resigned: fight this battle later, if at all. They turned away.

At the door the nun waylaid them. "I heard you ask about Ramona." Her black eyes were bright, her middle-aged face concerned. She still held the hand of the snaggletoothed girl, maybe twelve, who looked shyly at her shoes.

Nick said, "Yes."

"Do you know what happened? They wouldn't tell me. I just took Luisa here to a dentist I know, and we stopped by but couldn't get past the desk. And I saw her husband, but he was very short with me, poor fellow."

"My wife and I found her."

"Oh, glory be!" Something about her buck teeth gave her smile a delightful zaniness, as though Bugs Bunny had stepped from the screen into a convent. She tapped Sarah's nose. "And look at the little darling, fresh from God! Please, come sit a minute and tell us about it. You know, we'd gone out, and then I remembered my umbrella and came back and heard you ask about her. I'm so glad!" A stubby powerhouse, she pointed with her furled umbrella as she bustled them toward some plastic chairs that had just been vacated by the Hispanic family. "It's serious, they say," she prompted as they sat down.

"Yes. She was shot."

The black eyes squeezed shut in a sympathetic grimace. "Poor sweet! How did you come to find her?"

Nick sketched out the situation. She nodded gravely and asked, "She was unconscious?"

"Yes. Bleeding a lot," said Maggie. She took Sarah into her lap, where she began grabbing at Luisa's ear. Both children were highly amused.

"I hope the doctors can fix her up," said Nick.

"Yes. I'm so glad you two were there for her!"

"I keep thinking, if we'd just walked her to the restaurant," said Nick, despite his resolve not to play if-only. Maybe the sight of her habit aroused thoughts of confession. His sorrow and remorse still prickled very close to the surface. "I wish we had."

She offered understanding, not absolution. "So do I, child, but what do we know?"

Maggie said, "Sister, excuse me, but I wouldn't have expected Ramona to be a close friend of yours."

She chortled. "I wouldn't have expected it either! But you see"—she leaned forward and imparted the information with merry emphasis—"God is weird!"

Even Maggie was taken aback. "Yes, maybe so, Sister."

"Weird and wonderful. Beyond us mortals. We don't

know who we are or what we can do." She rocked back so vigorously that her chair creaked. "It was years ago that I met Ramona. I had just started at the shelter in South Brooklyn. Here." From the folds of her gown she handed Nick a soiled card. *St. Thomas Center*, it said, and scrawled underneath, *Sister Alphonsus*. She went on, "Ramona was sixteen. I'd seen her with some of the high school girls who came by, but she'd never stayed long. Then she appeared one night. Black eye, bruises, and a suitcase. 'Sister,' she said, 'I'm going to Times Square to be a whore!' 'Fine,' I said, 'and what do you want from me, a subway token?' "

They couldn't help laughing along with Sister Alphonsus's exuberant remembered mirth. Even shy Luisa was grinning at her shoes.

She continued, "Well, she was sixteen, didn't think it was funny. She threw her suitcase at me and broke a lamp, and I saw she wanted a fight. So I picked up a broom and chased her into my room and locked the door." She caught Luisa's amazed glance and nodded vigorously. "Yes, I did so! And you remember it, child! Ramona hollered a while and then settled down for the night. I slept on the lumpy old couch. Next morning she was ready to talk."

Nick had a sudden hunch. "Did you take her some cocoa?"

"Yes. Yes, I believe I did." She looked serious now, as much as her cartoonlike features allowed. "And she told me about her dad, who was alcoholic and alternated spoiling her and beating her. Her mother had long since been broken, but Ramona was tougher. Loved him but hated what he did to her. And she asked, what can I do? So I said, 'I'll tell you after breakfast.' "

"Good idea. Get some food into her," said Maggie the ever-ravenous.

"Oh, it wasn't that!" That tipsy grin again. "I needed time, you see! I didn't have the faintest idea what to do. I'm such a lamebrain, don't know why God chose me. I wonder about His taste, you know? But people are broken sometimes, and I'm sent the strength to help." She

gave an enthusiastic little bounce on the abused chair.
"Like that time with Ramona! See, during breakfast—
all kinds of people come to us, you see, and some need
breakfast—Ramona looked around the table and suddenly started clapping her hands. And she started singing
'I'm Gonna Wash That Man Right Outa My Hair.' Well,
I think she meant her dad. But that doesn't matter. The
point is, all the bums and even old sober Sister Catherine
Mary fell right under her spell. Clapping along with her,
grinning like fools. So God put Heck Callahan in my
head. We'd gone to St. Francis grade school together."

"I see," said Nick. Callahan had been a leading producer in the fifties.

"I called him and woke him up, I think, and told him
he had to look at this kid. And he swore at me and then
found out I'd become a nun, and he got so embarrassed
he said he'd do it. So after breakfast I asked Ramona
to think of her two favorite songs and go sing them for
Heck."

"And the rest is history."

The funny smile lit her face again. "A lot of people
forget. Ramona hardly ever came back. For a while I
think she was afraid of meeting her dad, and later she
was so famous. But she didn't forget. Twice a year she
sent money."

Nick said, "She told us you were her best friend."

"Oh, it's not me. Someone she sees through me and
won't admit." Sister Alphonsus nodded emphatically.
"And I see Him through her, and through the other
wonderful people I meet. I like this battered old world,
but it takes a lot of work, a lot of helping each other."
She glanced at Luisa. "Luisa's mom is working hard
now."

"At the detox," Luisa volunteered with a timid peek
at Nick. "Then she'll be better and get a job."

"But meanwhile somebody has to get Luisa to a dentist. Well, I think, hey, you with the buckteeth, you don't
want her to end up like you! So I get moving."

"Your center is for kids?" Maggie asked curiously.

"That's our focus. But sometimes the best way to

help the kids is to give mom a breather, or coax dad into finishing high school, or just get the whole family a square meal." She grinned. "Ramona is such a tease. Calls it Band-Aids for Broken Lives. Well, most people mend soon with a little help. We do need more family support for times when a family's life gets rough. Ramona hopes to help with that. And a few times I called her about some other kid she could help. She always razzes me. Says her big break came in *The Devil's to Pay* so it couldn't have been God responsible. But she always does what I ask."

Nick had a sudden vision of Sister Alphonsus, glorying in the huddled humanity of South Brooklyn, doling out a bag of groceries for this one, a set of braces for that one, a whole new life for the other one, all with the same loopy thankful grin. Maggie's questioning eyes met his, and he nodded. She thrust a twenty at Sister Alphonsus.

"Here, Sister. To get someone a Band-Aid."

"Oh, Luisa, look! It's the rest of Mrs. Hamed's rent money!" crowed Sister Alphonsus.

"Mrs. Hamed? Doesn't sound very Catholic to me," teased Nick.

"Oh, Catholic, schmatholic! If God wants us sorted out that way, He'll just have to do it Himself," she snorted. "You see, Mrs. Hamed's youngest swallowed four big buttons, so they had some expenses they hadn't expected. And their papers haven't come through, so they aren't eligible for medical plans yet." She stood up briskly. "We'd better go or Luisa's sister will start to worry about her."

"Yes," Nick agreed. They all went out into the cool evening. "Sister, I'm glad Ramona has a friend like you."

"Oh, I do hope she does all right! Well, she's strong, and I'll get everyone to pray for her."

"Good."

"Yes, God is wonderful!" She hooked her tightly rolled umbrella over one arm and reclaimed Luisa's hand, then glanced back at the hospital with a puzzled shake of her head. "But weird."

\* \* \*

Nick and Maggie had reached the hospital parking lot entrance when a gray limousine pulled out in front of them. The driver, tense, hunched over the wheel with a solemn Great Dane look. Nick leaped toward the car and banged on the windshield.

"Mr. Jenkins! Excuse me!"

"What the hell do you think you're doing?" Jenkins bristled through the two-inch gap where he hadn't closed his side window.

"I'm sorry. It's just that I'm a friend of Ramona's. I thought you might tell us how she's doing."

"My God!" he exploded, his spiky brows lowering. "First that little shit of an Englishman, and that nun, and now you! Don't any of you have any respect?"

"Yes. But we care about Ramona too."

"You care about her goddamn *money*! You're one of those goddamn actors, right?"

Nick felt his jaws tighten. "Yes, sir, I'm one of those goddamn actors, sir," he said mildly.

"Look, cut the sarcasm. I'm not interested in talking to any of you. Only one I want to talk to is that joe who found her at that construction site."

"At your service," said Nick. "Sir."

"What?"

"I'm the joe. I found her. My wife and I."

The haggard eyes shifted to take in Maggie for the first time. "That your baby?"

"No, we pick up strays as a hobby."

Jenkins ignored his words. "The police mentioned a baby. All right, look, hop in and we'll go talk." He pushed a button to unlock the doors. Maggie took Sarah around to the front passenger seat while Nick sank into the capacious back. Upholstery as soft as moss, the luxurious scent of thick leather.

"I'm afraid I can't talk long, Mr. Jenkins," said Maggie as the big machine glided, purring, into the street. "Have to get back to my work."

"You're not involved with this damn show, then?"

"No. I'm a statistician."

Jenkins scowled. "Financial? Never heard of you."

"No, consultant for people who want to analyze survey results, evaluate programs, that kind of thing. We work with corporations, academics, government projects. But that's not what you want to know from us."

"No, I—look, where are you going? I'll drop you there."

She gave the address and he shifted lanes. "What I wanted to know," he said, "was how the bastard got away. The police kept evading the question."

"They probably don't know," said Maggie. "I could give you our theory. We think that the kid ran through the building to the next street." She explained once again about the sheltering scaffolds, broken plywood walls, and the emptied handbag.

"Nobody saw him running away?"

"No. So our guess is that he ran back to the next street. There was a construction scaffold. Good cover."

"I see. Look, you said 'kid.' Why 'kid'?"

"Mr. Jenkins," said Nick, struggling to lean forward from the depths of the upholstery, "the police apparently haven't told you much."

"Damn evasive," Jenkins agreed.

"Well, you see, we'd like a trade," explained Maggie. "The police have been evasive with us too."

"Well, you were the last to see her! How can I know you didn't shoot her?"

"You can't," said Nick. He wished the seat weren't quite so deep and soft, engulfing him in yielding luxury that made movement difficult. He shoved himself awkwardly forward to balance on the round front edge of the cushion. "We can't know that you didn't shoot her, either."

But Jenkins seemed more astonished than offended. "Me? My God, why?"

"Quicker than divorce," explained Maggie drily.

"And you get her money," added Nick.

"Her money! Goddamn it, she won't die! And who the hell do you think wants the goddamn divorce? Not me!"

"That wasn't exactly a friendly discussion you had with her at rehearsal."

"That's none of your business."

"Maybe not. But she did tell us you were having an affair," Maggie said.

"God, that stupid woman!" Jenkins groaned. "And Ramona too. I wouldn't have expected her to be spreading that around. Yes, okay, I was seeing someone. But it didn't mean anything! It's just that Ramona gets involved in these projects and nothing else exists for her. I might as well be on the moon. So, okay, this time there was someone . . . well . . . available. And I thought I'd keep myself amused."

Nick had heard this story a hundred times: the devoted actor, obsessed with a role, neglecting everything else in life. And the bewildered partner reacting in jealousy against the loss of primacy, calling the reaction revenge or self-discovery or amusement, like Jenkins.

Jenkins repeated, "But it didn't mean anything."

"I guess it did to Ramona."

"I don't know why she couldn't understand! She's got all these Catholic hang-ups even though she hasn't been to church in years. I've explained to her before, when she got into these spells—but Ken Martin told me she was really over the edge this time. Really furious."

"She just found out?" asked Maggie.

"That idiot woman phoned her! Of course Ramona hit the ceiling. Ran straight to Ken to file for divorce. Didn't have any Catholic hang-up about that! He tried to talk her out of it, of course. Been my friend for years. But he couldn't."

"She was very upset," said Nick. The car bumped over a pothole and he slid helplessly back into the enveloping seat.

"But we'll work things out. Somehow. She'd promised to talk to me, that very night."

"So you want to save the marriage?"

"Of course I do! Ramona—well, she's special."

"You're right," Nick agreed, but wondered how much of Jenkins's disclosure was true. He watched the streetlights sliding past the rear window. "You think Ken Martin is helping you? And Ramona too? I don't understand."

"It's awkward for him, all right. But he's been the family lawyer for quite a while. It's not the first time she's gone sneaking off to him behind my back. You knew before I did that she'd roped him into this idiotic musical project. But he said he told her he'd insist on her getting someone else for a divorce action. She stormed around, of course, and . . . well, in the end he told me I might have to get someone else. But all this—what the hell difference does it make now?"

Nick hitched himself forward again. "Is her condition that bad, then?"

"She's—and those idiotic cops! Say they're doing all they can, but they won't tell me anything, and from what I can gather, they're convinced it was one of those men in the photos."

"And you're not convinced?" asked Maggie.

"Well, she was in such a mood after that stupid woman called her. I wondered if she'd got herself into trouble. If it was someone she knew."

"Such as us."

"Exactly."

"Well, it's true that she was ripping into us that day," said Nick. "You're right about the mood. But she didn't seem suicidal, if that's what you're suggesting. More like distracted. Maybe not as alert as she should have been. And the police seem to think there's evidence that there was a mugger."

"What evidence?" he asked, gruffly eager.

"Please, Mr. Jenkins, tell us how she is."

Jenkins glanced at Nick in the rearview mirror and shrugged. "Bad," he said brusquely. "Coma. Looks . . . well, she's full of tubes, wires. It's just not Ramona. She got a little better the first few hours, then something happened, a blood clot or something. Set off all their alarms. They added some tubes and she's stabilized again now. But the nurses . . . well, I don't know how to put it exactly." His voice thickened. "They all became more distant. More mechanical. Stopped telling me to buck up. Just told me occasionally to go get something to eat." He gave a sidelong glance at Maggie, who had hidden her face against Sarah's head, and said furiously, "Look, you asked!"

"Yes. We wanted to know," said Maggie, turning to look at him directly. "It must be hell for you too."

"God, if only—" Jenkins broke off, scowled out at the traffic. His hands tightened on the wheel.

Nick cleared his throat. "You asked why we said 'kid.'"

"Yes." Jenkins drew his thoughts back to the present. "Did the police show you photos?"

"Yes. They weren't kids," Nick confirmed. "But there was a witness, a woman who had been walking a few steps behind Ramona. She said it was a black kid. But she admitted she didn't see him well, just a glimpse as he dragged Ramona farther into the building."

"I see. A witness. What was her name?"

"I don't know," Nick lied, suddenly reluctant to expose Carlotta to Jenkins's inquisition. "Besides, she only caught a glimpse. The other thing is that I think the police found the man who stole her gun. One of the photos."

"But how did he get the pistol?"

"Maybe he's a small man. Maybe he's the kid's big brother. Maybe the witness was wrong."

"That's not what I mean," said Jenkins. "She'd hang on to her bag. He couldn't get the bag without the gun, could he? And he couldn't get the gun without the bag."

Nick pondered that. Carlotta had said nothing about a struggle or screams. But then she'd been running away, screaming herself, before the shots were fired. She might not have heard Ramona. He said, "Suppose the guy snatched her bag and she chased him. He happened to find the gun in the bag and shot her."

"Must have found it pretty fast," said Maggie dubiously. "Look, here's our corner, Mr. Jenkins."

Jenkins double-parked and Nick got out and took Sarah from Maggie. Maggie leaned back in and touched Jenkins on the arm. "Thank you. Take it easy, if you can."

He met her sympathetic gaze and his jowly face crumpled. "I'll never forgive myself!"

"She was upset, yes, but when you explain—"

"Oh, I know, we would have worked it out about the divorce. I don't mean that," he said roughly. "I mean, I bought her those goddamn pistols. For her goddamn fortieth birthday."

He was pulling away almost before she could shut the door.

Evening offered no relaxation. Nick fed and bathed his daughter as usual, but when Maggie arrived at nine-thirty he had to leave again instantly for a late appointment that his vocal coach had arranged. When he let himself back in, well after eleven, he found them in the bedroom rocking chair. Sarah was still nursing, drowsily euphoric at her mother's breast. Maggie too was dreamy, absorbed in the baby's happiness. Nick felt a wrenching at his roots, a surging primeval love for both of them. "Ahem," he said.

Maggie smiled up at him through mists of contentment. "She's almost done, love."

"I can change her."

"Good. I need a shower. Hey, *chouchoute*, you ready to go?" She sat the baby upright on her knee. Sarah woke up a little and belched.

"Go team," said Nick. Sarah noticed him and cracked that awe-inspiring grin of hers.

"Nick, how're you doing?"

He sat on the bed. "Okay. Made real progress on the Gladstone numbers tonight. But I still worry about Ramona."

"Yeah. So do I. Jenkins wasn't encouraging." Maggie handed Sarah to him and got out a clean diaper.

"Things okay with you?" he asked.

"Well, Dan's having some trouble at the office."

"What kind of trouble?"

"You remember that job we got from the Department of Corrections analyzing parole board decisions?"

"Yeah, I think so."

"They awarded it to us because I'm a whiz at multiple regression and Dan's a whiz at computers. When I told him how it should be set up, he thought it would be easy to adapt his regression program."

"And it wasn't?" Sarah was squirming. Nick propped her on his knee.

"We can't put in all the variables we need, it turns out. Program itself takes up too much room."

"I don't follow." Sarah was beginning to bounce on his knee. He held her delicately under her tiny arms.

"See, this program has a lot of options we don't need, and they take up core space. So Dan has to write a whole new program for this one analysis."

"Hey, look at that! You little Amazon!" Sarah had straightened her legs and was standing upright, her plump little body leaning into his supporting hands, her little toes kneading his thigh as she tried to jump.

"Yeah. Anyway, things are sort of at a standstill for my part of it," said Maggie morosely. "Until he gets the program done. Next week, he says."

Sarah's delight in the bouncing game was infectious. Nick was overwhelmed by her amazing trust in him, her joy in the developing abilities of her uncoordinated little body, her sheer glee in being alive and healthy and loved. After a moment he noticed that Maggie had said something. "What?" he asked, eyes still homed in on Sarah.

"Goddamn it, Nick, I'm here too! I asked you a question!" She jerked her bathrobe from a hook.

"Hey, c'mon, Maggie! Don't be jealous of your own daughter!"

"Yeah, okay. But I want to talk, and you're cooing to her."

"Well, it's nothing to get upset about."

"Isn't it? I thought maybe you, of all people, would understand!" She disappeared into the bathroom with a slam.

Dismayed, Nick stared at the door, then took Sarah to her table to change the diaper. "Your mother baffles me," he told her, worried.

"Ah-yah." Sarah grinned, not worried at all.

At the arrival gate, Elaine was pleased and surprised. Damn, she was a nice woman, thought Steve. So full of love and beauty. She exclaimed, "Steve! You didn't have to come!"

"I wanted to. Had to stay late at the office anyway. I've had quite a day too."

"Where's Muffin?"

"Home. With Rachel. No problem."

"Oh, I hope she's still awake when we get there!"

He grinned at her. "If she is, she'll be cranky."

"I don't care!"

"Listen, how's your dad?"

"He sailed through it. The doctor seemed pleased. Dad was awake and grumbling before I left. Made me promise to call when I got home. But Mom whispered that I'd better not, because she'd been told to give him a sleeping pill as soon as she got him home tonight."

"I knew he'd be all right," said Steve. Avery Busby was too tough to die. Occasional unworthy thoughts had crossed Steve's mind, especially after he'd lost the Japan job. But Steve had to admire Avery Busby, crusty as he was. A formidable father-in-law.

"How's your mom holding up?" he asked Elaine. She discussed her family and her trip as they drove home through the rain. It had been good for her to go, Steve thought, getting her out of her routine a little, seeing her parents, her roots. She was relaxed now, relieved that her father had had no problems. Thank God for that.

As they turned into their oak-lined street, he could see that there was something wrong. Elaine tensed too. "What's going on, Steve?"

"I don't know." It was hard to pinpoint. Past the tall hedge he could see Rachel standing out on their lawn, outlined by the light that streamed from her own living room window next door. Bob was patting her rigid shoulders. That was it, maybe, her stiff posture, hands clamped one in the other. Her usual relaxed good humor had evaporated completely.

"Oh, God," said Elaine. "Do you think it's premature labor? She was doing so well! And where's Muffin?"

"I don't know," said Steve. Something heavy and cold was growing in his gut. Evil things were in motion. He pulled up to the curb. Elaine was out almost before they had stopped, running across the light-streaked lawn to Rachel.

"Rachel, are you all right? Where's Muffin?"

"You don't have her? Oh, God!" Rachel sagged against Bob, whose arms went around her supportively.

"What the hell is going on?" Steve felt far away, as though he were watching the scene from the stars sparkling above. Rachel was sobbing, Elaine standing before her, alert and anxious.

Bob said, "Rachel went to pick her up, but she wasn't there. The woman said someone else had come for her."

"Someone else?"

"A young woman who said you had sent her."

"Have you called the police?" demanded Steve.

Rachel shook her head. "I didn't know what to do! I called your office right away, but you were out."

"Yes. I had to leave for a little bit," said Steve guiltily. Susan. He'd been with Susan while this was happening, while Rachel was trying to reach him.

"And I thought maybe you really had found someone else and then couldn't reach me because I'd already left. So I just came back here to see if you might be home. Tried to call you at your office again."

"I was probably on my way to meet Lainey by then."

Elaine was looking back and forth, not comprehending, maybe not wanting to. "What young woman? Where's Muffin?"

"Oh, honey, we don't know!" said Rachel. "I don't know what to do!"

"We call the police," said Steve. He bounded across the lawn and up his flagstone walk. The others trailed after him. He flipped on the hall light and hurried into the kitchen to pick up the phone. What should he dial? Local police? Manhattan?

"Steve!" cried Elaine. "Steve! Oh, God, stop!"

"What?" Still holding the receiver, he stepped back into the hall.

Elaine was crouched on the floor where the mail had fallen through the slot into a rough pile. She was holding a sheet of paper printed with large letters. Looked a little like an advertisement from here, Steve thought. But badly set, letters unmatched.

Elaine was looking up at him, dazed, like a shot animal that cannot comprehend what has happened to it. Steve dropped the receiver and squatted beside her, one arm around her shoulders. Gently he took the paper from her.

*This isn't real*, he thought, a bad movie or a bad dream. The words consisted of the cliché letters-cut-from-newspaper-headlines, as though already preparing for cliché tabloid emotions. But the message, cliché or not, went straight to the heart.

> We've got Muffin. Cute kid. If you want her back, pay us $500,000 by Friday night. We'll tell you where and how. We mean business. If we don't get the money, we'll send you her finger. If you call the police, we'll send you her ear.

*part three*

# A GRASSHOPPER'S UNCLE

*(Friday morning, March 9, 1973)*

# VIII

*Friday morning
March 9, 1973*

By morning Steve was beyond exhaustion, existing in a world of numbing fatigue and paradoxically heightened senses. For hours he and Elaine had been alternately bickering and comforting each other. They both felt panic; they both ached for their child; they both felt enormous, paralyzing guilt. And in this state of emotional chaos they had to hammer out a plan of action.

"Steve, we've got to be rational!" Elaine had sobbed last night after one bitter exchange of accusations. "Her life depends on it!"

"I know, honey." Steve had hugged her, his face buried in her hair, guilt washing over him again. How could he ever have believed that being with Susan was worth risking this? A giddy kid, now paying dearly for his irresponsibility. He couldn't add confession to Elaine's burdens now. But her pain was another knife twisting inside him. He said, "We'll be rational. Let's finish the finances."

They'd totaled it up. Most of their assets were tied up—the house, the cars, insurance. Bank accounts and stocks that could be cashed in before the Friday night deadline came to just over $100,000.

It was Elaine who finally acknowledged it. "We'll have to call Dad."

"Yeah. Damn."

She had called, near midnight, only to be reminded by her mother that Avery Busby was under sedation on doctor's orders. Elaine had refused to tell her mother the problem, but said she'd call back early the next morning. "Oh, I hope I didn't worry her too much," she'd said as she hung up.

"You were fine, honey."

"But do you think he can help?"

"Yes, but not till the banks open."

"Steve, how could you have let someone else pick her up?"

"It was Rachel, damn it!" Steve had just not been able to tell her about Maggie and Mrs. Golden. "You've left her with Rachel sometimes yourself!"

"Oh, God, why did I ever leave her?" Her anguish had shifted again, aimed at herself now.

"Honey, we can't do anything about what's already happened. We have to go on from here. Let's try to get some sleep."

A foolish suggestion; there was little sleep for either of them. Steve's thoughts were a maelstrom of worries —about Elaine, about Susan, about money, most of all about his daughter. Was she all right? Was she frightened? Would he ever see her again? The memory of her delicious dimpled smile knifed, clear as glinting sunlight, through the fatigued muddle of his worries. In the unfriendly darkness Steve put his head into the pillow and wept for his lost daughter.

But then Elaine, who with the aid of Valium was dozing a little beside him, awoke with a sob, and Steve blinked back his own tears so that he could try to comfort her.

Friday's dawn found them both ravaged by the night, but at least they could begin to act. They hurried first to the front door, to see if by chance a second message had already arrived, but nothing was there. Mechanically Elaine made coffee and toast. Only minutes later there was a knock on the door: Rachel, her belly enormous under a plush bathrobe.

"I saw the light on. Any news?"

"Nothing yet."

"I feel so guilty!" she sobbed. "If only I'd tried harder to check with you, Steve! If—"

"Rachel, please, it's not your fault. Anyway, I wasn't always by the phone."

"Oh, Steve! You shouldn't have come to pick me up!" Elaine burst out.

"Lainey, don't you think I'd do everything differently if I could?" Steve sat down helplessly, head in hands.

But her mind had already spun on to another question. "It's still too early to call Dad, I guess."

Steve checked his watch. "Maybe not. He'll kill us if we wait too long about something like this."

Elaine handed coffee to Rachel. "Really? It's okay?"

"Go ahead," said Steve.

Avery Busby was awake, all right. Elaine's mother put him on, and from across the kitchen Steve could hear the testiness in his "Hello?"

"Oh, Daddy, the most awful thing has happened!" Elaine was instantly a little girl again, pouring out her problem. She'd always be Busby's little girl. And Steve would always be the kid. Guilt twisted inside him; he had to forget his resentments now, to focus on Muffin's dilemma.

"Daddy, you've got to believe me! Listen, I'll read the note." Elaine picked up the paper and recited the ghastly words.

She listened a moment, then said, "No, of course we haven't called the police. Because of what the note said!" And in a moment she turned to Steve. "Here, he wants to talk to you."

Steve gripped the receiver. "Hello?"

"Is all this true, Steve?"

"I'm sorry, especially with your operation, but—"

"How much cash have you got?"

"Hundred and two, liquid."

"I'll get the rest. You call the police."

"No! The note said—"

"The police will know what to do. They're—"

"I don't care! The important thing is Muffin's safety!"

"Of course it is! All right, I'll call them. I've got connections."

"After she's back! Not before!"

"Look, Steve, they've got specialists. They'll know that getting her back safely and quickly is the important thing. They've seen this sort of thing before."

"I know," said Steve stubbornly. "But that note meant business. If they bumble things even a little, our baby might be hurt." In the background he could hear Elaine sobbing in Rachel's arms, and he hated Busby for forcing him to say these things.

But the old man was obstinate. "You're more likely to bumble on your own. In fact, I think I'll come up."

"But you can't travel yet!"

"Bill was in the medical corps in the Army. When did you get the note?"

"I don't know when it arrived. We found it about nine, when we got back."

"And you know she was safe at the school at five?"

"I called them to say someone else would be picking her up. They would've said something if there was already a problem then."

"Well, we've lost a lot of time already. We've got to get the police on it now."

"Please." Steve heard the desperation in his own voice. "Elaine is upset enough already. Damn it, so am I! We're just going to do exactly what they say until we get Muffin back. After that you can call in the FBI if you want. But not yet!"

"You're forgetting two things," said Busby acidly. "First, I won't let them hurt any relative of mine. I'll do what's best for the kid. Second, any kidnapper with half a brain wouldn't ask you for that much money. It's not your daughter who was kidnapped, Steve. It's my granddaughter. And so I'm going to run this show. I'll be there by noon."

"But—oh, damn." The line was dead. Steve slammed the receiver back into the cradle. Red visions of smashing Busby flooded his mind.

"Is he calling the police?" Elaine's hands clenched and unclenched jerkily.

"Yeah." Steve cleared his throat. "He's taking over. Damn, I should have known!"

"Well, maybe it's for the best," Elaine faltered, but her gaze strayed to the note.

"Look," said Rachel, concerned but a little more objective. "He's got the money, right? You can't do what the kidnappers say without him."

"That's true. Not by tonight," admitted Steve.

"So you need him, and he's going to help but on his own terms. What did you expect?"

"I expected some understanding of the problem! I mean—what they say in the note—"

"Well," said Rachel practically, "it's clear the police are going to be called. Better deal with that as a given."

"That's right," said Elaine. "You know how Daddy is."

"I sure do." Steve knew they were right. He'd just have to try to convince the police to stay out of it. Maybe the note would do it. "But what if the kidnappers are watching the house?" he asked. "I'd better call them myself."

He was forestalled by the imperious ring of the telephone. Avery Busby again. "It's all set," he informed Steve. "Their top specialist will be meeting you at the office at nine."

"The office?"

"Yes, of course. Your house may be under surveillance by the kidnappers. Much safer to talk to them at work."

"You don't think I'll be under surveillance there?"

"Look, they know what they're doing. This Lugano is the top man. Be sure to give him the note and a photo of Muffin. See you soon."

Steve hung up and turned to Elaine. "Okay, I'll do my best to keep them away," he said to her. "Honey, you'll have to manage the phone. Okay? In case the instructions come that way. And take care of your dad when he arrives. It'll be okay to call me if you need me."

"Yes." Elaine nodded.

"Do you want me to stay?" asked Rachel.

"Please," said Elaine. "Unless Bob needs you."

"I'll see him off and come right back." Rachel heaved herself to her feet and lumbered out.

Steve went for his tie and jacket. When he returned to the kitchen, Elaine had moved her chair near the telephone and was sitting dry-eyed, clutching Muffin's fuzzy brown teddy bear. Steve knelt before Elaine.

"Honey, it'll be all right. I'm sure it will," he lied. But the dazed grief in the lovely hazel eyes was beyond the reach of his words. He kissed her tense hand and, miserable, waited until Rachel returned.

On the way to his office he made plans about how to handle the police. Busby might insist on calling them, but the note had been more than clear: no police. Well, Steve would do what he could to keep them off the trail long enough for Muffin to be safely returned home.

When Myra Goodwin called to announce a Mr. Lugano, Steve went out to greet him. For a moment he was nonplussed—two men were sitting on the leather sofa waiting, both obviously businessmen in gray pinstripe suits and conservative ties. Steve asked the receptionist, "Myra, where's Lugano?"

"Mr. Bradford?" One of the two men stood up. Black hair, tanned skin, alert amber eyes like a lion's or jaguar's. "I'm Harold Lugano."

"Oh! Yes, glad to meet you." Steve shook hands.

"Glad you could work me in today."

"Yes, of course." In spite of himself Steve was impressed; effort and skill had gone into this act. "Do you want to come back to my office?"

"You know, I hate to admit it, but I had to miss breakfast. Do you suppose we could go out for a bagel and coffee?"

"I could send out for one, Mr. Bradford," Myra offered.

"Yes, why don't—" A fleeting frown in the amber eyes suddenly jarred Steve's exhausted mind to comprehension. "No, on second thought, I have an errand to do anyway. It'll save time to go to the coffee shop."

"Great," said Lugano.

"I'll be back soon," Steve told the receptionist, who nodded, oblivious to the tension in his voice, and returned to her typing and to her cigarette.

Safely in the bustle of the streets he asked Lugano, "Even my office is suspect, then?"

Lugano nodded. "I don't know any details yet, of course, but with young kids, kidnappings generally require inside information. Sometimes it's a complete stranger who watches the family routine for a while, but sometimes it's a trusted employee or friend."

Steve's head was pounding. "God, I never thought of that. You just sort of assume it's an outsider, you know? Listen, do you think we'll get my daughter back?"

"If we don't scare the kidnappers."

"Yes! Yes, that's what I'm worried about. Will anyone recognize you here on the street?"

"I've avoided becoming a household word," said Lugano with a slight smile. "Here, let's go in this place."

The coffee shop was just beginning to empty out a little from the morning crush. Lugano paused in the door, then apparently saw what he wanted as two men in a corner booth got up to pay. He headed for the booth and sat facing the main part of the restaurant. Steve slid in across from him. "We're lucky to find a private table."

"Those were my men," explained Lugano. A waitress arrived, and he paused until they had ordered coffee before saying, "Now, let's hear the story. Do you have the photo?"

Steve handed him the picture: Muffin grinning in a frilly spring dress her grandparents had sent her. "That's the best recent one."

"Looks good. She's two and a half, you said?"

"Yes."

"All right." Lugano pocketed the photo. "Do you have any ideas about who might have her?"

"None."

"Does your wife?"

"Look, Mr. Lugano—I mean, Captain? Or what?"

"Mister is best."

"Okay. Anyway, we don't know, and we don't want anyone checking into it yet, because of what the note said. We just want our daughter back!"

Lugano didn't answer; the coffee was arriving. When

the waitress had gone, he said, "So do we. You brought this note?"

Steve handed it over. "Here. You see how murderous they are!"

Lugano read the note and nodded. "I'm sorry to say this is pretty typical. They want to impress you."

"You mean they might not hurt her?"

"I don't mean that. We have to take them seriously."

"Yes, I thought so."

"Okay, now tell me how it happened." Lugano's notebook was ready.

"You'll promise not to go after them until she's safely back?"

"I promise not to endanger your daughter."

Steve drew a deep breath. "Well, my wife was out of town. Her father was having an operation."

"Yes. We heard from her father."

"I'll bet you did," said Steve grimly. "Anyway, she was only gone from noon to evening, but of course we had to make arrangements about Muffin. We thought it would be easy. Muffin goes to a Montessori school in the Village, below Washington Square."

"Isn't that unusual? Why not something in your own neighborhood?"

"We're only thirty minutes away. This school is run by one of Elaine's old friends, Mitzi Black. Also Elaine is a dancer, and she still studies with a teacher in the Village. So she'd bring Muffin about noon, have her own lesson, and then take Muffin home."

"I see. But not yesterday."

"No. She brought Muffin in as usual, but then went straight to the airport. Mitzi was going to keep Muffin till five, and I was going to leave work a few minutes early and pick her up myself."

"Okay."

The hard part loomed now. Steve was determined to keep the clever and efficient Lugano from getting close to the people who had Muffin. Lugano had promised not to endanger her; but there was a surer way. Steve said, "Well, it turned out that I had to run some errands, and there was extra work at the office, and—anyway, a lot of things piled up. Well, our next-door neighbor Rachel had offered to help. Muffin knew her. I hated to impose, but things were getting frantic, so I called her."

"I see." The predatory amber eyes flicked up at Steve.

"Damn, I feel guilty as all hell! But it seemed okay at the time!"

"Of course. Take it easy. Guilt won't help your daughter now. Facts will. What next?"

"I called Mitzi's to say someone else would be picking her up. Look, you're sure you won't go looking for these people?"

"I'll check MO in our files, in case it's someone we know. I'll ask cops on the beat if they saw anything yesterday. No questioning neighbors, no stakeouts, no all-points bulletins. Nothing to alert them that we're interested."

"Well . . ." Steve was still reluctant. Damn nosy Avery Busby. Once Muffin was back they could hunt to their heart's content. But for now it was best not to mention Maggie and the sitter, Mrs. Golden. Could Lugano find them without Steve's cooperation? If the detective broke his word and began questioning people, he would get a description of Maggie from the Montessori people, possibly a name, probably not an address or phone number. And if he somehow found Maggie, she could tell him about the pied-à-terre and possibly give him Mrs. Golden's name. But again, probably no address or phone number. Getting even that far would take time. And until Lugano reached Mrs. Golden, there should be no problem. Steve was convinced that Mrs. Golden was the one who knew where Muffin was.

Lugano asked, "Did the school know the person who picked up your daughter?"

"No. Tall, dark-haired, they said. Young. Not Rachel."

"Clothes?"

"I didn't think to ask. But please don't ask them! What if one of their people is in on this? We can't trust anyone, you said."

"I told you already, we won't be interviewing anyone. We cooperate, negotiate if possible, with the kidnappers. What does this Rachel look like?"

"Dark hair, strong features. Very pregnant."

"How long have you known her?"

"She moved next door last year. She and Elaine are good friends."

"Okay. Other good friends among your neighbors?"

"Sure. None that live so close. People we go sailing with and so forth." Steve frowned uneasily at the alert, poised policeman. "Look, you won't bother them? If one of them did it I don't want to upset him."

"We won't go near until your daughter's back. You might make me a list, though. Now, your receptionist."

"Yes. Myra Goodwin."

"She's been with you a long time?"

"A year and a half."

"Knows your routines?"

"Well . . ." Dismayed, Steve saw Lugano noting down Myra's virtues, which suddenly took on a sinister cast. "Look, she wouldn't do a thing like that!"

Lugano tapped the note. "People have done stranger things for less money."

"Yes. But she's not tall and dark-haired!"

"I have to be suspicious of everyone. Sorry. Now, can you add anything to what you've told me?"

"No. I guess I could ask Mitzi more about the appearance of the woman who took her."

"You've told her not to spread the word that she's kidnapped?"

"Of course. She's a friend of Elaine's. She'll cooperate. Unless—do you think she might be involved?"

"Anything's possible," said Lugano, "although a daycare outfit can't really afford the negative publicity of a kidnapping. I'd think they'd have more than this ransom to lose. We'll check recent employees of course."

"God!" said Steve. "Suddenly everyone looks guilty."

"Yes. You have to remember, most people aren't. Try to get a description of the woman and tell this Mitzi Black to tell people that your daughter is ill or something."

"Okay. Damn! Rachel and her husband know too. They were there when we found the note."

"They know not to noise it around?"

"Yes, I guess so. The one I'm not sure about is my father-in-law."

Lugano smiled faintly at the bitterness in Steve's voice. "He's not stupid. And we did impress on him that loose talk could be dangerous."

Steve nodded. Avery Busby was shrewd as well as cantankerous, and if anyone could convince him, it would be Lugano, with his quiet, competent manner. "I'd better call my wife. Make sure she understands she shouldn't tell anyone."

"Fine. Now, we'll be putting a tap on your phone. If the message is a note instead, call me at this number." Lugano gave Steve a card. "We'll instruct you on how to respond."

"I know how to respond," said Steve tightly. "We'll do whatever we have to do to get Muffin back. To hell with your instructions!"

"I didn't put that very well," said Lugano mildly. "We'll make suggestions, based on experience. If we've been able to identify the kidnappers, we may be able to advise you about what gets them nervous and so forth."

"Yes. I see. That would be helpful," admitted Steve. "Look, Mr. Lugano, I'm not trying to put you down. But I'm damned upset."

"Hell, don't apologize. I've got a kid too. We'll all do our best." Lugano glanced at his watch. "You'd better be getting back. We won't leave together."

"Okay. Uh, thanks."

"Talk to you soon."

Steve walked back to his building alone. The early spring sun had erased the last traces of yesterday's drizzle. He paused at a pay booth to call Elaine.

She answered on the first ring. "Hello?" Her voice was raw.

"It's okay, Lainey, it's only me. Are you okay?"

"Steve, hang up! What if they're trying to get through?"

"I'll be done in a second, honey. Just a quick message from the police. Don't tell anyone about the kidnapping. And make sure Rachel and Bob know not to tell, though I'm sure they know. Okay?"

"Yes. I see."

"We're all working on it. But the detective said we didn't want publicity."

"Yes. Okay."

"I'll be home early. Though I'd better stay here till lunch so it won't look suspicious. Call me if they call, okay?"

"Okay."

Steve returned to the office to stare unseeing at the papers on his desk. At ten-thirty Avery Busby phoned.

"I've arranged for the money. On my way now. Have you heard anything?"

"Not yet. We'll let you know the minute we do. Do you want to messenger me the money?"

"No. Lugano said they might contact me instead of you. He agrees it's my money they're chasing."

"Maybe so."

"I have a man on it here. We'll have to wait and see what they say. I'll be there soon."

"Right."

Steve hung up, unhappy. So what if Busby's money was what the kidnappers wanted? The note had come to Steve and Elaine. Why did Busby think the next communication might go to him? Self-centered old man. But as usual, they'd have to play the game his way. For a moment Steve daydreamed of breaking loose, defying Busby, besting him; but he pulled his thoughts back from such visions. Getting Muffin back was the most important thing. What was the next step?

Waiting, unfortunately.

He made a few meaningless marks on his papers and started home for an early lunch.

On Friday morning Derek was late to rehearsal, and before he'd said a word, they all realized that the news was bad. The little knots of people, casually doing warm-up stretches or vocal exercises, grew still as he stumped across the worn floor to the platform in the center. He stood silently, with filmed and vacant eyes.

Edith said, "Derek. Is it bad news?"

He forced himself to focus on her. "She's dead."

# IX

*Friday morning
March 9, 1973*

"No! That's impossible!" exclaimed Jaymie.

"She'd come through somehow!" agreed Edith.

"You mean she didn't make it?" Daphne's voice was disbelieving.

Derek stared at them blankly and didn't answer.

Larry said curtly, "So. Show's over." The foam coffee cup he held crumpled in his hand. Nick found his own hands clenched on the crown he was removing from the prop box.

"No!" protested Daphne. "It's not just her. It's a production company!"

"She'd want it to go on!" Edith agreed. "Derek, look, it's impossible! It can't be true!"

"Right." Cab underlined her point. "She wouldn't quit, Derek. Not quit a show. Even if she couldn't . . ." He trailed off.

Derek's eyes fastened on him, as though registering at last what all the clamor was about. "Look, mates," he said in a terrible, quiet voice. "Ramona is dead. The show is dead. All our bloody little dreams are dead. All of them!" He jumped down from the platform and strode for the door.

Larry caught his arm before he could open it. "Wait a minute! You can't just turn us out on the streets! You owe us—"

"Bloody hell, you sod! A great, wonderful star dies and all you can think about is money!"

"I'll mourn her on my own time, Derek. We all will. But we're legally entitled to two weeks' performance pay. You know that."

"I don't know a bloody thing except that it's all over! Now let go of my arm!"

"You can't just run out without making arrangements to pay us!"

"Let go!" Derek shoved at Larry.

Nick dropped the crown and nudged Cab, and the two of them stepped up to calm the combatants. "Let him be, Larry," said Nick. "He can't help us now. Derek, can you get that lawyer to meet with us?"

Derek rubbed his arm and remained silent.

"Derek, do you hear me? Ramona's partner, the lawyer. Ken Martin. He should meet with us."

"I—right, I'll do that." Derek started for the door again.

"This afternoon," Nick insisted. "Four o'clock. Or leave a note here where we can all check it."

"Okay. Right." He made his escape and clattered down the stairs. Larry turned away with a muffled curse.

Nick shouldered his gym bag. "He's just lost a hell of a lot."

"Oh? And the rest of us haven't? So we should smile sweetly and lose our pay too?" snapped Larry, picking up his jacket.

Nick was getting angry too. "Don't take it out on him!"

"He deserves special consideration?"

Nick followed him into the staircase. "You think you're the only one who had high hopes for this show? Larry Palmer in lights at last! Producers not giving your agent a moment's peace! Money rolling in! Film offers! A Hugh Hefner apartment full of Didis and Ramonas!"

Larry had reached the landing already. He laughed sourly. "Yeah, sounds great, all right. You and Derek have nobler dreams, I suppose. Rose-covered cottages, sweet happy little families, college for the kiddies, security, faithful dogs. Of course I don't understand all that, I'm too shallow."

Nick found himself off balance. "Look, Larry, anyone who can do Albert and Disraeli the way you do is not shallow. I know that. But why the hell can't you understand that Derek and I are hurting too? You've been trying to pick a fight for days."

"And you're ready for one at last?" Larry led the way into the delicious sunshine and turned east, past rusting and refurbished cast-iron facades.

"No need to keep it bottled up anymore, is there?" Nick asked mildly. "Emotion in a box, to be released when Dizzy and the Grand Old Man face off?"

Larry slowed and gave Nick an appraising sidelong look. "You work that way, do you? Yeah, so do I." After a moment he added, "You mentioned Didi."

"She's worried about you."

"And has some choice things to say about Ramona, no doubt. Like, wow, what a freaking bitch she is. And wow, what a freaking pig Larry is. Yes, Nick, maybe you and I have things to talk about after all."

"Okay," said Nick, curious about this handsome, hardworking playboy and wondering if they could get past their bristly working relationship. "Let's talk first. We can always fight later."

"You going home now to your sweet little family?" Larry was not quite ready for a truce.

"Pretty soon. Not yet." Nick decided to try bluntness. "Larry, was Ramona murdered?"

"What do you mean? She was shot, wasn't she?"

"We're supposed to think it was a mugger."

Larry nodded. "Yeah, I know what you're driving at. I've played around with the idea one of us did it, too."

"Yeah. There were a hell of a lot of emotions crackling around that last day. Ramona was doing her best to push us all to the breaking point."

"Well, she succeeded with me," said Larry easily. "I was furious when she cut my solo."

"I still don't think she meant it."

Larry shrugged. "Look, we've been through all that. Doesn't make much difference now, does it?"

"Except that Didi said you left her after a few minutes that night. She also said that Ramona was coming on to you."

Larry sized him up from the corner of his eye. "You're asking if *I* shot her?"

"It's just that it gives a different slant to things. Until Didi said that, I couldn't imagine a dedicated actor like you jeopardizing his big chance. Hell, even without the solo, your two roles would be great."

"You're right."

"And Didi said you were one hundred percent for your career."

"Sweet Didi. I wasn't sure she understood."

"She thought maybe what you said about Ramona chasing you was a fiction. A warning to her."

"Oh, no. Not entirely. Ramona really was on the prowl last week. Couple of rolls in the hay with Derek, she said. And rather obviously looking Cab over. Yours truly, her dear Prince Albert, didn't escape her roving eye."

"But you, of course, defended your virtue?"

Larry's dark eyes were opaque and cold. "I never screw anyone I'm working with at the moment. Matter of principle. It's bad for the show. Though of course I would have done the necessary to get my solo back, as clever little Ramona knew."

"And to hell with principle."

"Same principle, don't you think? My solo was good for the show."

"Yes, of course."

Larry looked at Nick shrewdly. "I can't believe she didn't proposition you, the way she laughed at your jokes. She did, didn't she?"

"Nothing happened," said Nick.

"Fidelity to your statistician?"

"Call it what you want. But I also happen to agree with your principle. Don't mess with the show."

Larry nodded. "Too bad Ramona didn't subscribe

to our old-fashioned morality. She made it tough those last few days. But you can see that I wouldn't risk the high point of my career. I can't afford to let personal feelings get in the way. Either way."

"Okay, I'm not accusing you. But I was curious."

"Curious. Fine. My turn now. How about you? Did you shoot Ramona?"

"No. You're thinking that I was one of the last people to see her alive?"

"Right. Opportunity. We know you were nearby. And she'd been needling you too." Larry had stopped, his back to a graffiti-adorned doorway. They had left the cast-iron district and were in the middle of a dingy block in the Bowery.

"Didn't cut my solo," Nick reminded him.

"She would have if you'd had one, woolly mammoth. And there's another thing. You have a wife. A cute little baby. And Ramona was coming on to you too. A lot more awkward for you than for a fancy-free bachelor like me."

The words were cutting; but there was a strangely bitter note in Larry's voice. Nick admitted, "Well, that version hangs together."

"Better than your story about me!"

"Depends on how much you care about Didi, right? She thinks your actions told a different story from your disclaimers."

"Damn Didi!" Larry jerked a thumb angrily at the building behind him. "I don't invite people to my place. But I can see there's no getting rid of the jealous, tied-down family man till he can ogle my famous Hugh Hefner pad." Without waiting to hear Nick's protests he unlocked the door and bounded up the stairs. Nick, half ashamed, followed. Peeping Tom O'Connor.

It was on the fourth floor of a dingy building, a walk-up with questionable neighbors and ancient plumbing. The hallways hadn't been painted for years, except with graffiti. So when Larry unlocked his own apartment door, it was a striking contrast. Small, yes; but painfully neat, no pictures on the plain white walls, simple furniture, a chaste gray carpet. In the narrow corner that the land-lord probably billed as the kitchen, an ancient refrig-

erator and sink and tiny stove gleamed white. Above, on
an oak shelf, white mugs and plates were symmetrically
arranged. A murderer's obsessive neatness? Nick pushed
the thought away. An oak table and chairs and a trim
bed with a tailored gray twill spread stood against the
wall. The only note of extravagance was the collection
on the simple oak nightstand: an ornate Victorian lamp
with stained-glass shade, a photograph in a gold frame,
an enameled Italian box, a stack of books.

Larry stowed his things in the closet and turned back
to Nick with a mocking bow. "Well, what's the verdict?
Would Hugh Hefner be proud of me?"

"Hardly. Gandhi might be."

"Yes. I too have simplified."

Nick thought of his own house. If murderers were
neat, he was off the hook, with the chaos of half-stripped
wallpaper, mounds of laundry that despite their stren-
uous efforts continued to accumulate, a kitchen en-
crusted with spilled baby food, a stepladder waiting for
someone to find a minute to finish scraping the ceiling,
piles of diapers and baby seats and mobiles and toys,
days that were brimful with a demanding baby and an
active dog and a rantipoling wife. "Wish I could sim-
plify," he said wistfully.

Larry motioned him to one of the chairs and sat on
the edge of the gray bed himself. "Really? I thought you
wanted the prototypical Don Juan."

"And instead I find the prototypical Thoreau," Nick
admitted. He wondered suddenly, who was the prototypical dad? Who was the Don Juan of diaper changes,
the Thoreau with drool on his shoulder? The Lone Ranger
who walked the baby instead of sleeping with his wife?
Where were the heroes he needed now?

"If you're wondering how Didi and the others fit in,"
Larry continued, "they don't."

"A man of compartments," said Nick. "Sex over there,
home over here, work somewhere else. All separate. But
suppose she likes your soul as well as your body?"

"Her problem. Look, you needn't be so protective,
Mr. Family Man. Didi agreed to the ground rules. Just

a fling, no commitment. She understood. I made her recite it back to me."

"Okay, okay. She recited it back to me too."

"Well, it's not my fault if she decides later she wants to change the rules. Play a different game that I won't play."

"Crawl out of her compartment?"

"Yes, exactly!" Larry flung himself back on the bed. "I suppose you find it blissful to have a woman in all of your compartments?"

" 'Blissful' is too peaceable a word for chaos," Nick told him. "But—'joyful' maybe. Sometimes."

"Lucky you," mocked Larry.

Nick said gently, "You might find it joyful too, Larry." With his forefinger he nudged the photo on the nightstand: Larry, youthful and tuxedoed, with a pretty brunette in a pink prom gown.

Larry glanced at the picture, said, "Hell," and lay back, his forearm across his eyes. After a moment he said, "Yes, I thought she was all I needed in any compartment. But I couldn't fill all of hers. She had this great gaping compartment labeled 'Security.' Liked my acting but couldn't stand my unemployment. What would you do, Nick? If it was your work or your family, what would you choose?"

Nick rubbed his bald head. "Love versus duty?"

"Yeah. What would you choose?"

"God, I don't even know which is which anymore. If I ever had to choose—well, whatever my choice, I'd end up with compartments, I guess."

"Yeah." Larry moved his forearm from his eyes and squinted at Nick. "I tried to pretend it was just a delay, that I'd get a break in a year or two, make enough money for Beth to live on, live happily ever after. Doesn't work that way."

"You're working pretty regularly," said Nick.

"Doesn't count. You know that, Nick. This aborted show that we just finished could be the last job either one of us will ever land. I hope not, but it's possible."

"True. And you're afraid Beth won't wait?"

Larry laughed grimly. "Not Beth. Two years ago she married our hometown Westinghouse dealer. Secure as all get-out now. Baby on the way."

"I'm sorry," said Nick awkwardly. Stumblebum O'Connor, roughshod over people's emotions again.

"She wanted me to go into real estate sales. Act as a hobby." He rolled onto his side, back to Nick. "But sometimes . . . you know, I wonder if she might have come round after a while. If I'd done things her way . . ."

"I don't know. I do know that marriage is hard work even when you both approve of this ridiculous profession."

"Yeah." Larry waved an arm at his chaste room. "But you have to give up the world, you see. Or at least taste it in compartments."

Nick's life was not in neat compartments. Far from it. More a tangled mess. But perhaps the alternatives were no better. He said to Larry, "That's probably your best answer, for now anyway."

"It's the only answer that doesn't drive me mad." Larry sat up abruptly. "Look, we both better switch compartments. Get out there and make the rounds."

"Right. Job-hunt time again," Nick agreed.

But after he left Larry, the first thing he did was call Maggie.

She was coming in early anyway, she said, and met him at Canal Street. Sideways, to avoid hurting Sarah, she gave him a hug. "I'm sorry, Nick. Poor Ramona."

"Yeah. We're all pretty shaken up. Half expected it and still believed she'd pull through."

"I know. Same with me. So you're back to making rounds, then?"

"I'll see George. Visit a few casting directors. And I have to check back at the loft to see when Ramona's partner is talking to us." He removed Sarah's sticky little hand from his *Back Stage*.

"God, I'd hoped so much she'd make it."

"Yeah. Never came out of the coma, I guess. By the way, your idea about Derek and Ramona was right. Larry

says so anyway. On the prowl this week, he said, soliciting
every male in sight. Even old bald married ones."

"They ain't so bad," said Maggie calmly. "Look, do
you have to see George instantly?"

"Pretty soon, so he can tell me what auditions are
coming up. But maybe not instantly. God knows I don't
like making rounds. What did you have in mind?"

"I wanted to visit Buzz's apartment. I'm worried about
Muffin."

"That's why you came in early?" Nick found himself
annoyed.

"Partly. Mostly to see if you needed bucking up."

Their eyes met. Hers spoke of love, worry, fatigue,
determination. He said, "Damn, why can't the world
leave us alone for a little while? Two careers and Sarah
and marriage and a house renovation and a dog is enough
to juggle."

"The world is seldom considerate."

"I know. Damn, I'm depressed, Maggie."

"Yeah." She gave him another of those unsatisfying
sideways hugs. "I'd help if I could."

"Yeah. Let's go to Buzz's apartment." Maybe it would
give him a few minutes' respite from the anger and guilt
and discouragement of a friend's cruel death, of the loss
of a wonderful part.

The front door of the building was propped open
today, and they could hear hammering and the whine of
electric tools to the right as they entered. Nick already
regretted coming; there was so much else to do. Or maybe
today he'd regret doing anything. They climbed the stairs;
though mostly unfinished, the upper floors were quieter.
Maggie said, "Let's go around behind, just in case someone's in the apartment."

The building was C-shaped, with an entrance cen-
tered in each section. Most of the apartments were on
the outside wall, but a few small ones opened onto the
ten-foot central airshaft between the wings. The apartments along the south hall were finished, their walls cutting off the hall from the light of the outside windows,
but those in the north were just framed in, with workmen's supplies and piled lumber in the halls. Maggie led

the way to the fourth floor and around to the unfinished
wing of the building. There were only two small apartments on the inner side of the hall, Nick could see; their
windows would afford a view only of the airshaft and the
other apartment windows ten feet away. Maggie went into
one, picking her way around the stacks of two-by-fours
and wallboard, and looked intently across the airshaft.

"That's the one," she said, pointing at the window
directly across from them.

"Can't see a thing," said Nick. What the hell was he
doing here? He should be calling his agent, or finding
out when Ramona's partner would be meeting them, or
something.

"Guess they're gone," said Maggie. "I'm going to
check." She started out again.

"Can't you just call him and ask?"

"I tried. Couldn't find any Buzz Hartfords in any of
the directories."

"The sitter, then."

"Yeah, he told me the agency name. Maybe I will."
But she still led the way around to the opposite, finished
wing of the building. At the apartment door she paused,
listened, then fiddled a moment with the lock. The door
opened quietly.

No one was there. The apartment was as she had
described it: small, two windows onto the airshaft, furnished with cheap new furniture. A brief wall of small
kitchen appliances, a door to what was probably a bathroom. Maggie looked in it, checked the closet, then picked
up a wastebasket and shook her head.

"What have you found?" asked Nick, impatient.

"Nothing," said Maggie, removing Sarah's fingers from
the wastebasket and putting it down. "And that's the
problem. Muffin had a satchel with the usual kid
supplies—paper, crayons, fruit juice, and so forth. And
I threw away the note that had this address on it. Threw
it right in here."

"So Mrs. Golden is neat and cleans up."

"Yeah, but it seems maybe too clean." She frowned.

He tried to stifle his irritation. "It isn't necessarily
sinister to clean up, you know. Granted, you and I

haven't sighted our own baseboards for months, but out in the real world it is done."

She grinned absentmindedly. "Yes, I've heard of such bizarre primitive practices too."

"On the other hand," added Nick, "it usually *is* considered sinister to break and enter."

Her eyes darkened but she said evenly, "Yeah, you're right. Let's get out of here."

As they descended toward the front entrance, they heard a voice from the hall where the workmen were clustered: "Be with you in a sec, Dino. Left my saw on the front stairs."

Nick and Maggie hurried back up a flight and through the second-floor halls to the far staircase. Emerging into the side street, Maggie gave a disdainful jab at the insecure doorjamb. "Buzz isn't very security minded. You could pop that lock with a butter knife."

"The local burglars probably aren't as refined as you. Don't carry butter knives."

"That's all that saves him." She stroked Sarah's drowsy head and sighed. "God, Nick, I'm tired."

"Well, why the hell aren't you home taking a nap?" he erupted. "That's why we arranged this crazy schedule to begin with, so you'd be rested! Why are you meddling in Buzz's goddamn affairs here, when you don't even have time for yourself?"

"Myself?" Like lightning finding the earth, her frustration answered his. "Which self are you worried about? The cow who spends four or five hours a day nursing your baby? The washerwoman and char? The friend who comes in early to hold your hand when you're down?"

"Yeah, full of comfort, aren't you? A regular madonna!"

"Look, I'm trying to sympathize, Nick. I'm also trying to earn our mortgage payments and take care of our baby." She hugged Sarah a little closer.

"Golly, ma'am, is it a thank-you note you want? What with bathing Sarah and collecting my minuscule check, I clean forgot! I'll put one in the mail tomorrow. Or do you want one for each of your talented selves? Madonna, mom, and moneymaker?"

They were standing under filth-encrusted fire escapes and a sliver of ridiculously cheerful blue sky, their voices seething with pent-up outrage. "You're forgetting one for the moo-cow!" Maggie stormed. "And for the meddler. That's part of me too, like it or not! And for the ex-mistress. Though I can see why you'd—"

The pulse in Nick's temple was seismic. Sarah whimpered. He bellowed, "You're upsetting her!"

Maggie glanced down at the baby's unhappy, crumply face, spun away from him, and strode down the street. Nick wanted to strangle her.

Her; or maybe himself.

# X

*Friday, late morning*
*March 9, 1973*

Susan's flight was in the afternoon. Calling from a booth at Penn Station, Steve caught her just before she walked out the door. "All packed?" he asked.

"Long since. Just chewing my nails about this new job!"

"Don't worry," said Steve. "Once you get a concrete problem or two on your desk, you'll see you can manage."

"I hope so. God, I'll miss you, lover!"

He closed his eyes against the ugliness of the station, the horror of his worries, and murmured, "Same here. But we'll see each other again. Somehow."

"Sure you can't play hooky and come see me off?"

"No, I . . . well, things have come up. But I wanted to say bon voyage."

"Thanks. It's been good, Steve-o."

"It sure has."

But hanging up, turning from the brief magical haven of her voice back to the gritty everydayness of the station, Steve was swamped again with the enormity of his problem. It wasn't just Muffin, though of course he agonized over her. Was she frightened? Were her unknown caretakers kind? Competent at least? But he could do nothing about that. He could just make sure that he got her away as soon as possible, back home. And he must make sure the return was not jeopardized by the police or by stubborn Avery Busby. All that responsibility fell on him. And a mistake could—well, he wouldn't think about that. In crisis, said the white hunter, best not to think. *Precipitate into pure happy action.*

He was home again by eleven. "Have you heard anything?" he asked Elaine. She was sitting in the chair nearest the phone, neatly dressed, her perfect face sagging. Rachel, sympathetic and uncharacteristically quiet, was curled on the sofa, changing position occasionally to shift the weight of her belly. A radio droned in the background.

"No. Except Daddy's on his way. What about you?"

"Nothing. I've got our money. And your dad called me too, said he was bringing his."

"Yeah." She passed a hand across her forehead. Her hair straggled across her face; her skin was blotchy. For an instant Steve was pulled out of his own mass of worries to focus on her. His beautiful, impeccable wife, Muffin's joyful mother, Busby's elegant daughter—all had disappeared into this tense, exhausted despair.

"Lainey, honey, it'll be okay!" Stooping to hug her, he wished he could undo yesterday. If only he hadn't been with Susan, if only he'd never even met Susan! He held Lainey's sweet, ravaged head against his shoulder. "Really, honey, we'll manage! She'll be back and everything will be fine!"

"Oh, Steve!" she sobbed. "You know, I keep wondering, maybe I wasn't meant to have a child!"

"Oh, Lainey, don't be silly!" Steve was on the verge of sobs too. He looked at Rachel in appeal.

"Elaine, you know you're the world's best mother," said Rachel. To Steve she added, "She's been like this all morning. I wish there were something she could do besides wait."

Steve realized that it was true; he at least had had the police to handle, the money to gather. He said, "Now, listen, Lainey. Your dad and I will get her back. Believe me, we will. Your job is to think of what she'll need when she's back. I don't think they'll mistreat her, but she'll be pretty confused, and—"

"But the note said all that about her finger!"

Damn that note. "They just said that to warn us, honey. And we're warned, and the police have agreed not to take any action that will endanger her. Really. And the note also said she was cute. Remember?"

"Yes, but—"

"So they like her too. They won't hurt her as long as we do what we're supposed to do. She'll be fine. But you should be ready to give her a lot of reassurance when she gets back."

"He's right, Elaine," said Rachel, seeing his drift. "She'll need you more than ever."

"Yes. I see." A little determination was coming back into her expression.

"And it'll really be up to you," Steve continued, "because I have to be away at work so much. Especially since I'm not getting much done now."

"Oh, Steve!" She touched his arm contritely. "I know you're worried too."

"Yeah, nothing else seems important," said Steve. "Listen, Rachel, did Elaine mention that the police said not to talk about this?"

"Yes, but we knew anyway. Listen, I brought over some sandwiches but Elaine hasn't touched them. You want some lunch?"

"I haven't even thought about food. But you're right, maybe I should have a sandwich." He paused; they'd all heard the shuffly sound of the mail sliding through the slot. Rachel was closest and reached the hall first. She handed the stack to them.

There were bills, advertising circulars, and a fat padded envelope. First class. No return address. Steve opened it. Inside was rolled a child's pajama bag in the shape of a teddy bear, an ugly dusty purple color, with a zipper on its belly and one eye missing. That was all.

"What is it?" asked Elaine apprehensively.

"Some kind of symbolic message?" asked Rachel, shaking the padded envelope to be sure no note was enclosed.

Steve unzipped the bear. Inside it was a paper, covered with cut-out newspaper letters as before.

Money goes in here. Unmarked hundreds and five hundreds. Bear bag goes next to other bears on shelf at Ming Bazaar on Canal Street before 5 P.M. today. If no police show we'll ring with news of Muffin before 6. If anyone causes trouble you know what will happen.

Steve looked at Elaine. For the first time there seemed to be a glimmer of hope in her eyes. But all she said was, "Daddy will be here any minute."

Nick felt like a grasshopper's uncle.

Oblivious to people passing on the sidewalk, he trudged on, wrapped in confused shame. *Who's who and what's what*, Gladstone's rantipoling wife used to ask when things were bewildering. What was Maggie's problem? Where had that lightning bitterness come from? For that matter, where had his own come from? It was easy enough to say that his friend had died, his job—no, more than a job, his current obsession—was lost. Easy to say anyone would feel glum. But why lash out at Maggie? She'd offered support. Not exactly comfort; there was no comfort at a time like this. But she'd come. And he'd attacked her for it.

Love versus duty. At the rate he was going he'd end up with neither. No conflict because nothing worthwhile would remain in his life.

Somehow he'd lost touch with her. It wasn't just grief at Ramona's death. Nor the bitterness of losing the exhilarating work—that happened all too often in his bumpy profession. If there was anything he'd learned to cope with, it was being out of work. No, the problem was newer—and more profound—than that.

The problem was Sarah.

Her arrival had turned his life jagged: new peaks of unexpected joy, new chasms of frustration. He and Maggie had both wanted her; they both adored her. And they'd both been muddling along pretty well, he'd thought, sharing the sleeplessness and dirty laundry with good-humored grousing, building on the sturdy bond that had linked and enriched them both for years. They enjoyed Sarah, enjoyed each other's enjoyment. Watching Maggie nurse her, the two of them floating in that state of euphoric communion, he was filled with powerful new emotions. Love, pride, and more. He'd thought that Maggie shared those feelings.

But she'd called herself a moo-cow.

So it was more complicated than he'd thought, for her too.

Moo-cow. What had he missed? They'd always shared a quick instinctive comprehension, reading each other with ease even when no one else could follow. Like the Dr. Rank scene: little games that symbolized a deeper oneness. Sarah had curtailed all those things. Games. Talk. Music. Sex.

God, was that his problem? Sulking because he missed his nookie?

Gladstone had wrestled with that problem too. An energetic, lusty man, he'd struggled to maintain lofty moral standards, as Victorian as Victoria herself. But his beloved rantipoling wife had borne eight children in a constant cycle of pregnancy, nursing, tending children in their illnesses. The relished marriage bed had soon created its own restraints. Gladstone's answer to the frustration had been to enjoy the children, to work harder, to preach to prostitutes, to become prime minister of the world's most powerful nation. The People's William, they called him. The Grand Old Man.

And Nick's answer? He'd lost his job. Attacked his wife. What a neat guy. The Grand Old Prick.

His unguided feet had brought him back to the rehearsal building. He should check to see if Derek had posted a note about the meeting with Ramona's partner. He opened the door and plodded up the stairs.

Working up a part, you looked carefully at every word your character said, at every word he reacted to, at every word said about him, for clues to the deeper currents that motivated him. There had been words, all right. Meddler, he'd called her. Well, okay, they were too busy now to waste worries on someone else's child, but that wasn't the real problem. Maggie's curiosity and lively sense of responsibility had always been part of the joy of living with her. Calling her meddler didn't mean that he wanted a change, just that he was irritated. No news there. The kind of quibble that could usually be settled quickly, rationally.

Madonna, though—there was a word to unpack. He'd called her madonna too. What had he meant? Beautiful, yes. Nurturing. Comforting.

And asexual, of course. With her baby a unit, whole and holy.

No need for little Joseph, who hovered anxiously in the background, wearing his sainthood like the after-thought it was.

But he wasn't Joseph! No sirree. Not Nick the red-blooded. Hell, the Army had made a man of him long since. And the theatre too, for that matter. Three beer commercials, right? And a pickup-truck spot. On tele-visions all over the nation, Nick's flickering image was an emblem of masculinity. Any day now they'd be asking him to carry Scarlett O'Hara up those stairs. Or maybe be the next Tarzan. Beating his hairy chest. Snacking on raw tiger. Uprooting trees.

Attacking his wife.

Damn.

Madonna, he'd sneered. Because she was so involved with Sarah that she'd forgotten him? Or because some-thing in him was reluctant to defile one so sacred as a mother?

Mm. Better leave that one for now, Nick old man.

But her other words had been pretty weighty too. Moo-cow, she'd said. Ex-mistress. He didn't like that "ex." What the hell was happening to them?

For minutes he'd been staring at something, unseeing. He focused on it: Derek's note, scotch-taped to the locked door of the loft. Four-fifteen, it said. Ramona's partner, Ken Martin, would bring final paychecks. He glanced at his watch. A little over five hours.

Nick turned to the phone and called his downstairs neighbor.

"You want me to put your blasted dog out again?" she demanded. Julia was nearly seventy, feisty and brac-ing as a splash of astringent. She tried hard to hide her fondness for Maggie and Nick and Sarah and even the blasted dog.

"No. I need advice, Julia."

She picked up the seriousness in his voice instantly. "Maggie told me Ramona Ricci died. I'm so sorry, Nick. Your job too."

"Yeah. But this is a different problem. I think it's different. Julia, when you had your babies, your marriage didn't disintegrate."

"The wind's blowing that way, is it?" she asked thoughtfully.

"Well, did it?"

"Not exactly. But I disintegrated, and so did Vic. Temporarily. Took us months to notice what was happening to the other one."

"Yeah."

"Silly to have honeymoons after weddings and not after babies, you know. Just as much happens to you. 'Course, it's hard to get away from the blasted baby. Nursing and all that. And even if you find an hour, home's no good. Too much work to be done. Distracting."

"Right," he agreed glumly. "So there's no answer?"

"Sure there's an answer. First, you're both exhausted and you will be for a while. So don't dream up any fancy theories about problems that can be explained by being bone-tired."

"Yeah, I see."

"For the rest, talking and hugging is the answer, as usual. The difficulty is finding time for it. You have to schedule it. A little honeymoon, in small weekly doses. Vic and I used to trade time with my cousin. Do you have anyone you can trade with?"

"We don't have many friends with kids. But I'll find someone."

"Good. Now, for the immediate problem. Do you have any money?"

"Some. Final paycheck today."

"You know I don't baby-sit," warned the fiercely independent Julia.

"Hey, I'm not that much of a clod. But I had to ask

someone who'd understand. We'll find someone to trade with."

"You know, though," said Julia, who admired Dorothy Parker, "I've always dreamed of staying in the Algonquin. Even if it means playing nanny a few hours. One time only. Sunday afternoon would do."

"Julia, you're such a hustler!"

She chuckled and hung up. Nick made his arrangements and then sat down on the steps to study his *Back Stage*. He started a list of casting directors he could visit before four, and was debating which one to try first when he heard voices.

"Take it easy!" That was Daphne. "Look, the light's off, see? It's over, honey."

"Oh, God! What'll I do?" Voice breaking, Jaymie ran up a few steps, staring at the darkened transom of the rehearsal loft. Then she noticed Nick.

"Hi," he said.

"Are the others coming? Will we start again?" asked Jaymie, bright-eyed.

"No." He gestured at Derek's note. "Final paychecks."

"Oh, God." Jaymie ran up the remaining distance lightly, read it, and sagged onto the steps. Daphne hurried to her and was pushed away.

"Can I help?" Nick asked her uneasily.

"No." Daphne glanced sadly at Jaymie, then descended a few steps to sit near Nick. "God, I don't have time for this crock! Gotta dress for the hearing, meet the kids—and suddenly Miss Chicago here freaks out. She's coked up. Suddenly got the idea there might be a rehearsal after all. Came charging over. She feels awful."

"Yeah. We all feel rotten."

"Not as rotten as she feels." Daphne lowered her voice, adjusting her African print skirt over her knees. "A week ago she heard that her mom had to go into a nursing home."

"God!"

"They're real close. Her mother sent her to Juilliard, you know, gave her lessons with Madame, everything. But Mrs. Price told Jaymie not to come see her now.

Told her to work on this role, it was the big chance they'd both been waiting for. But it must be serious, going into a home."

"A home!" Jaymie had overheard. "A *home*, they call it! What you do is, you give them all your worldly goods, and in exchange they stick you in a cubbyhole on some long gray corridor!"

"And care," said Daphne. "They have good nurses, she said."

"Yeah. Good nurses. Oh, God, why did she die?"

"Did she—oh, you mean Ramona," said Nick.

"Yeah! Yeah, Ramona! Look, I was doing okay. My mom wanted me to succeed! She backed me up, paid for my apartment here, everything, just so I could—" Blindly, Jaymie yanked a handkerchief from her big tan shoulder bag but didn't use it, just gazed at it musingly as she remembered. "When I was little she gave me lessons, took me to contests. I won them too. Cook County Junior Princess. Singing on the radio. Dancing in the *Nut-cracker*, the Mouse King, when I was very small. But Daddy left anyway. And then we couldn't afford Loreen any more, and she left too. Mom found a high school where I could get training. Said we'd show Daddy. Got me into Daphne's class, and the Juilliard program. Every time—" She pressed the handkerchief to her nose. "Oh, God, why do they have to fire us? After all Mom did!"

"I'm sorry," Nick said.

"Yeah. Even though it turned out to be so long before I got a chance. She always wanted to be a star herself. But Dad picked her out of a chorus line and he was too rich to pass up, she said. But she always missed it terribly. After he left she tried to go back, but by then she was in her thirties. She was so happy when I decided to act."

"My mom was horrified," said Nick.

"God, mine too!" agreed Daphne, looking surreptitiously at her watch. "Look, Jaymie, I have to run along now, to meet—"

"No! Daphne, please! Daddy left and Loreen and Mom— I can't talk to her now, don't you see?" The drug had worn off, and Nick could see how ravaged Jaymie

felt as she tugged at her handkerchief, dark bangs drooping over sad eyes. "I can't tell her it's over. Not now. I
can't let her down now. What can I do?"

"Lie," suggested Daphne unkindly, standing up; but
a glance at Jaymie softened her voice. "Honey, I'll talk
to you later, okay? I have to rush to the studio to change,
and then back to meet the kids at Anna Maria's so we
can plot strategy for the hearing. Don't you see?"

Jaymie came down the steps. "I'll go with you!"

"No way, honey!" Daphne held up a firm palm to
fend off Jaymie's bedraggled, overwrought approach.
"We'll talk later, okay? But today is for Callie and Mellie.
We're going to go into that hearing looking like Saint
Coretta Scott King in three assorted sizes. Blow their
little social-worker minds. And you see, a rich white girl
kind of spoils the image."

Jaymie whispered, "All right." But tears were welling
up again.

Exasperated, Daphne checked her watch again. "Okay,
tell you what, you pay for my taxi and I'll help you come
down now. But just for a few minutes. Then I've got to
go."

Jaymie nodded mutely and Daphne sat back down,
pulling her a little roughly down onto the step beside
her. "Now, look at Nick," she coaxed. "He's checking
*Back Stage* for casting calls. That's what you should be
doing too."

"Is that what you'll do, Daphne?" Jaymie was a little
calmer.

"Nope. What I'll do is go back to work for Madame,"
declared Daphne firmly. "Should have stayed there to
begin with. That's why I'm in trouble with the goddamn
social workers now, you know. Quitting a steady job.
They came sniffing around to see if they could get the
kids away. 'Course, I knew they would, and if it had
been anyone but Ramona—"

"You'd worked with Ramona before, right?" asked
Nick.

"Oh, we go way back together," said Daphne with a
humorless smile. "I was in the chorus of *Devil*. Quite a

coup for a black girl in those days, but they probably figured the honkies would expect to see us dancing in hell. Anyway, one night Ramona popped a toe and thought she couldn't go back on. I poked it back in place for her and she finished the show, even the last dance. Must have appealed to her professionalism, I guess, because after that there was no end to the favors she was ready to do for me. Though she accused me of being a voodoo queen and claimed she'd never miss a show if I was around." She shrugged a slim dark shoulder and added bitterly, "Well, shows you how much use I am as a good-luck charm!"

"It would have been a good show," Nick said.

"Yeah! Yeah, it would have been, wouldn't it? I guess it was the right choice to sign on. Ramona would have put us over. But I feel rotten about the old gal. And it's just so goddamn disappointing."

"The school will take you back?"

"Natch," said Daphne. "They complained when I took time off for this. I've got a way with teens, Madame says. Old slave driver."

"Well, she's right," said Jaymie. "You should see her manage those kids, Nick. Or manage me, for that matter."

"Hey, babe, you're no teen anymore! Yeah, I do like working with them. 'Course, after all the work you end up with nothing but a roomful of sweaty kids. If you're lucky one of them might be half as talented as you or Jaymie, the rest just lumps."

"No Baryshnikovs?"

"Not on my watch. Not yet. Well, I work for the ones with a little something. But I'd hoped to get into more choreography. This job would have opened doors. Freed me a little from Madame."

"I've taught acting in a college," said Nick. "Kids are so enthusiastic. And it felt good to have a solid job."

"Oh, I know. It's got its good side. Even Madame—well, she's a tough, sour old bitch, but I admire her for that when she's not cursing me personally. How about you? Any leads yet?"

"A couple of the calls might be interesting. Mostly I'm going to drop by the casting offices, let them know I'm alive."

"They forget awfully quick."

"They sure do." Nick stood. "Do you want to look at my *Back Stage*? I'm finished."

"Yes!" said Daphne, accepting it purposefully. "Now, Jaymie, we'll run through this and make you a plan. Then you can start making rounds while I'm off at the hearing."

"God, I can't believe I have to start all that again!" Jaymie eyed the newspaper glumly.

"Come on, buck up! Your mother wouldn't want you to be a quitter!" urged Daphne.

"I guess not," she murmured, and took out her appointment book.

Nick glanced back up the steps before going out. They were huddled together at the landing in the gray light from the filthy window. Daphne's maternal arm stretched around Jaymie, dark as the *Victoria R* death gloves.

## XI

*Friday, 11:15 A.M.*
*March 9, 1973*

Nick saw Maggie as soon as he emerged from the loft building: stricken blue eyes fixed on the entrance, one hand patting Sarah on the back, the other holding a fresh disposable diaper. She waved it at him. "Truce?" she offered.

He almost felled a passerby as he bounded across the sidewalk to engulf the two of them in a huge hug. "You bet!"

"I didn't really mean—" She was trying to hug him too.

"No, no." He put a finger on her lips. "Don't take anything back. We really did mean something. Both of us. We need to figure out what."

"Yeah. But I can't even figure out me!"

"Same here. Except for one thing. I've figured out that you are definitely not a moo-cow."

"But I'm so flabby!" She pulled away a little, not looking at him, playing with the zipper on the baby carrier. "I try to work out but there's no time. God, I don't know how you could stay interested."

"Oh, I'm interested. Exhausted sometimes, but interested." He should have guessed; trim and lovely as she seemed to him, her lactating body could not come up to her own gymnast's standards just now. He added,

" 'Age cannot wither her, nor custom stale her infinite variety.' "

Maggie snorted. "Yeah, that's all very well for Egyptian queens who travel on golden barges. But I'm just a slob who rides the subway and oozes all over the goddamn sheets."

He grinned. "They say that Cleopatra too stayed beautiful by bathing in milk."

Her startled eyes met his, then she whooped with laughter. "Nick, you're a delicious man! But don't poke fun. I'm serious!"

"I'm serious too, love. We've got a problem but it's not your body, which is obscenely attractive. In every sense."

A smile flitted across her face, but she turned her attention to the zipper again. "It's just . . . well, you're surrounded by gorgeous people. Ramonas and Didis, and—" She peeked quickly at him before finishing timidly, "And Lisettes."

Dear Lisette. Nick's first wife had been a dazzler, true enough. Beauty, talent, vulnerability enough to make men swoon. He certainly had. What could he say now to Maggie, he who had spent the day savaging her tenderest overtures? Attila O'Connor. Well, Attila, try the truth.

"We've both had some good yesterdays, Maggie," he said gently. "But our ghosts are mostly benevolent ones. They don't interfere much with building a good today. I don't think they're the problem now." She gave a tiny nod and he shrugged. "But hell, I know I can't wave a wand and make you not feel like a dud. I feel like a dud myself."

"Really? You?"

"I can't seem to live up to my own standards anymore."

"Yeah." She nodded grim agreement and absentmindedly jiggled Sarah, who was whimpering. "Nick, I get so ashamed of myself! I mean, you were right the other day, that's why I got mad. You said I was jealous of my own daughter. Goddamn it, I kick myself, but I can't help feeling that way! She needs you, and I want you to pay attention to her. I really do! But when she distracts your attention from me, I'm jealous. Do you know what I mean?"

"Yeah. Same here."

"And even worse." The blue eyes locked on his were dark with shame. "I'm jealous when you distract her attention from me."

A shock of recognition: Madonna came clear. Double love; double envy. Nick nodded slowly. "Yeah. I watch the two of you when you're nursing her or playing with her, all wrapped up in each other. And I'm full of love and joy, like a good and noble daddy. Right out of *The Waltons*. But you're right, I'm also jealous as hell. Of both of you."

"But you—"

Sarah, her whimpers ignored, escalated to a screech. Maggie burst into tears. "Damn it! Not now!"

"Lunchtime?" asked Nick. It was eleven-twenty.

"Yes," sobbed Maggie. "Lunchtime. And then dinner. And then bedtime. And then breakfast. On and on, while everything else disintegrates!"

"Hey. C'mere," said Nick. He led his wailing ladies back across the sidewalk to the loft steps and settled them in the corner. Sarah set greedily to work, impervious to the storms about her. Maggie, whose needs were more complex, continued to snuffle.

"Is that you again, Nick?" called Daphne. She and Jaymie were still huddled at the landing of the stairs, near the light. "Is everything okay?"

"Yes, except the baby's hungry," said Nick.

"Oh, okay." They returned to the notices in *Back Stage*.

Nick sat on the step above Maggie's and leaned forward to murmur into her ear. "We can talk Sunday afternoon."

"Why should Sunday be any different?" she snuffled. "Same as every other damn day. She'll be hungry just as often. Crap just as often. The laundry will be just as dirty. If Dan gets the program debugged, I may even have to go in to work."

"Have to? This is a serious proposal, lady. I want a date."

"Well," she amended, a flicker of curiosity in her tearful glance, "he says it probably won't be ready till Tuesday. But I want to get started the minute he's done. It's so frustrating, wasting the few hours I have to work."

"This won't be a waste of time. I've just splurged half my last paycheck on two rooms at the Algonquin Sunday."

"Two rooms?"

"Different floors. One for you and me. One for Julia, who will take Sarah as soon as you finish nursing so you can slip away for a few hours. I think she plans to teach Sarah all the best Dorothy Parker quips."

Lively interest glowed now in the blue eyes. "And just what is it that I'm slipping away for?"

"For whatever we decide we need. An uninterrupted talk. An uninterrupted fuck. Maybe even an uninterrupted nap."

"God, Nick!" She had bowed her head over Sarah's.

"Is there a problem?" he asked anxiously. "What are you thinking?"

She managed a damp little after-tears grin. "I'm thinking—just in case—I ought to buy some black lace bikinis."

Nick felt like a triumphant gladiator. He let his lips brush her ear. "Maggie one, moo-cow zero," he murmured. She chuckled.

Madonna, he knew, might prove a little harder to vanquish. A tough broad, that one, rooted in childhood taboos. But black lace was potent too. There was hope.

Daphne was standing up. "Zero hour, kid," she said to Jaymie. "I'll see you later." She started firmly down the stairs.

"Maybe," said Jaymie melodramatically.

"Hey." Daphne swiveled on the steps, one foot higher than the other, and raised an admonishing finger. "You're going to be okay, honey. I so decree! But Callie comes first. You understand?"

"Yes." Jaymie's hands clenched on the strap of her bag. "I understand."

Daphne surveyed her an instant, then said gruffly,

"Well, okay, come along and help me get a cab now. You promised." She started down again.

Jaymie jumped up and clattered down after her. Daphne had paused to admire Sarah, who was sunny-tempered again now that her gluttony was sated. "Hey, look at that gorgeous kid!"

Sarah gave her a gummy grin. Jaymie, joining them, smiled too. "Hi, baby," she said, and then sang softly, "Twinkle, twinkle, little star, we'll show Daddy who we are! Up above the world at night, that's my Jaymie's name in lights . . . I mean . . ." Her brows contracted in confusion.

"Boy, your mama was ready to do anything to get back at your daddy, wasn't she?" Daphne laughed. "Come on, babe, let's move out."

"Okay." As they went out the door, Jaymie slipped her appointment book back into her big bag. A small, dark, well-bred volume, not the huge tooled-leather book Ramona had sported.

Ramona's book.

Something clicked.

Nick turned to Maggie. "Hey, Ramona's book!" he exclaimed. Hawkshaw O'Connor. Nick the dick. "It wasn't there!"

"What?"

"Her appointment book. It should have been in the stuff dumped out of her bag in that building."

"You're sure it wasn't under the bag or something?"

"I don't think so. The billfold and the gun would interest a mugger. But a half-used appointment book wouldn't appeal much, would it?"

"Not to me," she said, right with his thought. "Not unless my name was in it, at the wrong place and time."

"Exactly. So it's important that it wasn't there." Nick went up the stairs two at a time.

But Sergeant Perez, when he answered the phone, was not very impressed. "We'll ask him about it," he told Nick.

"Ask who?"

"The suspect."

"The guy who had her gun?"

"Yeah."

"Look, don't you see? If the appointment book is gone, it may be because someone's name was in it. Someone Ramona knew."

"That's only one of many possible explanations," said Perez wearily.

"Yes, but shouldn't you check?"

"Look, Mr. O'Connor, if we thought it was someone in the play, we'd still be grilling you. You especially, you were right there. No one else knew where she'd be. But we've got evidence on this guy. He hangs out in that area, drugged out half the time. He's got a record of violence. And he had her gun. That's solid."

"Has he confessed?"

"You want miracles? Who confesses? He told us he found the gun in a trash can. You wanna guess how many times we've heard that one? But we'll check out this appointment book thing."

"Okay. Thanks." Nick replaced the receiver.

Maggie had come up to the landing and was grinning at him. "Meddler," she said.

Nick drew himself up indignantly. "No, no, you don't understand. When *you* do it, it's meddling. When *I* do it, it's good citizenship." He rubbed a hand over his bald head. "Anyway, I keep coming back to the same problem. We all had everything to lose and nothing to gain."

"Nothing obvious."

"Yes. And if Perez has got the guy with a gun and a record, I should quit worrying about it."

"Tell you what, fellow meddler. You quit worrying about who killed Ramona, and I'll quit worrying about Muffin, after we do one thing."

"Okay. What?"

"Call the baby-sitting service for me and find out how I can reach Mrs. Golden. I'll call her, and then I promise to quit worrying and we can get to work on our own lives."

"Which are worrisome enough. Okay, it's a deal. What's the name?"

"Carstairs, he said."

Nick called directory assistance and dialed. "I'd like to speak to your Mrs. Golden," he explained. "Can you tell me how to contact her?"

"Mrs. Golden? No, I'm sorry." The voice was youthful.

Maybe they were just protective of their employees. He said, "Well, can you pass on a message to her? She can get in touch with us."

"No, I'm sorry, it's not that. We don't have a Mrs. Golden working here."

"You don't?"

"No."

"But a friend said he hired her through you."

"I'm sorry. Perhaps he made a mistake. Or perhaps she misrepresented her affiliation. Is there a problem?"

"No, no. She, um, seemed very competent. Thank you."

Maggie was frowning up the stairs at him as he hung up. "What's the trouble?"

"The trouble is that they claim Mrs. Golden doesn't work for them."

"Oh, hell."

"Any other way to find out what you want?"

"Of course! Montessori! I should have thought of them first. Muffin will be back in school today. C'mon, *chouchoute*, your dad will change you." She carried Sarah and a clean diaper up from the landing, thrust them into Nick's arms, got the number from information, and dialed.

"Hi!" she said brightly when someone answered. "I've been trying to invite Muffin to a birthday party, but I can't reach her mother. Could you tell me . . . Oh, I'm sorry to hear that. I hope it's not serious. . . . Oh, no, I wouldn't dream of it! Thanks so much for your help!"

She replaced the receiver and turned to Nick and Sarah, one eyebrow quirked like a blackbird wing. "They say she has a cold. Isn't in school."

"Maybe it's true." But Nick found himself uneasy too. He concentrated on getting the clean diaper around Sarah's squirming little body. Not an easy task with her on his lap.

"They seemed upset. Said not to bother the Brad-fords while their little girl was sick."

"Don't bother who? Didn't you say Hartford?"

"Mrs. Golden said Hartford."

"Mrs. Golden said Hartford. And she told Buzz she was from the Carstairs Agency, which she's not. Why is she lying?"

"Maybe she misheard his name?"

"And he misheard the agency name? Are you sure he said Carstairs?"

She squeezed her eyes closed, trying to remember. "He just mentioned it in passing as he was tearing off the addresses from his memo pad—hey! There was a logo on the pad!"

"A logo? How does that help?"

"Let's find the yellow pages, Nick. He works down-town here somewhere. Finance or law, from the way he dresses. If I can spot the logo we can call him at work maybe. Ask if she's okay."

This was beginning to sound like a lengthy project. Nick frowned. "He'll probably just tell us she has a cold."

"I know, but—look, Nick, we statisticians are paid for guesswork. We take fragmentary information and use it scientifically to make guesses about the unknown truth. Obviously we'll be mistaken sometimes, and so we think a lot about the cost of our mistakes. If I guess something is true, and it's not, what's the cost? Or if I guess it's not true, and it really is, what's the cost of that? Part of my job is minimizing the cost of mistakes."

"Thanks, Prof, for the lecture in the philosophy of statistics," said Nick gently. "But please tell me what's in your gut."

She perched on the step next to them and held out a finger to Sarah, who seized it, as fascinated as if she'd never seen it before. "Nick, I took a little girl from school, because a man who said he was her father seemed to be in trouble. I gave her to a woman who might have been a baby-sitter, and might have been named Mrs. Golden, and might have made a mistake about Mr. Brad-ford's name, and might have been from an agency."

"Or might not," said Nick.

"Buzz might be her father, or he might be Mrs. Golden's partner. And if he is her father, and if there is a problem, he doesn't know how to find me. And maybe it's silly to worry, but goddamn it, people should take care of little girls! Even other people's little girls!"

That passion ran raw in her, he knew. And he could empathize now. On the few occasions when they had left Sarah for a couple of hours with a friend, she had always been clean and coddled on their return. But if anyone ever frightened her or hurt her . . . He pushed aside the image of his own hypothetical rage and hugged Maggie with the arm that wasn't holding Sarah. "You're right, love. This thing is damn fishy. And I see the point of your statistical logic. If she's really not in trouble, and we investigate, the cost is a bit of our time. Precious time, granted, but only time. On the other hand, if she is in trouble, and we can help but don't bother, the cost to her may be terrible."

Her eyes were alight again. "Okay, team. Let's go hunting."

Anna Maria next door let them borrow the yellow pages in exchange for being allowed to hold Sarah. Maggie looked through Lawyers, then Commodity Brokers and Financial Planners before she hit Investment Securities and said, "That's it!" A big block *B*, the two interior half-circles transformed into a fat dotted *i*. "Busby Investments. Look, World Trade Center. He could walk here in half an hour, even with a crutch. Or get a cab."

"Busby Investments," said Nick. "Buzz."

"Hey, right! I'll call." She copied the number and they went to Anna Maria's pay phone.

"Hello. May I speak to Mr. Bradford? . . . Yes, hello, may I speak to Mr. Bradford?" There was a long pause. "Oh, no, no message, but could you give me his home phone? It's rather urgent. . . . I see. Well, I'll try back later." She hung up and turned back to Nick.

"Not there?" he asked.

"She said he went home. They don't give out home information, but when she asked someone in the background where he was, I heard him yell 'He's in Garden-port.' "

They looked at each other. Nick rescued Sarah from Anna Maria's cooing and grumbled, "The cost of this possible mistake is going up every minute."

"I'm sorry, Nick. Is it too high?"

He sighed. "Not yet, I guess. Not unless it interferes with taking care of our own little girl and our own lives. Which includes picking up my check here at four-fifteen."

"Here I go, then." She held out her arms for Sarah, her eager gaze once again as vibrant as in the first days he'd known her. Nick smiled and shook his head.

"No. Here *we* go. The three musketeers."

From Canal Street, Penn Station was three stops away, and by racing they caught a train just about to leave for Gardenport and points east. Gasping, they flung themselves into their seats. Sarah, delighted by the gallop, was crowing.

"You suppose we're raising her to be a meddler too?" asked Maggie, laughing at her.

"How can she help it?" Infected by Sarah's glee, Nick too was grinning like a fool.

"Guess she can't." Maggie sobered. "And speaking of meddling, I want to know why you were so excited about the thought that Ramona's appointment book was missing."

"No good reason. I mean, Perez is right. None of us want Ramona dead."

"Also, they've got a black guy with the murder weapon. And Carlotta said the killer was black."

"Yeah, but that doesn't bother me."

She raked her fingers through her curls thoughtfully. "Daphne? She's the only black connected with the show, isn't she? It's true, she's slim. Carlotta did say it was a kid."

"Maybe Daphne. Maybe Daphne's niece—she was there too. Or maybe someone else. I told you about the death scenes in the play, didn't I? How we pull on the black gloves to symbolize death?"

"God, that's right!" Maggie snapped upright, fastening on this idea. "A murderer would want to avoid fingerprints anyway. And Carlotta only saw the arms. And for someone theatrical—that's perfect!"

"Also, there's our assassination scene," Nick went on. "Based on a real event. Someone tried to assassinate Victoria, fired two shots. Neither worked."

"Two shots. You mean maybe Ramona's killer wasted the second on purpose, so it would match the show?"

"Oh, I know it's farfetched."

"But theatre people are a farfetched lot. God, Nick! I see why that missing book looks ominous!" She leaned back, mulling over his words.

Nick looked out the window. They had emerged from the long tunnel, and late winter sunlight struggled to cheer up grimy factories and rail yards. He shook his head. "But I keep smacking up against the fact that none of us wanted Ramona dead, no matter how much she might have been bugging us that one day."

Maggie nodded and glanced at Sarah, who was subsiding into sleep to the lullaby of clicking wheels. "Even so—tell me who she was bugging. Derek, I suppose. Maybe threatening to tell his wife about their affair?"

"Yes, that's one possibility. But it's obvious that he's committed to this show, more than the rest of us, if that's possible. And—"

"I know. But forget the counterarguments for a minute. You're right to be bothered about all those parallels. Just tell me who else was upset."

Nick squinted at the windows across the aisle, where the glittering skeletons of the World's Fair were sliding past, and cast his mind back to Ramona's last rehearsal. "God, who wasn't? You mentioned Derek. She cut Larry's solo and insulted him in front of Didi. She told Jaymie it was a good thing she'd never get a chance to go on as understudy. She threatened Daphne with bad references, insulted her choreography. Insulted Callie too. The niece. For that matter, she insulted me. Also did her best to get me in trouble with you. Hell, Larry's right, I've got as good a motive as anyone."

She grinned and waved her hand airily. "Fortunately, you've got a terrific alibi. Me. Also, you had a lot more reason for wanting her alive. You loved the show. Loved your part. Didn't mind getting paid."

"Yes. But that's true of everyone else. I suppose you could say Jaymie doesn't need the money as much as the rest of us, but the real need is psychological and she's as desperate to act as any of us."

"So you agree with Perez. No motive."

"I have to."

She pondered a moment. "The husband? Jenkins?"

"Yeah, that's true. Though the rest doesn't fit him as well."

"Still—well, I really thought Perez was right. They've got the guy. But now I'm not so sure. Keep on the case, meddler!"

"Okay. Though I don't know what to do next."

"Yeah." She looked out the window at a sparkling bay coming into view. "God, Nick, I hope Muffin's okay. Wish this train would hurry."

In fact the Long Island Railroad transcended its reputation and delivered them to Gardenport in the advertised thirty-one minutes.

The area around the station was chiefly a parking lot on a commercial street of upscale coffee shops and dry cleaners. A single cab was parked by the station.

"Library?" asked the cabbie, with a glance at the three elderly women in bright plaid blazers who were waving at him from the station behind them. "Sure, I could take you there, but you'd hate me. It's close, this side of Northern Boulevard. Couple of blocks."

"Thanks," said Nick. They followed his pointing finger, leaving him to the doubtless more lucrative use of the three women laden with Saks Fifth Avenue bags.

The directory and maps were clear: Steven M. Bradford lived on Garden Lane, four blocks the other side of the station on the hill that sloped down to the bay. They walked along oak-lined streets past tall evergreen privacy hedges, exotic specimen trees still bleak in March, dormant lawns, wide-spaced imitation Tudors and imitation colonials and imitation ranch houses clashing in their varied attempts to evoke other places and eras. The

Bradford place was one of the Tudors. A magnificent silver limousine was in the driveway.

"Well. Shall we ring the bell?" asked Nick. They had paused across the street by a shaggy hedge.

"No. Let me think. The woman at Montessori was so urgent about not bothering them. And I don't know for certain that Steve Bradford is the guy I talked to. So I'd like to scout a little first. I mean, if Muffin really is there with a cold, there's no sense—wait!"

As one, they ducked into the hedge. Five people were emerging from the front door of the Bradford place: a handsome man younger than Nick, though there was a touch of gray at his temples; an older man in a wheelchair pushed by a muscular black in a business suit; and two women—one willowy, caramel-blond, beautiful except for the raw anxiety that tightened her face; the other far advanced in pregnancy, with dark hair pulled back to a clasp at the nape of her neck.

"The younger guy is Buzz," Maggie murmured.

"So he checks out. But I don't see Muffin."

"No. Of course if she's sick in bed—look, he's leaving."

Steve/Buzz shook hands with the old man, picked up a briefcase again, and strode off toward the station. The pregnant woman hugged the blonde and then crossed the lawn to the gray clapboard colonial next door. The older man looked up at the blonde, his tanned, weather-beaten face softening a moment as he squeezed her hand. Her hauntingly tense expression did not relax, but she kissed him automatically on the forehead. He signaled imperiously to the black man, who trundled him across the lawn and into the car backseat, then stowed the wheelchair, took the wheel, and eased the big machine into the road.

It slowed by their hedge. "Who's there?" demanded the driver.

Nick murmured, "I'll field this." He flipped open his notebook and stepped out, looking startled. "Huh?"

"What the hell are you lurking there for?" demanded the sun-crinkled old man in the backseat.

"Just counting pledges." Nick was all earnest inno-
cence. "We're having a local fund-raising drive, and I'm
only a thousand dollars or so from my goal today. Would
you like to—"

The old man's hard eyes skimmed over Nick. "Anh,
he's all right, Bill. Just some do-gooder. What're you
collecting for, son?"

Nick cast about for an innocuous cause. "The YWCA,"
he said proudly. "We're trying to raise money for—"

But the old man exploded. "The YWCA! Bunch of
anti-Americans!"

"Oh. I'm sorry, sir." Nick backpedaled. "It's actually for swimming lessons, here locally, sir."

"Yeah, yeah, I know. You're going to claim you're
not responsible. Second Amendment in shreds, Russians
on the borders, the goddamn YWCA inviting them
in for tea! You're not responsible for that either, I
suppose?"

"I certainly hope not, sir!"

"Well, you just get the hell off my daughter's street.
And tell your namby-pamby YWCA to keep out of mat-
ters they don't understand. And tell them *my* money's
going to the Sportsmen's Alliance. Every penny." A spasm
of pain crossed the wrinkled face and he closed his eyes
and leaned back in the seat. "Get moving, Bill. I've got
a plane to catch."

The limousine pulled away. Nick, shaken by the dia-
tribe, managed to stay in character. He made a show of
looking hesitantly at his notebook, then at the Bradford
house, then at the retreating limousine. Out of the corner
of his mouth he muttered to Maggie, "Sorry. Didn't mean
to choose such a subversive charity. What the hell is the
YWCA doing to the Second Amendment?"

"I think I read somewhere that they support handgun
registration."

"Ah, of course. The primrose path to a Russian take-
over."

"Well," said Maggie pragmatically, "at least you convinced him you weren't interested in his family especially."

"Only in selling out my country. He'll probably turn me in to the CIA."

"Right. What now?"

"Let's not bother the blonde if we can help it," said Nick. That tense face haunted him.

"Yeah," agreed Maggie soberly. "If Muffin's sick, I have a feeling she's very sick. But I still want to scout a little here. We can always catch Buzz in Manhattan, now that we know where he works."

"Okay. Game time. I play private eye, interview the expectant friend. You and Sarah play Peeping Tom, see if you can spot Muffin through a window. Okay?"

"Fine. There's lots of foundation shrubbery. Plenty of cover."

"Looks like plenty of money," said Nick, helping Maggie tuck the flaps of the carrier around Sarah's head for protection against branches.

Maggie mused, "Think we'd look like plenty of money if we bought shrubs to plant in front of our brownstone?"

"No need. We can just transplant the mold in the fridge."

"Luxurious." She grinned, then pointed at the house where the pregnant woman had disappeared. "Give me two minutes to slip over to the side away from Buzz's. His front lawn is more open, so I'd rather work along the hedge there and around from the back. I'll meet you back here when we're both done."

"Sarah, you're going to love this," said Nick.

He watched them disappear into the hedge, Maggie agile and solicitous of the bundled baby, and remembered Maggie when he had first met her, winging among the catwalks high above a college stage. She had always loved action, games, justice, jokes. Had always felt responsible for friends, for children. Had never flinched from adventure. Sarah may have diminished the opportunity, but she hadn't damped that life-embracing curiosity.

And hell, admit it, Nick, you old meddler. You enjoy a spot of adventure too. Why else would you stick with

such an idiotically risky profession? Anyway, this was
better than brooding over lost jobs.

He checked his wallet and selected a library card
with official-looking print, assumed his best Philip Mar-
lowe air, and strode to the door of the colonial. Indian-
red door against gray clapboard and white trim. He rang
the bell.

# XII
## *Friday, 1:30 P.M.*
## *March 9, 1973*

At close range the young brunette who answered was heavy but attractive. She had strong features with a lazily humorous cast, and thick, gleaming hair.

"My name's O'Connor. Private investigator," he said, flashing the library card at her.

Her eyes darted to the Bradford place as she said, "Jesus, who the hell sent you?"

"Busby Investments," improvised Nick.

"God, that old fart! So that's why he was talking to you out there!"

Not the answer he had expected, but an interesting one. He said, "I just have a couple of questions. About the Bradfords."

"Well, get the hell inside before the whole neighborhood sees you." With a disgusted gesture she waved him inside. "Have you talked to Steve and Elaine?"

Elaine. That must be the tense blonde. Steve's wife. The old man's daughter, whose street Nick was to get the hell off of. Nick said, "I had a couple of minutes with Steve. That's all."

"Will you have to talk to Elaine?"

She was a bit bristly. Protective of her neighbor. Well, the Montessori woman had been too. And Nick's own glimpse of that lovely taut face made their attitude understandable. Muffin had more than a cold, he knew already. He said, "Elaine's very upset, I understand. So I won't bother her if I can get the information elsewhere. One reason I'm talking to you."

She relaxed, resting her hand against her swollen belly. "What a mess. But if old man Busby sent you, who am I to complain? You know that Steve and Elaine think he shouldn't even have called the police. And now you! Steve must have hit the ceiling."

"Yes, he did." Was this a police matter, then?

"But you take orders from the old man no matter what Steve says?"

"Who's paying me? But I'll try to be discreet."

She gave him a wry look. "Well, off to a great start, aren't you? At least the police had the sense not to come banging on the front door!"

He put on an abashed face. "Gee, you want me to try again, I'll come down the chimney."

This evoked a quick laugh. "Oh, hell, come on back and have some coffee." She led the way through an early American living room, some authentic old pine pieces there, to a modern kitchen with a clutter of expensive breakfast dishes still stacked by the sink. The place smelled clean, spray wax and fresh coffee. Once, before Sarah, Nick's house had sometimes smelled like that. She asked, "Cream and sugar?"

"Black's fine."

She poured two mugs, arranged her spreading body in a caned Breuer chair at the round oak table, and motioned Nick to take another. "Okay. What does old Busby want to know?"

Nick pulled out his notebook, filled with casting directors' names. "It's usually best if you tell me in your own words. So I don't put ideas into your head." As though he had any ideas to put there.

"You look for discrepancies, huh? And then whirl and point your finger at me and announce, 'Hah, Rachel did it!' "

Nick grinned at this pleasant, mocking mother-to-be. "Wow. Sounds like fun. Maybe I should change my technique."

"It's not like that, huh?"

"It's usually sitting in a car for hours going numb while some guy goes to work and to business meetings instead of having the affair his wife thinks he's having. Or it's sitting at a typewriter for hours attempting to compose a report that won't put the client to sleep too. Hell, you're the high point of my week!"

She laughed again. "Poor little man! No one ever said that to me, not even when I still had my figure!"

"Shucks, no one ever said it to me either. And my figure's as good as it ever was."

She looked over his broad build with unconcealed amusement. "Yeah, we're a couple of battleships, aren't we? Okay, you want my own words on this, you say."

"Right." Nick found a clean page in his notebook.

"You mean just the part I was involved with? Because Steve or old Busby must have told you about the kidnap note."

Something icy clamped in Nick's chest. Worse than a cold, indeed. But he stayed in character. Coolly professional, Nick the private eye replied, "Yes. But tell me about it in its proper place. And why Steve and Elaine are worried about police and detectives, because so far I only have Busby's side."

"Steve was short with you? I thought so."

"Very short."

"Okay." The coffee mugs were expensive and Danish. She held hers in both hands as she sipped. "Let's see. Begin at the beginning. Elaine had to go to Palm Beach because your employer was having a prostate operation. Hah, bet he didn't tell you that detail!"

"No, he didn't," said Nick truthfully.

"Yeah, wouldn't fit his image," she said with satisfaction. "The old fool came up here personally with the money, dragging that male nurse. Pardon me for insulting your source of income, but he really is antediluvian. Big money, big game. Elaine says he's got lions, rhinos, et cetera. A whole herd of heads looking down at you in his billiard room. How could he shoot those beautiful creatures just for his billiard room?" She regarded him belligerently.

"Gives him a sense of achievement?"

"Achievement! No doubt it makes him feel all male and primeval. Except he needs about a million dollars' worth of technology for killing to bring him up to the ability of one of the animals he shoots. How primeval is a rifle or a jeep? Listen, I'm boring you, but I don't like hunting."

Nick tapped his notebook. "Yeah, I've already put you down as pro flowers and puppies."

She grinned her lazy grin. "Pro motherhood and apple pie too, as you can see. Okay, so Elaine took Muffin to school and then flew off to help restore her dad to manhood. I'd offered to help with Muffin, but Steve said no need, he'd pick up Muffin himself. Then, Thursday afternoon—God, that's just yesterday, isn't it?—he called. Some big job had come up at the office, and he hated to bother me, but could I pick up Muffin after all? Okay, no big deal, a thirty-minute train ride. So I went waddling off to the big city. Hi, I say brightly, I'm here to get Muffin. Oh, sorry, she says, Muffin went with someone else."

"I see." Nick was scribbling in his book, trying to imagine Rachel at Steve's little SoHo apartment with the voluble Mrs. Golden. "Who did she go with?"

"Tall, curly black hair, a baby of her own. Seemed bright and competent, and Muffin took to her, she said. So it didn't occur to her that Steve had meant me instead of her."

"I see." Nick hid his dismay by chewing on the pencil. Was this story leading where he feared?

Rachel leaned forward earnestly. "It's got to be someone at Steve's firm, don't you think? How else would this curly-haired woman have known to cut in line ahead of me? But if someone overheard his call to me, they'd know it was their chance to get the baby. Might have planned it a long time ago and waited till a chance like this came up."

"Makes sense," said Nick slowly. He was right, damn it; Mrs. Golden had told Rachel that Maggie had taken Muffin! And they'd already failed to find Mrs. Golden, who had left no traces. Poor Bradford was doubtless in the same situation and had only her false references.

Had he seen her face-to-face? Possibly; but Nick remembered that Maggie had delivered the envelope with the pay. Perhaps Rachel was the only one who could identify the woman, if she could be found.

Rachel; and Maggie.

Who was the prime suspect until the truth was found.

There was another possibility, he realized. Could Rachel be lying? Must be someone at Steve's firm, she'd suggested, someone who had overheard Steve's arrangements with her and could send the kidnapper ahead. But she, Rachel, also knew the arrangements, also could send someone ahead. And she knew intimate details of the Bradfords' life, the source of their money, where they spent their time and when. Everything a kidnapper needed. In that way, perhaps a more likely criminal than Mrs. Golden.

Rachel said, "You're big on thinking, aren't you?"

Nick pulled his thoughts back from theory and shrugged. "Well, when I started out I used six-guns instead. But I'm a low-budget operation and bullets cost more than thoughts."

She smiled. "In every way."

"Anyway, I think you're right about the coworker," he said. "They probably had a plan made up waiting for the right situation to come along. And of course I'll be checking out the firm, though not openly. Busby insisted."

"I'll bet."

"Okay. What did you do when you heard someone had already taken Muffin?"

"Well, I didn't know what to think. She was so sure about it. Said Steve had mentioned a baby. I told her he probably just meant I was pregnant. Right? But she gave me this funny look and I realized she really believed the curly-haired woman. And furthermore, she thought I was a kook! Well, I am, but not that kind. I tried to call Steve but he'd already left the office. I decided maybe he'd found someone closer but by the time he'd tried to call me back I'd left. So I went home and waited for Steve and Elaine to arrive from the airport. Worried as hell."

Nick had finished his coffee. He pushed the mug aside. "And rightly so."

She nodded, the lazy grin gone now. One of her fingers traced the design on her Danish mug. "They found the note when they got home. It was terrible. Ugly stuff about cutting off fingers—God, I've had nightmares about it! About my baby. . . . Anyway, it said specifically, no police."

"Yes," said Nick. "Steve Bradford was worried about that too. I'll do my best." Steve would have told him about the note too. So he asked obliquely, "And they've followed the instructions in the note, he said."

"Right. Steve left just a few minutes ago to deliver the money. The guys have a weird sense of humor. Wanted the money delivered in a toy bear! There's one for old Busby's billiard room!"

Nick grinned. "I'm not supposed to laugh at him. He's my employer."

"Oh, I know." She grew serious. "I suppose he thinks he's doing right. And it's his half-million bucks the kidnappers want, we all know that. Steve and Elaine can hardly tell him off. I mean, they're like us and everyone else on this street, mortgaged up to their ears. This burg is a Chase Manhattan company town."

"God, looks pretty comfortable to me."

"Oh, yeah, can't complain. Unless Bob loses his job, or one of us gets sick, or the baby. Then we drown without a trace, and Chase Manhattan finds a rounder peg to drop in this little hole."

"Not much danger of that, is there?"

She lifted her shoulders an inch, frowning at her empty mug. "I've been lucky. I worry what would happen if we lost Bob's income for some reason. I mean, here I am, seven months committed to having this kid, and no job of my own, no way to pay off this huge house. Not like Elaine. Steve is pretty well set because it's her dad's business. And if Daddy dies, then it's her business."

"So why are they mortgaged?"

"Oh, I told you Busby was antediluvian. He thinks it builds character or something to owe money to the bank." She leaned back, stroked her blouse smooth over her distended belly, and mused, "I think they would have built enough character with all the trouble they had having a baby. That's tough on a person."

"Fertility problems?" he hazarded, hoping to keep the information coming. Rachel, less secure financially than her friend, had obviously given some thought to ways in which she was more fortunate.

"I guess so. And miscarriages. Elaine says once Muffin was born Steve treated her like a goddess or something. We were sitting by the dock one day, and she said, 'I bet it would be fun to do it in the sailboat.' And I said, 'God, you mean you haven't?' And she told me how she was sort of on a pedestal." Her cheeks colored. "My God, I shouldn't be telling you this!"

"No, you're right. It feeds into the whole kidnap situation. Better to hear it from you than to have to ask Elaine."

"Yeah, you better not ask her about this." The lazy grin came back. "Thank God my Bob doesn't respect me that much!"

*Ah, shrewd and lusty lady, you'll find that being three is far more complicated than being two.* Nick felt a stirring of sympathy for Steve. If Sarah, quickly conceived and smoothly borne, could wreak such emotional havoc, how much more complicated it would be if she also symbolized a long-sought prize! But Rachel wouldn't understand yet. So he just smiled and said, "So long as Bob respects the mortgage payments, right?"

"Yeah. Bottom line. And listen, Mr. Private Eye O'Connor, if a single word of this last stuff gets back to Busby, I'll personally slay you."

"I know. I'm not an idiot. Merely a paid brute."

"Well, brute, I only told you so you wouldn't be bugging Elaine." She still felt guilty.

He hastened to reassure her. "I shouldn't have to now. Tell you what, when I leave I'll go inspect your hedges. You can tell people I'm a landscape contractor bidding on a job."

"Good idea. But listen, try to make old Busby understand." Her dark eyes pinned him with their earnestness. "This is not a big game hunt. This time the quarry is a little girl, not a rhino. And we want her back alive. So tell him to quit making the kidnappers nervous. To quit sending guys like you around."

"Yes." She could be right. Or, he reminded himself, she could be warning him away because she herself was involved in the plot. He almost hoped she was; his presence might panic a kidnapper into doing something rash, but if Rachel was involved, she seemed cool, witty, not rash at all. Still, better keep her thinking that he liked her theory. He said, "I won't be doing much until the little girl is home safely. After that I'll check out Steve's coworkers."

"Good."

Nick decided to risk another question. "Also, he sent me packing so fast that I didn't get the address of the woman who gave Muffin to the kidnapper."

"Mitzi's address? Sorry, I don't know. But you can get in touch with her at Montessori any day. But—"

"I know, I promised! Not until after the little girl is back. Thank you," said the private eye automatically, closing his notebook. But Nick's mind churned as he walked back through the house.

Rachel said she had gone to Montessori to pick up Muffin.

Not to Mrs. Golden.

And that put a different and even uglier slant on the case.


The one-eyed bear stared glumly at Steve.

Steve stared at the bills. Hard to believe how much it was.

Busby, fuming about the tight schedule, had grumbled that they'd only had time to mark the five hundreds. Fifty thou. Steve pulled one out of its bundle, squinted at it, finally spotted the little extra curlicue on McKinley's portrait. Idiotic old Busby. A professional kidnapper would see that instantly. Well, he'd fix that—or rather, Busby Investments would. Banks were pulling these larger denominations out of circulation, and Busby Investments, a good-citizen firm, would cooperate fully and change them for hundreds. They were going to follow the instructions in that note, damn it, whatever the old man thought! Busby didn't care about Muffin, he only cared about revenge on people who tweaked his nose.

But Steve had to stay cool, move calmly, so the secretaries wouldn't ask premature questions. The rest of the bundle would be as safe here as anywhere. He unlocked his top left drawer and slid the bag and the bear inside, next to his gun. Beautiful, tiny gun. He frowned at it a moment, then loaded it. He'd feel better carrying the gun when the time came.

The bear looked at him from the drawer.

Steve slid the gun into his pocket, along with his new passport. That had cost money too. But it was completely confidential, his expensive contact had promised; and the man was real, or had been, with a birth certificate on file somewhere in Chile and probably old school records, in case anyone checked. José Santos, he was called. Blue-eyed, like Steve. A few years younger. But the photograph in the passport was Steve's.

His plan was complete. He'd change the bills and wait here at the office, calm and respectable, until late afternoon. Then he'd leave, call Elaine from a booth. He'd talk in a funny voice, high-pitched, to tell her that the ransom had been received. And he'd give her the address of the Douglaston day-care center where he'd told Mrs. Golden to take Muffin today.

Then he'd catch the JFK Express, anonymous in the crowd, and be in time for the evening flight. Steve Bradford would never be seen again.

But José Santos, lucky man, would turn up in Caracas tomorrow, with half a million in his pocket and Susan on his arm.

*part four*

# THE SHORT HAPPY LIFE OF JOSÉ SANTOS

*(Friday afternoon, March 9, 1973)*

# XIII

*Friday, 2 P.M.*
*March 9, 1973*

Even being chief suspect in a kidnapping was not enough to dull Maggie's appetite.

"It's almost two o'clock," she complained. "And they haven't told people about it, if they don't even want the police to know."

"That's assuming Rachel is telling the truth. At least hide the curly black hair, okay?" suggested Nick. "I'll carry the baby. Not much we can do about your height."

"You could keep putting off lunch. I'm shrinking already," grumbled Maggie. She was scraping her hair back and tying her scarf over it tightly. But despite her complaints her eyes were lively again, anxiety and fatigue driven out by excitement. The pleasure of the hunt, of having a concrete problem instead of amorphous unease? Nick found it hard to imagine her an untouchable madonna now, with the imps back in her eyes.

But at the moment the highest priority was getting her out of the Bradford neighborhood, though she refused to go any farther than a café on the parkway not far from the Long Island Railroad station. Maggie sank her teeth into a cheeseburger and mumbled, "So somebody's lying. Who? And where have they hidden Muffin? Because there wasn't a sign of her around the Bradford house. Elaine Bradford was sitting in the kitchen. Just sitting, staring at the telephone. God, Nick, I want to throttle somebody! But who?"

Nick arranged Sarah's blanket. She was sound asleep on the seat of the booth beside him. "Three possibilities," he said. "Mrs. Golden, for starts. If she kidnapped Muffin, she's done a good job of hiding her tracks. Told Bradford the wrong agency. Told you his name was Hartford."

"Yeah, but how did she know I didn't know his name?"

"True. Still, it was worth a try. If you'd corrected her, she could have pretended she misheard. Anyway, maybe she lied about her own name too."

"Yeah." Maggie looked glum but didn't stop chewing. "God, I knew there was something not quite right there. I hope we end up with more identification of her than whatever Identi-Kit portrait I can make."

"You think they'll let you try, if they arrest you?"

She shook her head. "I just wish I could remember some of the other things she said. Maybe one would lead us to her somehow." The cheeseburger was disappearing fast. "Okay. Number two, maybe Rachel is lying."

"She's certainly in an ideal position for a kidnapper," said Nick. "She lives next door, and she's pregnant so she has a good excuse to ask questions about the details of Muffin's life."

"That's true." Maggie chewed thoughtfully a moment. "And the parents seem to trust her. She's even been told about the progress of the case. Knows about the ransom and the stuffed toy. But why would she tell you? And if she took Muffin from Mrs. Golden, why would she claim that she went to Montessori? It's so easy to check."

"Well, maybe she did go to Montessori, to throw the police off the scent, and then went to Mrs. Golden later."

"Won't wash. Because Steve would have told her where to pick up the kid, and he'd remember."

"Which brings us to possibility number three," said Nick.

"Steve my-friends-call-me-Buzz Bradford." Maggie waved the waitress over and asked for pie and a second glass of milk. Then she continued, "But that won't wash either. It's his own daughter."

"Still," mused Nick, "it's simpler if he's the one who's lying."

"How do you mean?"

"If Steve told you the truth, both women have to be lying—Mrs. Golden about the agency, Rachel about where she went to pick up Muffin."

"Yes."

"But he's the one who told you the name of the agency. He's the one who told Rachel where to look for Muffin. He's the one who didn't give his full name or tell you how to reach him in case of trouble."

"Or ask how to reach me in case of trouble. Right. And he's the one, maybe, who told Mrs. Golden his name was Hartford."

"Yes."

The pie arrived, looking machine-made and aged simultaneously. Oblivious to its provenance, Maggie set to work on it. "I believe it with my head. But it can't be true!"

Nick, contenting himself with coffee, asked, "Is it that you can't believe such a successful guy would set you up?"

"Hell, no! For half a million I'd consider setting someone up myself! But Nick, it's his own *daughter!*"

"Hey, you know parents aren't all great. Kids get beaten, abandoned—all kinds of terrible betrayals. Look at Jaymie. At Ramona."

"Yes," she said stubbornly, "I know there could be stresses in his life. But we've all got stresses. Right now, if Dan can't adapt his program, we'll lose money on the Department of Corrections bid. And you're back to making rounds. Stress, right? And yet Sarah's the only part of my life that I know for sure won't be sacrificed. Whatever happens."

Nick nodded.

She waved in the general direction of Gardenport. "That sister from South Brooklyn told us about families with real problems. How could Steve Bradford have that much stress? All that money makes this place look like Oz to me."

Nick took her hand. A bony, strong, hardworking

hand. He said, "Gladstone was in politics for the money. Lots of mouths to feed, the family estate to maintain. He rose to the top, ran the greatest empire of its day. It's hard to imagine a more perfect citizen of the world— loyal husband, devoted father, great statesman. But he was always tortured, pulled in one direction by his zeal to reform the world through religion, another direction by his oratorical talents, yet another by his taste for prostitutes."

"You think maybe Steve got pulled too far in some direction? And wasn't strong enough to resist? But his daughter—"

"I know. I can't imagine anything in the world that would lead me to hurt or frighten Sarah. But it's always a balancing act. Hell, Maggie, you know that from your own life! Maybe he's got gambling debts, or a black-mailer." He remembered what Rachel had said about Elaine's being on a pedestal. "Or maybe he's just noticed he's middle-aged and life is passing him by."

Her thoughtful gaze met his and sharpened, searching for a personal meaning. "What the hell do men think life is?"

"Hey, we're all given these little idealized pictures— even Gladstone liked to visualize himself as a religious reformer. But it's damn hard to find idealized exciting images of fathers to emulate. I mean, who are the famous fathers? Lear? Rigoletto? Montague and Capulet?"

"Don't you dare emulate them!"

"Well, there are a few good guys famous for being dads, but they're such wimps. Saint Joseph, or the Wal-tons."

"Yeah. Don't emulate them either." She was smiling at him now, intrigued by his observation.

"Or look at history," Nick continued. "George Wash-ington, father of his country but not of babies. Jesus was not a father. He's defined as son. And His father is pretty hard to emulate."

"True."

"Or go back into the Old Testament. Good old Father Abraham. Remembered for his readiness to sacrifice his son for the sake of an ideal. Are we to emulate him?"

"You're suggesting Steve is emulating him?" said Maggie, then suddenly her eyes flared open with excitement. "Oh, God! Abraham!" She sprang to her feet.

"What's up?"

"Abraham! He lives in Bay Ridge!" She was sprinting to the back of the restaurant toward the telephones.

"Long way from the Holy Land," muttered Nick to Sarah, who slept on.

Maggie was a long time on the phone. When she returned she looked grim and didn't sit down. "*Espèce de salaud*," she said, snatching up the baby carrier and strapping it on. "Let's go!"

Hastily Nick picked up Sarah. "Um—mind bringing me up to date? In English, please."

"We're going back to the station. That son of a bitch! Where the hell is our bill?"

"Coming, I think," said Nick as he slid Sarah into the carrier. The waitress, alarmed by the obvious signs of hasty departure, was scribbling on a pad and in a moment had brought it to them.

Maggie was already at the door. "Okay. Hurry. Let's see if we can catch the quarter to three."

Outside he had to stretch a little to match her long, angry strides. "I can tell it's serious," he said, "because you're swearing in French and because you left half your pie. Is it Steve?"

"Yes. Unless Mrs. Golden is the best liar ever. Which is still possible, I suppose."

"You spoke to her? Father Abraham appeared in a vision and gave you her phone number?"

They had paused grudgingly for a light, but Maggie started across the street as soon as the traffic thinned. "God, Nick, bear with me! I'll try to be coherent. First, it's not Father Abraham. It's Nephew Abraham. Jerry Abraham of Bay Ridge, her sister's son. Jerry wasn't home, but his wife was, and she gave me Mrs. Golden's phone number."

"Golden is her real name, then?"

"Unless this is a more elaborate setup than seems probable. I called the number Mrs. Abraham gave me, and there she was. Chatty as ever."

"What did you say?" he asked nervously.

"Well, in case she's involved in the kidnapping, I didn't want to let her know that I knew about it."

"Right."

"So I told her I was the one who brought Muffin to her yesterday. She might have recognized my voice anyway. I said I'd just discovered Muffin's sweater among Sarah's things, and I wanted to give it back and needed the parents' phone number. Did she have it? No, she said, Mr. Hartford said he'd be at a lot of different numbers in his job, so he'd call her."

"Hartford again?"

"She was sure. He spelled it for her on the phone."

"Hartford for her, Buzz for you—looks damning. Let's jump to the punch line, okay? Where's Muffin?"

"Douglaston. Two stops down the line from here. There's a church drop-in baby-sitting service near the main street. Mr. Hartford called her last night and said he'd been held up, please keep Muffin overnight at the apartment. He said he'd add a hundred dollars to her fee. So she said fine. Then early this morning he called again and told her to take Muffin to the drop-in center in Douglaston. He or his wife would pick her up. She objected a little, but he said he'd already messengered a package there with her pay. She went, the package with her pay was there, so she left the little girl and took her money back home."

"So we call Elaine Bradford."

Maggie shook her scarfed head. "Not unless Muffin is really there. If she's not, if Mrs. Golden is lying or if Steve has moved her again, the cruelest thing we could do to that woman is raise a false alarm. Look, here comes the train. Sarah and I will get off at Douglaston and see if we can locate Muffin, and you—"

"Maggie, you're already a suspect! You should stay away from her!"

Maggie found a set of seats facing each other, flopped into one of them, and propped her feet on the one across. "I'd send you, but you don't know what Muffin looks like. Besides, you have to get back to the loft to collect your paycheck, right? That was our deal."

"We could call the police. Anonymously."

"This is quicker. You saw Elaine Bradford's face, Nick. Muffin probably feels the same way."

"Shouldn't I at least take Sarah?" The train was easing out of the station.

She smiled, almost apologetically. "I'm afraid it's nearly moo-cow time again. Nick, really, I'll be careful. I'll keep my hair hidden and do my best not to look like a shifty-eyed kidnapper. But if Mrs. Golden was telling the truth, and Steve Bradford did this—well, we can't wait! We can't give that son of a bitch the chance to get away with it."

Nick knew that determined look: Maggie as Valkyrie, as pursuing Fury. There was no stopping her now. And he had to admit that he agreed—however pure Bradford's motive might be, even if he was trying to get the half million for his family, the pain suffered by that woman and the little girl was too cruel, too high a price. Nick almost hoped Mrs. Golden was lying. But he was still uneasy. "Look, I'll be back at the rehearsal loft in less than an hour. Call me there, okay? Before you contact Elaine Bradford, before you call the police, before you go after Mrs. Golden if Muffin isn't there. If you haven't called by four o'clock, I'll call out the Mounties."

"It's a deal," said Maggie.

But it was still with a sense of foreboding that Nick watched them leave the train at Douglaston.

Even on the street outside the loft building he could tell that something was wrong. A young police officer, pale and squinting in the unaccustomed sun, was standing in front of Anna Maria's window. He watched sharply as Nick entered the stair hall. A second officer, older, black, with profoundly sad dark eyes, was waiting on the landing, gazing up toward the door of the rehearsal loft.

"Excuse me. Is it all right to go up?" Nick called.

The dark eyes cataloged him, swiftly and professionally. "You involved with this show?"

"Yes. An actor."

"Go ahead, then. We're about to leave."

Nick climbed past him and opened the battered door

to the loft. The dismal tableau that greeted him increased
his misgivings. Daphne, dressed neatly in a navy suit and
a white blouse, armor for the upcoming hearing, no doubt,
stood proudly near the center of the room, head high,
tears rolling silently down her thin cheeks. Derek, be-
wilderment clear in the helpless gesture of his arm, was
asking, "But what did she say?"

A black girl in a pink dress, little Mellie, gripped the
hem of Daphne's jacket. In a tiny voice she said, " 'What
kinda motherfucker are you? We just kids.' But then I
was running cause she said run. So I didn't hear no more.
Only—only—" She turned her face into Daphne's jacket.

Daphne laid a protective hand on the small head.
"Enough of this," she said, her voice rough. "Derek,
you'll do that thing for us?"

"Of course. Call me when you can. Daphne, I'm so
very sorry."

"Yeah." Daphne took the girl's hand tenderly and
hurried out. Nick held the door for them, but in her
distraction she didn't even say hello. At the landing she
glanced at the mournful officer and said, "Let's go." The
three disappeared around the turning.

"What's up?" Nick asked Derek.

"God, I don't understand! She said—but I'm not
very clear, Nick. It's a nightmare, a dream. Ever since
they told me about Ramona, nothing seems sensible. It's
as though everything is ticking along underwater." He
spread his fingers, frowned at his hands. "I do things
physically and it's as though someone else is doing them."

"Yeah. Everything loses its real meaning."

"It's so hard to concentrate . . ." He gazed at the big
window with vacant eyes. "Ken Martin will be coming
about four, you know that?"

"Yes, that's why I'm here. I came early because I'm
expecting a phone call. Um—what happened with
Daphne?"

"Oh, right, you didn't hear. She was at Anna Maria's,
and the children were to meet her there. But—"

The door opened and Jaymie demanded, "What's
happened? I saw Daphne out there and she won't talk

to me!" Distractedly she fingered the strap of her tote bag. "There were policemen!"

"Yes," said Derek. He passed a hand back across his dull hair and concentrated on his listeners. "What happened was this. The two kids were coming to meet Daphne. They were meeting her at Anna Maria's for an after-school bite before they went to the hearing. But apparently when they got off the A train at Canal Street, someone accosted them underground."

Nick felt chilled. It was a station of tunnels and corners. He'd just come from there himself. Maggie and Sarah would be there soon. In a voice that was suddenly hoarse he repeated, "Accosted?"

"Went for them, the little sister said. The fellow had a ski mask and a gun. Callie told her to run, so she did. But apparently he'd grabbed Callie's arm and she yelled at him. Cursed him and said—they were just kids." Derek looked away suddenly and swiped at his eyes with the cuff of his sweater.

Jaymie sank onto a folding chair too, trembling.

Nick cleared his throat and asked, "What happened?"

"He killed her."

Tough, outspoken little Callie. Nick blinked at the grimy floor. *Mine eyes dazzle; she died young.*

# XIV
### Friday, 3:30 P.M.
### March 9, 1973

On his way back from changing Busby's marked bills for unmarked at the bank, to let everyone see that things were normal, Steve paused to discuss the weather with two of his subordinates. Then he returned to his own office suite. "I'm back, Myra," he called.

"Oh, Mr. Bradford! Mr. Lugano is here. You didn't have any appointments so I let him go on back to your office to wait."

Damn. Well, he'd just have to get rid of him. Steve managed to smile and say, "Thanks, Myra."

Lugano was sitting behind the desk. He stood with a polite smile, but Steve had already seen that the drawer was open. Damn, why hadn't he locked it?

"Hello, Bradford, good to see you!" said Lugano genially. "Do you have time to discuss our offering now?"

"Why, yes, why not?" stammered Steve. He saw then that Lugano was pushing a neatly printed note toward him.

"Don't delay the ransom delivery! I'll explain," read the note. Damn! How had he found out about the ransom? Busby, no doubt. Aloud, Lugano was saying, "Would you mind walking across to our lawyer's with me?"

Belatedly Steve remembered that Lugano thought the office might be wired. "Yes, um, of course."

"Here's a summary." This was cover for a second note: "Ransom is $50,000 short."

"Oh. Thanks." Steve hesitated, then pulled the unmarked bills from inside his jacket. He had to look cooperative until Lugano left. "I was just—ah—cleaning up some details."

Lugano understood. A shadow of disapproval flitted across his face, but he accepted the packet and added it to the others. "Don't forget your briefcase." The amber eyes were sympathetic as he slid the plastic bag of money into the tired plush toy and held it out to Steve. Helping out the foolish, rattled parent.

"Of course not. Here it is," said Steve. He was rattled, in fact. He tucked the sagging bear into his briefcase and squeezed it closed again. Thank God he was already carrying the little gun and the passport, he thought with an inward shudder. What if Lugano had found them too?

Halfway down the hall Steve paused. "Damn! Forgot my pen," he said. "I'll be right along." He hurried back into the office and came out again instantly, sliding the pen into his pocket.

Lugano's face was still sympathetic. "Your briefcase," he reminded Steve gently.

"Oh! Right." Steve dodged back to pick it up again. So that wouldn't work. Silly to try, he realized now. He'd better not push his luck; those sympathetic eyes could turn predator, he knew. Well, okay, Steve, play it by ear. In Venezuela, José Santos would be improvising all the time. Better find a way now. Good practice.

But outside he couldn't help asking, "Did my father-in-law call you?"

"Yes. On his way out of town." Lugano was brief. "I know you're worried. But it would be invaluable if we could see the pickup. We really would like to catch these fellows."

"But I want my little girl home safe!"

"Of course. Don't worry, with an open-air exchange on Canal Street we can stay completely hidden. But we want photos."

"I see. You won't go after them?"

"I promise. When we hear that your daughter is home safely, then we'll start working. Seriously, Bradford, our goals are exactly the same as yours."

Not quite, thought Steve despairingly. He said, "I know. But I'm damned nervous. Couldn't you pull back? Stay out of it, just as their note demanded?"

"You have to trust me a little. We'll be watching. But it will be from a building across the street from the Ming Bazaar. Cameras only. No sharpshooters. What I want to stress to you now is that you shouldn't wait. I've known kidnappers to get nervous, to . . . ah . . . do stupid things, when it got close to the deadline and the ransom wasn't there yet."

"Oh. I didn't realize. I thought . . . well, it's only a quarter to four. You know, with the money just sitting there, what if someone else got it by mistake?"

"It's a risk. But these fellows have thought of it too. I imagine they're ready to pick it up almost as soon as you're safely out of sight. And they did choose a rather shabby bear. Not likely to be pounced on by eager grannies looking for birthday presents."

"Well, okay, thanks for telling me."

"Fine." Lugano continued to stride beside him.

Steve stopped. They were only two blocks south of Canal Street now. "Um—we shouldn't be together, should we?"

"We won't be. Just thought I'd give you a little moral support."

"Well, thanks. But I'd really feel a lot better if you weren't there."

"Of course. Go ahead, then. Don't be nervous. We'll have our eye on you." He crossed the street.

Don't be nervous. Steve walked on, heart galloping. This was not supposed to be happening! He had invented the details of the ransom drop casually, choosing the Ming Bazaar on Canal Street only because he'd bought the pajama bag there, a week ago. Now, suddenly, everything depended on his ability to improvise a plan from this chance decision.

Venezuela will be like this, he told himself. José Santos will have to keep a cool head. Analyze.

Okay, given number one: Lugano was watching.

Which led to given number two: He had to put this bear onto the shelf with the others. Could he remove the money somehow first? But as he turned onto Canal, even in the crowd, he felt exposed. High-powered binoculars were trained on him at this very moment. He walked stiffly along, self-conscious, awkward as a kid giving a speech. No, removing the money was not an option. If only he'd thought of it back at the office! If only he'd—

Too late now. *Analyze, Santos.*

Given number three: The money, because it was in the bear and could not be removed in view of the police, had to be left in an open-air stall on Canal Street. If only he had another bear! But that was not an option.

And yet—he suddenly saw a slim hope. There was one other purple bear, stuffed fat with crumpled newspaper, on a low shelf. Could he move it up? No, not with Lugano's eyes fixed on him. But maybe he could take the second bear. After all, a real kidnapper might find two bears confusing, right? That's what he'd tell Lugano if he asked: he was trying to avoid confusion. He showed his bear to the Chinese proprietor as he entered. "Can I exchange this? I didn't notice the eye was gone."

The proprietor, in the middle of a sale to three young black women, gave a curt nod. Steve, still feeling the police eyes on him, set the bear in its place with exaggerated movements. Then, subtly, he removed its two-eyed twin from the lower shelf and squeezed it into his briefcase. It was wildly unlikely—but maybe he could exchange it again somehow later. The proprietor eyed him as he left but didn't complain.

Half a block away, across the street, was a bar. He dodged inside, sat down near the street window, and ordered a bourbon.

His heart was pounding like a jackhammer. Could he really survive this life of adventure? Was his doctor right about middle age? Did he really belong in Venezuela?

*Come on, Steve*, he told himself sternly. *It all depends on who you are.* And he'd found he was definitely not a staid middle-aged commuting investment counselor. Hadn't he?

He sipped his bourbon and stared morosely across the street. Half a million dollars stared back, one-eyed.

The rehearsal loft still gloomed with the shadows of Daphne's grief. Nick shoved up the window sash with some primitive notion of letting in the sunshine, but of course it didn't help. Derek's way was better. Methodically the little Englishman was sorting through the rehearsal props—toy crowns, canes, water pistols. Nick joined him. "Can I help?"

"Just keeping busy," said Derek. "I don't know what you Americans do with rehearsal props when you're done. There are so many regulations. But I thought sorting things wouldn't hurt."

"True." Nick could remember sorting things, too, after Lisette died; a good way to direct the energy of helpless rage, to keep yourself from screaming and smashing down walls—to keep yourself from thinking very much.

Derek said, "Ken Martin should be here in half an hour or so."

"Good." Nick turned to the pile of rehearsal costumes: long shabby skirts, wigs, top hats, gloves. He arranged them more neatly in their box. There were the large men's gloves, used first by King William IV and later by Albert to symbolize their deaths. In the corner, Queen Victoria's long slender pair. Straightening them, images flashed into his mind: Daphne's dark arms around Jaymie; dark arms pulling Ramona into the shadows.

And here were the water pistols, the double shots that had not killed Queen Victoria. Bang, bang.

The phone shrilled in the hall, jolting him from his musings. "I'm expecting a call," he told Derek, and bounded out to answer it.

"She's there," announced Maggie as soon as she heard his voice. "I'll call Elaine Bradford and then come right in and tell you about everything."

"No!" Nick was vehement. "You've been set up, Maggie. Don't get in any deeper. Did they see you at the day-care center?"

"No. I got sunglasses and a huge blue plastic sun hat on sale at a place called Aline's, and put Sarah in the shopping bag. Then I sauntered past the windows. Luckily no one asked why my shopping bag was wriggling."

"Not bad. Now, the call to Elaine Bradford will be from a man."

"Well, be quick, man. Muffin is sitting in a corner, past crying. Big eyes just staring at this hostile world. They look like good people at the center, but she's out of their reach. I wish I could have asked about her, but of course I didn't."

"I'll hurry. Directions?"

"The center is right next door to the church. Red brick, colonial-style." She gave the address and Elaine's number.

"Okay," said Nick. "And be extra careful on the subway because—"

"Sure. Now call!" she said urgently, and hung up.

Uneasy because he had not been able to tell her about Callie's death, but anxious to help the sad little girl in Douglaston, he dialed quickly.

"Hello?" Anxiety crackled across the line.

"Mrs. Bradford?" Nick found himself sinking into character one last time: courtly, British, Gladstonian.

"Yes, this is Mrs. Bradford."

"This is Mr. Merrypebble." It was Lord Clarendon's nickname for Gladstone. "I'm most happy to inform you that everything has been resolved. Your daughter is at the day-care center in Douglaston. It's next-door to the church on Main Street, red brick, colonial-style."

"You mean I can—I can get her now?"

"As soon as you wish, Mrs. Bradford. The people there have nothing to do with our business. Best not to ask too many questions."

The woman's relieved sob pierced through his role to a deeper reality of love, pain, gratitude. "Oh—oh, thank you, thank you!"

He swallowed, pulled the tatters of his invention about

him again. "I served to the best of my ability," said
Merrypebble gravely as the line went dead.

And make-believe or not, it was not a bad final scene
for Gladstone, Nick decided. The Grand Old Man would
approve.

Steve was on his fifth bourbon.

It had been over an hour since he'd delivered the
ransom. Every time a customer approached the store
across the street, he'd stiffen. José Santos, jungle-tough
and city-smooth, preparing to arrange a cool deal for
half a million. Keen as a jaguar stalking his prey.

He'd thought of a plan. Not ideal, but José Santos
—and jaguars—knew there was little in this world that
was ideal. The secret was to keep alert, keep trying, stay
ready to improvise.

What he'd do was this: First, he'd move out of this
bar and farther down the street, hugging the buildings
to stay out of sight of the monitoring police, moving
nearer the subway stop. A coffee shop, say. Then he'd
find someone to help him. A regular solid-citizen type,
a Good Samaritan type. He wouldn't ask much. He'd
just explain that he'd bought this very special color of
bear for his little girl, and had just noticed that its ear
was torn. Actually he'd surreptitiously torn it himself a
few moments ago. Just a little. And he'd explain to the
Good Sam that he'd sprained his ankle and had trouble
crossing streets rapidly, had just noticed the tear, and
would the Good Sam please go across and exchange the
bear for him?

And the clever part was this: The Good Sam would
notice that the only identical bear had only one eye,
would decide *not* to exchange it, and would come back
to the coffee shop with the original toy and lots of advice
about how he could easily mend the little tear in the ear.
The police, of course, would follow—discreetly—thinking that the bear the Good Sam was carrying held the
ransom. Meanwhile Steve, aka José Santos, would be
slipping behind their backs across the street to purchase
the ransom bear and disappear into the subways.

Sure, it wasn't perfect. It depended a lot on the reactions of a stranger. But Steve could read people pretty well. Look how well the arrangements with Maggie and Mrs. Golden had worked. It was only cantankerous Avery Busby who had caused a problem by pulling in the police; but even that was not irreparable. He'd already successfully laundered the marked bills. Steve would prevail yet.

And the helpful stranger would not be in bad trouble. The police would probably follow the fellow to the coffee shop, watch him look around for the long-gone Steve, eventually follow him home. Muffin would be back with Elaine soon, of course, and then they'd close in on the Good Sam. At that point they'd probably discover the mistake, or at least when they checked the fellow's alibi. They'd realize then that Steve had been behind it. But Steve didn't care. He'd always known they'd figure it out eventually; what he needed was time to catch the plane safely. By the time they'd worked out what he'd done, he would have disappeared without a trace. All he needed now was a few hours.

The Good Sam could furnish him with a few hours.

He paid his tab and moved, not too fast, into the street again, hugging the building facades. He had to cross a street; police eyes might see him, unless— He could improve his chances a little: he waited in the shelter of the building until he saw a small knot of customers pause at the shop across the street, then crossed as swiftly as he could without attracting attention, keeping to the side of the crosswalk that should be invisible from fifth-floor windows. Unless Lugano's people had broken their pledge and were hanging out the windows, they wouldn't see him. Fine. Half a block now, not even that, to the coffee shop. He'd pick some sympathetic person who didn't seem to be in a hurry, and—

Maggie. Emerging phoenixlike from the subway stairs ahead.

José Santos didn't stop to plan. The limp returned instantly, instinctively, quicker than thought. He hid his steely eyes behind a frank, open, boy-next-door gaze, noticed without surprise that she veered toward him, and said, "Oh, damn!"

"Well! Buzz!" she exclaimed in greeting. The baby was strapped to her breast, half asleep.

He looked up from the bear in innocent surprise. "Maggie! How are you? Hey, I didn't have a chance to thank you for helping me out!"

She patted the baby's back thoughtfully, studying him. "Don't thank me. Muffin is a darling. How is she?"

"Fine. Tip-top. Listen, could you by any chance do me another favor? And Muffin too?"

"I'd love to do something for Muffin. But I am in a hurry right now." Still, he could see the curiosity in the deep blue eyes.

"Well, it's still the damn ankle. I bought Muffin this bear pajama bag. See the store over there?" He pointed out the Chinese shopkeeper. "She loves this crazy color, so she should like it. And it's a good price. But I didn't notice, the ear has a little tear. I want to exchange it, but the ankle keeps throbbing. The doctor was right, I should have stuck with the crutch. But I hated it." He grimaced, waiting for her sympathetic response.

"I see. You want me to run this bear across the street and exchange it for one in better shape?" She took the fuzzy toy from him and inspected it. "Ugly little fellow." Sarah, despite her mother's comment, made a drowsy grab for it.

"Yeah, if it hadn't been that Muffin loves this color, I wouldn't have looked twice either. Listen, would you mind if I sat down?" He gestured at the coffee shop.

"Tell you what," Maggie said. "Your ankle needs a rest, and I'm in a hurry to take Sarah to her dad. Why don't you stay there while I take her, and then on my way back to the subway I'll exchange the bear and then bring it to you in the coffee shop? Shouldn't take more than a few minutes."

"Maggie, I just hope I can pay you back someday, somehow! You're a regular Good Samaritan!"

Her radiant smile beamed full on him. "Hey, glad to help, Buzz!" She tucked the bear in her briefcase and flew away down the street.

Steve really did stumble as he limped into the coffee shop. Maybe he should get some caffeine. He was weak with nervous excitement, thrilled at how smoothly the José Santos side of him was taking over, overcoming obstacles. Steve Bradford would never have been so ruthless. Steve Bradford's plan involved a bystander who could prove himself innocent within hours. Not so Maggie. In one smooth, instinctive reaction Santos had added an inspired touch to the crude plan: the same unknown person who would be identified as the kidnapper by the Montessori staff was now picking up the ransom! It would create not just hours, but days of confusion! Steve congratulated himself.

Or rather, he congratulated José Santos.

Of course it was frustrating to have to wait for Maggie to take her baby to wherever she was going; but even so, this idea was brilliant.

In the coffee shop he ordered a cup, black.

Ramona's lawyer, Ken Martin, turned out to be a tubby, red-faced giant who would have looked more appropriate in jeans driving a pickup truck in rural Appalachia than in his Manhattan lawyer's pinstripes. It was clear from his sour expression that he hadn't wanted to bring Simon Jenkins, who stood bristling at his side. "Now, just wait here, Simon," he soothed the glaring Jenkins. "This won't take long."

"Don't give them a thing!" Jenkins's voice was blurred with grief or drink. Probably both, Nick decided.

"Just what we have to," Martin agreed. "Now, sit down, Simon. We'll be done soon."

Nick glanced around the loft. Everyone was here except for Daphne and Jaymie. Too many sorrows today. He was suddenly very eager to be done with this, to start something new, to get away so he could grieve in quietness.

Martin addressed them crisply, his concise phrasing at odds with his comfortable farmer's voice. "I know we are all deeply upset, so I'll try to make the situation clear in brief. I have your checks. They are the last obligation that the producers have to you. You have already completed the last obligation you have to the producers. We wish you well. Are there any questions?"

Edith voiced the secret wild hope that they all had. "Mr. Martin, this is such a good show. Ramona believed in it. Don't you think, with the right replacement, she'd want us to go on?"

Jenkins started to erupt but was stopped by Martin's imperious hand. "The right replacement?" Martin bellowed. "For Ramona Ricci? My God, there is no one on this earth who could replace her!"

Taken aback by the unexpected attack, Edith could only gape at him. Martin drew a deep breath that traveled the long length of his pudgy shirtfront. He continued calmly, efficient again, "The producing corporation exists only to produce a musical, *Victoria R*, starring Ramona Ricci. So you see, a different legal entity would have to be created in order to do what you suggest. We can't do that now."

"You don't think she'd want it to go on?" faltered Edith.

"What I think and what you think is irrelevant," Martin rumbled. "In fact, what Ramona wanted is irrelevant. There is no suggestion in any legal document that this show is to continue. Are there any other questions?"

Derek pushed a strand of pale hair from his eyes and asked incredulously, "Nothing in the will either?"

This time even the massive Martin was unable to keep Jenkins in his seat. "You greedy little bastards! Isn't it enough that you killed her? You want to take all her money too?"

Derek was short, pale, usually self-effacing, but today he leaped to his feet so angrily that Nick and Larry both grabbed at him to restrain the little Englishman, an enraged bullterrier charging unflinchingly at the snarling Great Dane. "If anyone in this bloody room killed her, it was you, Simon Jenkins! You think I didn't hear about your plots to keep her off the stage? Your affairs that broke her heart? And when she tumbled to your little games, you had the bloody guns already planted for your revenge, didn't you?"

Ken Martin had grasped Jenkins's arm with both hands and was hauling him away from the livid Englishman, but Jenkins raged on. "Damn right I wanted to keep her away from the likes of you!" he stormed. "You think it's easy for a man to see his wife run off to mingle with scum like you people? Ramona is a star! A goddess! She doesn't need to wallow in the mud, doing a trashy two-bit show like this! I tried to tell her you only wanted her money. Tried to reason. But there was something—" Suddenly he seemed to run out of energy. Martin dragged him back to his chair, and Jenkins allowed himself to be pushed down, shaking his head, looking mystified at the scuffed floor as Martin made motherly clucking noises. "It was like a fire in her," Jenkins murmured plaintively to Martin. "I'd think it had been put out, that I'd made her happy, and then it would flare up again."

"I know, Simon." His hand still resting on Jenkins's shoulder, Martin turned back to Derek, who still stood fuming, held by Nick and Larry. The lawyer said, "In answer to your question, there is no provision in her will about the show, other than the stipulation that her debts be paid. Once that is done, the residual amount, which is to be divided equally between family and charity, is very small. Probably in the hundreds." Derek, hopeless again, fumbled his way back into his chair, but Martin continued relentlessly. "There are commitments to costume designers, publicists, many others that must be paid. Your own union requires payments to your Welfare Fund and the Pension Fund. We have to pay you your rehearsal salaries, and also two weeks' performance salary, though you never performed. It all adds up. Ramona invested her entire personal fortune into this show, but since there was no chance to recoup any of it through ticket sales, it has effectively vanished."

Nick leaned wearily against one of the peeling columns. Was this what Ramona's death meant, this sad haggling over money? But it was not just the money, he realized; it was the hopes and dreams they shared with her that had vanished. That was the real tragedy. Now she could never see her beloved show succeed, never give her husband the forgiveness he craved, never help the bucktoothed nun in Brooklyn save other young Ramonas. It left a sour taste in his mouth.

"Let's have our money, then," said Larry, tossing his jacket over his shoulder and straightening. Nick could almost see him switching compartments: close up the grief-for-Ramona compartment, concentrate on the financial one. But it took energy to keep life so neatly divided. Larry's jaw muscles were knotted tight despite his relaxed stance.

"Very well," said Martin.

Derek said, "Daphne couldn't be here, and Jaymie isn't here either. I'll take their checks for them."

"The hell you will!" burst out Simon Jenkins, but this time he didn't stand up.

"Daphne asked me to get it for her!" Derek was on the verge of attack again too, his hands clenched.

"I'm sorry," said Martin smoothly, a wary eye on the explosive Jenkins. "I can give checks only to the people named."

"Well, Daphne will come to me for it!"

"You'll have to tell her it's at my office, then, Mr. Morris."

"Lovely," muttered Derek; but he leaned back in his chair.

Martin called out their names and distributed the checks, then arranged with Derek for the return of tapes and scores that Ramona had in her possession. At last he escorted the glooming Jenkins from the loft. Nick glanced at his watch as the others dispiritedly collected their things and began to plod out. Four-forty. End of chapter. Time to move on.

# XV
### *Friday, 4:45 P.M.*
### *March 9, 1973*

Maggie's glowing eyes and airy step contrasted so with the departing tide of the disheartened cast that she seemed to have arrived from a different, more ethereal, world. He had to smile. "O spirit of love! How quick and fresh thou art!"

"Quick is right! Nick, hurry, take Sarah! The game's afoot!"

"What game?"

"You did reach Elaine Bradford?"

"Yes. She should have Muffin back by now."

"Well," said Maggie, "Mr. Bradford-Hartford wants me to run another errand. I'm to take this bear and trade it for another one, and then deliver that bear to him."

"Damn, Maggie, you don't mean to do it!"

"Of course I do! Here, take the baby."

"Maggie, you idiot!" Grabbing her arm, he led her out of earshot of the few remaining people. "This is the ransom pickup!"

"I know! Nick, listen, it's clear—well, mostly clear —what he's up to. He tricks me into picking up Muffin and tricks me into picking up the ransom. I pass it to him, and he disappears while the police follow me."

"So why the hell cooperate?" Automatically he was strapping on the baby carrier.

"Well, suppose instead I follow *him*? The police track me, I track him, and we all find out what he's up to. Whatever it is, he's got to do it soon, because once Muffin is back and the police pick me up for questioning, he knows it won't be too long before they'll want to question him."

"Maggie, I don't like it. You've been set up—"

"Nick, I've got to! Look, that prick tricked me into helping kidnap a helpless little girl." Her eyes flamed blue with anger. "And he's going to pay for that!"

"Let *me* go, then!"

"No, he'd know there was a problem if I didn't show up. Tell you what. If I run into trouble, I'll head back here."

"I'd rather watch."

"But Sarah mustn't be there. The Ming Bazaar is only a block and a half from here. If it looks like Steve knows I'm following him, or if anything makes me uneasy, I'll run right back here, okay? You can hang around and be ready to do your famous U.S. Cavalry impersonation if I come running. Otherwise I'll just quietly track him and lead the police to his lair. Wonder if it's that apartment?"

"You're making me lose faith in the good sense of the American mother," grumbled Nick.

"Yeah, I was thinking about that," said Maggie cheerfully. "Maybe if I weren't a mother, I could just say, 'Ooh, how awful,' and forget it. But little girls are important."

"Yeah." Nick had taken Sarah, who was half asleep, looking around dopily. He needed no convincing; this blinking, drooling creature was possibly the most important thing there was. And then there was Maggie. Not your ordinary American mother or wife or statistician. She was unique, unpigeonholed. A woman who relished love, duty, and adventure, all three. A woman who could even relish marriage to an actor. Who could understand the fire inside that baffled Jenkins, because she had fires of her own. "Well," said Nick, "I'll be watching. I insist. But from a distance. And we'll meet here if things get iffy."

"Okay."

"But before you go, there are a couple of things that I wanted to ask about."

Suddenly focused on him, she searched his face, the eager anticipation of her plan switching to concern for him. "Nick, I'm sorry. Something else has happened, hasn't it?"

"Callie was killed. Daphne's niece."

"Oh, God! The older one, right?"

"Yes. She was bringing her little sister to meet Daphne, to go to the hearing. Someone in a ski mask shot her in the subway transfer tunnel."

"*Merde!*" Maggie sagged into one of the folding chairs, long legs stretched before her, brow contracting in grief and dismay. "Why? Why the hell would anyone shoot a kid? It looked like a mugging, I suppose?"

"Yeah. But . . ." Nick shrugged.

"Exactly: But." Maggie leaned forward, pulled her feet under her, put her elbows on her knees and her chin in her fist. Rodin. "Nick, it's too unlikely. Maybe she knew something—she *was* here the night Ramona was shot."

"Right." Nick detached Sarah's fist from his nose and set her carefully on the platform to coo at the ceiling. "And I wonder if it fits with something else I thought of. About Ramona. I saw the toy pistols for the assassination scene in the prop box and remembered that Victoria wasn't killed. I wondered if maybe we were going at things the wrong way around. I mean, maybe the shooting was on purpose, but not the killing. Maybe she was only supposed to be wounded."

A breeze from the open window, cool in the late sunlight and bearing tidings of bacon in Anna Maria's coffee shop downstairs, stirred Maggie's dark curls. "So the waist really was the target!" she exclaimed. "To get her out of the way, but just temporarily. So she wouldn't cut the solo, maybe. Or would rethink filing for divorce."

"Yes."

"That's good, Nick. That explains a lot. And Callie —well, suppose she noticed something. She was here that night. She'd become a serious danger for the gunman when Ramona died and the charges became murder."

"Just what I was thinking. Yesterday she was bragging that she knew something about Ramona, but Daphne shut her up." He shook his head. "But this idea doesn't explain how the man Perez is holding got the gun."

"Found it in a trash can, I imagine, just as he claims. Even junkies probably tell the truth sometimes. In any case he couldn't have killed Callie if he was locked up." She glanced at her watch. "Nick, together with what you were saying about the black gloves—well, we've got to talk about this soon!"

"Right. After you've done your foolish jaunt for little-girldom. If that doesn't land us all in prison. But the prop box gives me another idea. Here." Leaving Sarah on her pad on the platform, he crossed to the box and pulled out the blond wig Edith had used to rehearse Baroness Lehzen, the youthful Victoria's German governess. "Take this along. Just in case things get tough and you don't want the police to be making connections between the ransom pickup and the little-girl pickup at Montessori."

Maggie clapped it on her head with a grin. "Great! Do I look like Jean Harlow?"

He cocked his head, considering. "No. More like a Valkyrie. Or Alice in Wonderland. I can't decide which."

"Part Alice, part Valkyrie—Nick, what peculiar taste you have in wives! Well, see you soon. Here I go!" With a toss of the blond curls she pranced toward the door.

It sprang open and Jaymie hurtled in, trench coat flared open, tan tote bag bouncing beside her. "Where's —where are the checks?" she gasped.

"I'm sorry, Jaymie," said Nick. "You missed him. He said—"

"Missed him?" There was such a depth of pain and exhaustion in her cry that Nick hurt too. He was glad to see Maggie spontaneously hug her.

He said, "The lawyer told us he'd hold the checks at his office for you and Daphne."

"Oh. I—I ran all the way." She was still panting, speaking in little bursts between breaths.

"You can get your check soon, Jaymie," Maggie soothed her. She looked frivolous in the flaxen wig, but Jaymie seemed too distracted to notice.

"But it's Daphne, you see. It's my only chance. I have to give Daphne her check."

"But he wouldn't let us do that," Nick explained gently. "Derek offered to take your checks to you, but the lawyer said he wouldn't give a check to anyone except the person named on it."

"Then it's all over! If you love someone, they leave you!" Jaymie raised her hands to her face hopelessly. "Oh, God, I want to die!"

"But you'll get the check soon!" coaxed Maggie, flashing a puzzled glance at Nick. "So will Daphne."

"But she won't talk to me!" Jaymie pulled away from Maggie, walked to the window, and leaned her hands on the sill, staring out at the grimy kitchen roof below. "She said, 'All I want from you assholes is my check!' "

Understanding began to flicker. Nick said, "Daphne is sad and angry right now, Jaymie, but I'm sure she'll want to see you soon. It'll take a while for her to get back to normal, because she loved Callie very much."

One of Jaymie's hands made a fist and she thumped the windowsill rhythmically, as though trying to pound away her thoughts. "More than me, more than me," she murmured.

"Callie was her niece," Nick tried to explain. "Of course she was attached to her."

"But I need her! Mama, Daddy, Loreen. All gone away. And now Daphne. I'm alone. Forever alone." She gave a little sob and shrugged her shoulder bag forward, clasping it across her chest with both arms. "And I did everything for her."

"I know it's hard—"

"And she's gone anyway! Oh, God!" She twisted away from the window, head turned toward the left, neck arching gracefully, hand to her temple. In the hand was a little gun.

"Jaymie, no!" The tremor of horror in Maggie's first syllable modulated instantly to a soothing tone. "Things seem bad now, that's natural. But wait, they'll look better soon."

"I did everything! And still—"

Maybe it was Jaymie's theatrical pose against the backlight of the window that inspired him, maybe the whimper from Sarah on her pad, maybe just the sight of Maggie's frizzy blond wig as she moved toward Jaymie. Nick opened the piano, soft-pedaled, and began to sing gently, "Vickelchen, nap in your wee elfin cap, sleeping happy with never a tear."

The gun at Jaymie's temple wavered, and drooped. Maggie glanced at Nick. He nodded and she eased her arm around Jaymie again while Nick crooned on, "I know a charm that will keep you from harm, and disarm all the demons you fear." Powerful demons indeed that poor Jaymie was wrestling in her despair. But now she was sinking to her knees as in the show, clutching Maggie's skirt with her left hand. Maggie, half-sitting on the windowsill and stroking Jaymie's glossy hair, had succeeded in catching her right hand, gently easing the gun loose and into the bag again. Despite the chill that suddenly gripped at his heart, Nick sang on, "Life, like our stories, has goblins and glories. It's gentle and hard as a stone. But I'll be beside you to keep you and guide you. You won't have to face it alone."

Jaymie was sobbing as the last chords sounded. She tensed, groping at her tote bag. Nick went back to the beginning of the lullaby and she relaxed again, almost hypnotized by the childish tune and the gentle hand on her hair, sliding into the role as she had at rehearsals. Maggie's foot crept out and nudged the tote bag away from Jaymie and back along the wall.

"Things will be better, Vickelchen," she murmured as the last chords sounded, instinctively improvising to keep Jaymie in the character of the compliant Princess. "I'll take care of you. You won't be alone. Now, come, I want you to find something for me." She stood, very slowly, and coaxed Jaymie to the costume box. "Where's your wee elfin cap?"

Automatically, a little-girl look of wonder on her face, Jaymie pulled out the cap.

"Good." Maggie, all comfortable earth-mother, tied it under Jaymie's chin. "We have a special treat today, Vickelchen."

Sarah whimpered again and doubt flitted across Jaymie's face. But Maggie's words soothed her. "We're going to go out now, and we're going to get you a cuddly bear!"

"No!" exclaimed Nick involuntarily. Maggie couldn't know, might not have guessed. That gun in Jaymie's hand had been Ramona's.

And in Jaymie's disintegrating half-fantasy world, who could guess what she might do next? Little Hedvig, shooting herself for fear of losing a father? Annie Oakley, who might shoot anything? But that gun was not a prop. They had to keep her away from it, to call the police somehow, to get Jaymie into professional hands.

Maggie was smiling at him serenely. "Yes!"

"But—" But how could she still be concerned about the kidnapping now? How could she suggest taking a killer away with her?

"It's all right, you see. People should take care of little girls." She was patting Jaymie's shoulder, but Nick's mind jumped at last to comprehension. Maggie was protecting Sarah by taking the dangerously unpredictable Jaymie away. Protecting Jaymie by separating her from the gun in the tote bag. And calmly, still acting the solicitous governess, leading the unsuspecting Jaymie to the team of police who were doubtless watching the ransom pickup.

He nodded his understanding and Maggie picked up her briefcase and led Jaymie away.

The closing door seemed to renew Sarah's fussing. Nick checked, discovered that she'd thoroughly messed herself, and reflected a moment. He couldn't do anything this minute anyway, because Maggie needed time to get Jaymie down the stairs and out the door. He mustn't follow yet, mustn't even call the police from the phone on the top landing until they had left. In any case he couldn't be too close to the activity with his beloved, yowling, vulnerable infant. Potential hostage, potential victim. He'd have to trust Maggie and the police. Meanwhile, might as well see if he could reduce the yowl factor.

In record time he rushed through the diaper change and got Sarah mobile again in the carrier. Then he trundled her out to the hall phone and called Perez.

"Sorry, sir, Sergeant Perez is not available," a chipper young voice informed him.

"Well, tell him that I've found Ramona Ricci's second gun."

"Okeydoke. Who are you and where?"

"Nick O'Connor. Tell him it's at the rehearsal loft."

"Sure thing!"

"It's a homicide case," said Nick, suddenly dubious about the knowledgeability of a police officer who owned such a cheery outlook on life.

"Hey, natch, it's Perez, right? Thank you, sir," said the voice.

"Okeydoke," said Nick, and hung up with a worried look at the receiver.

He walked Sarah back into the loft and looked at Jaymie's tote bag. Might be a good idea to be sure that gun was unloaded before people began poking around in the bag. He took Sarah back to the piano, arranged her carefully on the side away from the bag, and then went back to open it gingerly.

The reflected sunlight from the window was strong. He needed it; the bag was chock full of the necessities of an actor's life. A scarf on the top. Hairbrush. Umbrella angling up from the lower depths; don't touch that yet, in case it in turn touched the gun. The first few of many lipsticks and makeup pots. A script for *Victoria R*. The appointment book he'd seen her use for casting notices. Curious, using the scarf to keep from obliterating fingerprints, he opened the dark leather cover and flipped through the pages. Here was February, here was March. March 6.

*5:30, RR—L'Étoile.*

Somehow he hadn't fully believed it till this moment. Jaymie, so sweet-faced, so hardworking. How could she? And yet—what was it she'd said of Daphne? *I did everything for her.*

Ramona's death had been an accident, then, as they'd conjectured. The shot had been fired, not to kill her, but to keep Ramona from retracting her letters and harming Daphne's court case, to keep her temporarily out of the way. How stricken Jaymie must have been to hear of Ramona's death—but yes, he could remember her anguished cry: that's impossible! All day she'd been struggling to cope with the sudden horror, the shock that an action meant only to delay instead had killed. She was right; she needed Daphne, needed mothering, needed someone to get her to the help she needed.

But Daphne, floundering in the pain of her own problems, could not respond; not only the loss of Ramona, of the job, but also the tension of the court hearing, and now—worst of all—Callie's death.

Callie's death.

Goddamn it. A weary certainty flooded through Nick even before he pulled the ski mask from the bag. He could remember Daphne's brusqueness: "Callie comes first. You understand?" And the desperate tears in lost Jaymie's eyes: "I understand."

Thank God they'd got the gun away from her!

But where was it?

Carefully he pulled out the rest of her things. Then he checked for other compartments. Nothing.

One by one, he replaced the objects from the pile beside him. Still nothing.

He jumped to his feet, hunted in burgeoning panic along the wall, and then all over the loft. Nothing.

He remembered Jaymie groping for her bag while they sang the lullaby.

Then he snatched Sarah from behind the piano and frantically strapped her into the carrier.

Maggie had gone out there, cosily hand in hand with a deranged killer.

And the killer was armed.

# XVI
*Friday, 5:10 P.M.*
*March 9, 1973*

Steve looked at his watch. Five-ten. Where was Maggie?

He had left the coffee shop where he'd told her to meet him and was back at the bar. It would be easy from here to cross the street and get the bear as soon as she'd lured the police away. But where was she?

Could she possibly suspect him? No, there was no way she could have found out about the kidnapping. She didn't know his name. She didn't know Muffin was missing. Even if for some reason she had tracked down Elaine or Mitzi, they knew to say that Muffin had a cold. No, Maggie was the ideal Good Samaritan. José Santos had been right.

But then where was she? There were four women at the Ming Bazaar: one with a stroller, one inspecting house slippers, and a tall blonde talking to a dark-haired friend, then leaving her to nod to the Chinese vendor. Steve squinted at the friend. Trench coat, yes; was it Maggie? But Maggie did not droop that way; she moved gracefully, breezily, like the athlete she was. Nor did she wear a frilly cap. Steve scanned the street again. No one. Then he glanced back at the shop and froze.

The tall blonde had moved to the shelf of pajama bags and was looking carefully at the purple one.

She turned and called to the vendor, and Steve realized that it was Maggie. Damn! Why the hell was she wearing that wig? Now Lugano would think the pickup had been made by a blonde! But, his José Santos side whispered, it was not vital; the important thing was that she distract the police. Blond or black-haired, she would lead the police to the coffee shop where he'd said he'd meet her, then to her job or wherever she went next. That was all Steve needed. And she was doing the right thing, carefully comparing the two pajama bags, noting that the one with the torn ear was in better shape, preparing to keep the one he'd handed to her.

Time to call Elaine, said the plan. Hands shaky with anxious anticipation, Steve dialed. As it rang he stepped out of the booth, receiver tight on his ear, so that he could peer out at Maggie. Elaine said, "Hello?"

Why that blond wig? And who was the other woman? He was so rattled that he forgot to disguise his voice. "Hello," he said.

"Oh, Steve! Thank God! I didn't know how to reach you!"

"I've been leaving the ransom," he said, desperately attempting to cover up. Damn, now he'd have to call back in a minute, in his high-pitched voice, to tell her where Muffin was.

But Elaine was bubbling, unaccountably delighted. "I know you have! Steve, she's back! We just walked in the door!"

"What?"

"She's fine! She's not hurt. Keeps hugging my skirt, but I keep hugging her too."

"Muffin's back?"

"Yes! Listen, maybe this is a clue. I haven't had a chance to call the police yet. The man who called had an English accent. Called himself Merrypebble or something. Said he had the money and told me where to find her."

"Where to find her?"

"Oh, honey, you can't believe it, can you? Here, Muffin, say hi to Daddy."

And the unmistakable voice piped, "Dad-dee!"

"Hi, Muffin." Steve had never felt so numb.

Muffin home.

That meant the police would not wait, they'd follow Maggie immediately, even arrest her, as soon as they heard the news. He had to get the money. Now. Instantly. Before Lugano heard. He replaced the receiver and sprinted to the door of the bar, ready to go for the bear as soon as Maggie started for the café.

But Maggie had gone berserk. Not only was she wearing that wig, but she was taking the wrong pajama bag! Horrified, Steve saw her wave the one-eyed bear at the vendor and smile radiantly at his nod.

And then she didn't head across the street to the café! Instead she glanced back at the woman who had come with her, her smile suddenly fading. Steve looked too. The droopy woman had pulled something from her head, the little lacy cap, and now was looking around distractedly, slapping at her own hips as though looking for a bag. She had no bag, he realized. She wheeled away suddenly and raced back the way she had come, with amazing speed for someone who had so recently seemed half asleep.

And Maggie, damn her, darted after her, around the corner toward the cast-iron buildings!

Steve leaped from his shelter in a black fury. He didn't know what she was doing or why. But of one thing he was certain: she was winging away with his new life tucked under her arm. The life he had sacrificed wife, child, and reputation to gain. *What would jaguars do for such high stakes?* whispered Santos.

Steve charged.

Nick lunged for the door, ready to run out to find the police, to warn Maggie, to gallop to the rescue, when he heard the downstairs door bang and a clatter of footsteps on the stairs. He braked and peeked out. Jaymie was rounding the corner of the landing. Clutching Sarah against him, he dove back to take cover behind the piano.

Ramona's little derringer was in Jaymie's hand.

Crouching behind the sturdy upright, Jaymie's tote bag in one hand, Sarah's supplies and his own gym bag slung over his other arm, Nick huddled protectively over his daughter. Maybe Jaymie was merely looking for Daphne again. Maybe she'd leave as soon as she saw the loft was empty. He heard her pause at the door, then stride straight to the window. A terrible question knifed through him: Where was Maggie? But he pushed it away. He had to watch Jaymie. From low in the shadows behind the piano he could see her squinting along the wall. "Damn," she muttered, and turned to survey the loft. Frowning, she approached the costume box.

Looking for her tote bag, Nick knew.

The bag with the ski mask in it.

The bag he was holding.

Better rearrange things, get some distance. He eased the bag onto the floor at one end of the piano, then crept silently all the way to the other end. Jaymie stirred around in the costume box for a second, her dark hair swinging about her lowered face.

Nick looked longingly at the door. Too far. The window was closer, but still not near enough to escape without—

Sarah sneezed.

Jaymie whirled into an Annie Oakley stance, the little gun ready, her eyes sliding wildly around the big room. "Who's there?" she shrieked.

A clammy sweat soaked Nick's shirt. Come on, old man, get on stage. He swallowed, hummed a bar of Lehzen's lullaby, broke off, and said, "Hmm?"

"Who's there? Nick?" Her voice was strained. She was racked on her interior agonies, nerves stretched to snapping.

"Yeah. Just me changing Sarah," said Nick soothingly. He pushed his gym bag onto the top of the piano, and when she didn't shoot, straightened just enough to look over it at Jaymie. "How was your walk?"

"Nick." Disappointment in her voice, and suspicion. The gun still trembled in her clenched hand. Her knuckles were white. "Why are you behind the piano?"

"That's where the diaper bag was." Smoothly he pulled his head down again, desperately hoping his improvisation would work.

"Bag," repeated Jaymie. He wished he could see her. "Where's my bag?"

"I don't know. Where did you leave it?"

"You've got it!" There was that hysteric note in her voice again.

Nick said hastily, "Maybe it's under the piano. Here, I'll move it over a little so you can look." He grabbed the upright posts of the rear frame, and trying not to bump Sarah in the carrier across his chest, he heaved the massive instrument nearer the window, angling it for better protection. He heard Jaymie scurry for the tote bag and sneaked a glance back to see if she was distracted enough for him to slip out the window. He had to find out what had happened to Maggie.

But she was not looking at the bag; she had clutched it under her left arm and now said accusingly, "You looked at it!"

"No, no," soothed Nick mendaciously. "Maybe I pushed it over by mistake when I got Sarah's diaper, that's all."

Alone, he might have risked a dive across the sill and onto the flat roof a couple of feet below the window. But with Sarah he couldn't. He'd have to go through, trunk upright. Sit on the sill, then lift his feet over and out, before he could crouch below the sill and scramble out of danger. They couldn't afford to be targets that long.

Try to soothe her, then. He began to hum the lullaby.

"No," said Jaymie, hitting at her temple with the heel of one hand, "not the music. I have to think—"

"And you have to take care of your cuddly bear!" came a new, melodious voice. Maggie! Awash with relief and concern, Nick peeked around the piano and saw her coming through the door, proudly extending the ugly purple pajama bag at Jaymie.

Jaymie half-turned and stared at it, bewildered.

Nick barreled over the windowsill and dropped to the relative safety of the tarred roof. Sarah cooed in delight.

He peeked back through the corner of the window. Jaymie was shaking her head as Maggie approached her. "No, no, I'm not Vickelchen!"

"Of course not. You're an actor. You're very good. Here, take your little bear!"

But Jaymie shook her head.

Maggie tossed the bear into her hands and dove behind the piano. "Vickelchen," she said, managing somehow to keep her voice calm and soothing, "let's sing to the bear. Okay? . . . Vickelchen, nap in your wee elfin cap."

Jaymie still shook her head, but she was clutching the bear, confused. Then her eyes snapped up and she stared at the door.

Maggie continued to hum softly, but in another second Nick too heard what Jaymie had noticed.

The drum of running footsteps on the stairs.

# XVII
*Friday, 5:25 p.m.*
*March 9, 1973*

Steve pounded up the steps, panting, furious. A ruddy fire-eater. Everyone had betrayed him. Maggie was running away with his money; Lugano had set police to watching; even little Muffin had somehow gotten herself prematurely home.

And yet there was something purifying in his rage, a sort of elation, a sense that finally he was at liberty to act, to reach, to test himself. Like Avery Busby, he was free. Angry, of course; and angriest at Maggie. She'd taken the wrong bear and run in the wrong direction. Some Samaritan! Well, Steve would get it back. Snatch the bear, dive into the subway, let Lugano pick up the pieces. Enough was enough. These obstacles only whetted his appetite. He was more keen than ever, riding the wings of his anger, *precipitated into pure happy action.*

There was a door at the top of the steps, cracked open. He could see the blond wig on the floor. What was she up to? He slipped his hand around the gun in his pocket and edged up to the door, cool and fearless. *He that dies this year is quit for the next. Damned fine.*

But when he looked in, his rage bubbled over. He could see Maggie silhouetted against the window, hugging the bear, crooning to it. Her voice cried, "Steve! Look out! There's a gun!" She was threatening him! And in her hand, yes, a stubby gun.

José Santos didn't have to think. In one smooth action he aimed, fired once, twice, and bounded in to rip the bear from Maggie's collapsing body and—

It wasn't Maggie.

A flood of cold surged numbingly through Steve. His unfeeling fingers let loose the bear and the gun, then crept as though in slow motion to his mouth, tried to stop the gagging moan. His eyes refused to unglue themselves from the young woman on the floor: trench coat, yes, but straight hair. And a shattered eye socket. Blood welled up, flowing through the dark hair and onto the dusty floor.

Real blood.

Steve staggered toward the open window but didn't make it. The world contracted to a throbbing agony of nausea. His stomach heaved, again and again.

After a while—short or long, he couldn't tell—he became aware of a voice, cursing. Was the woman alive? He dragged his eyes back to look again. No, she still lay crumpled on the floor, the blood still pooling about her head. But someone was kneeling over her, holding her wrist and swearing in a soft, hopeless voice. Through the tides of shock and nausea he recognized Maggie.

In a moment she laid the wrist down gently and stood up, her head still bowed toward the still form on the floor. Then she seemed to feel his eyes on her and looked up. "You shit-brained idiot," she said dully. He saw that her face was streaked with tears.

"I didn't mean—it just happened," said Steve miserably. He felt naked, stripped of the armor Santos had provided.

"Yeah, sure it did." Scorn animated her voice. "It's not enough to kidnap your own kid, torture your own wife, steal from your own family! You've got to get yourself a gun too. Go rampaging through the world like your goddamn father-in-law! Was that it, Steve? You wanted to prove you had balls, like the old geezer?"

"No!" Her words stung like a splash of acid. He shook his reeling head. "It was Susan—"

"Ah. Another woman. Clean break, right? Muffin would never see you again? Well, Buzz old pal, I've got news for you. Even without this murder your illustrious daddy-in-law would have tracked you down like a wounded trophy animal. Anywhere in the country."

"Not in South America!"

"South America. I see." She looked down at the crumpled young woman again. "What a nice little script. Steve Bradford, intrepid he-man, blasts his way to adventure, wealth, and romance, slaying dragons as he goes. Or had you maybe cast her as a herd of rhinos?"

"I didn't mean to! I didn't know!"

She sighed. "Well, this kid had a gun too. Accidentally killed someone, just like you. The second time—oh, God, I don't know. Once I thought I knew what justice was. This one needed help, not justice." The fire-blue eyes locked on Steve again. "She had a hell of a lot of problems. One of them—maybe important, maybe not—was that her dad abandoned her without a backward glance. I won't let you do that to Muffin, Steve."

"But—" Images swirled in his head: Susan, Busby, Elaine, jaguars, Muffin, Lugano. The dead woman. He covered his face with one hand. His mind wouldn't work.

"Listen, Steve!" Maggie was next to him, shaking his shoulder roughly. "Pay attention! I don't give a damn what you work out with your wife. She's adult. But don't hurt Muffin!"

"But—"

"We don't have time to argue. The police will be here any minute. Here's your story: You chased her because you thought she kidnapped Muffin. She was standing there with the bear and a gun. You shot in self-defense. Got it?"

Steve's mind was beginning to work, a little. He turned over her plan, tried for alternatives. He just wanted out. Suppose he cleaned things up, wiped the fingerprints from his gun—where was his gun? Oh, yes, across the room by the door, where he'd dropped it. He could run out again, into the subways—

But then he heard the door open, far below.

Police.

He looked wildly at Maggie. "It really was self-defense! Wasn't it?"

"Yeah. In a way. I can tell them so if they ask me."
She had lowered her voice. "See, no one will much blame
a father who tries to shoot his daughter's kidnapper."

"Yes. Yes, that's right!" he whispered gratefully.

"You may even be a hero." The blue eyes on him
were ice cold, magnetic. "Muffin will admire you. Elaine
will admire you. Old trigger-happy Busby will admire
you. Unless, of course, they figure out that you were the
kidnapper."

A lurch of fear. "Maggie! You won't tell!"

"I won't if you won't," she agreed briskly with a
glance at the door. "It'll be better for Elaine and Muffin
if they never know. Do you have your ticket to South
America on you?"

"God! And the passport!" He snatched them from
his pocket.

Maggie took them. "Good."

"But I can't keep you out of it," he whimpered. "The
police had telephoto lenses."

"I'll tell them it was Jaymie's project to pick up that
bear. She's the kidnapper, remember? Anything else?"

"Mr. Bradford?" Lugano's voice. Cautious, still far
below.

"I—no, nothing else, but—I don't understand," he
whispered urgently. "How can I trust you? How do I
know you won't tell the police?"

She was picking up her briefcase and edging toward
the window. "You trust me because you've got no choice.
This passport plus explanatory notes will be in my
bank safe. But you can trust me not to tell, for two
reasons. First, Muffin. She needs a dad. Not a prick
who uses her to skip the country with his bimbo." She
looked down at the body and brusquely swiped at her
own streaked cheek. "A little girl shouldn't have to deal
with that."

Steve gazed out the window. Somewhere out there
Susan was winging her way across blue waters to a new
life.

But for him—well, Maggie was right, there was no
choice. His prints were on the gun, Lugano was ap-
proaching the door. And she had the tickets and passport

now. "And for Muffin you'll keep quiet?" he asked unbelievingly.

"Yeah. For Muffin, and for half a million bucks."

Impossible! Steve's eyes squeezed shut. But his reeling mind thudded again and again into the same closed doors. He whispered, "Okay."

When he opened his eyes, Maggie was gone.

Only the body remained.

"Mr. Bradford?"

"In here, Lugano," called Steve shakily.

It all depends on who you are.

# XVIII

*Friday, 5:35 P.M.*
*March 9, 1973*

Mr. Merrypebble, his rantipoling wife, and his dozing
baby had slipped quietly through Anna Maria's kitchen
and out to the street. They were strolling casually toward
Canal Street, past the policemen hurrying into the loft
building they had just left. But despite her convincing
saunter Maggie was shaken. "God, Nick! What a goddamn mess!"

He didn't feel all that steady himself. "Yeah. Acci-
dental judgments, casual slaughters, purposes mistook
and fallen on the inventors' heads—"

"Yeah. And I'm the idiot inventor!" She slapped her
chest in disgust.

"Hey, no!"

"Look, a minute ago I was preaching to Steve because he'd tried to live out his silly teen-male fantasy.
Tried to force me to take a role in it. And Jaymie was
in that strange destructive scene of her own. Casual
slaughters—" She shuddered. "But God, I'm no different! Trying to get Jaymie to play a little girl instead. And
now I'm forcing Steve to stick with his kid. To play my
script instead of his."

"Or instead of the cops' script," Nick pointed out.
"If he got what the law prescribes, he'd be ruined."

"More to the point, the family would suffer. But even

so . . . I don't know, it just sickens me." She glared
unseeing at a pink plastic bag blowing across the sidewalk. "I was feeding Jaymie's fantasy too—"

"It was the only way we could get through to her,
Maggie. We had to control her."

"Okay, but controlling her is the point! What right
do I have? And look at what happened!" A quick inhale
to block fresh tears. "Some control!"

"Yeah, I feel rotten about it too," Nick admitted.
"Morally grubby. But she'd killed two people. She was
troubled far beyond any help we two could have given
her."

"Maybe. But . . . oh, hell, Nick, I saw a suicide once.
You know how that haunts me. And we'd calmed her
down once. I was hoping—"

"Maggie, she had a gun. Whatever scene was in her
head, or yours, that gun was real. That had to be the
priority."

She mulled that over a moment, then viciously kicked
a Bud can into the gutter. "Yeah. I guess so. But I still
feel like shit." Her grieving eyes met his. "Sunday I may
not be much of a date, Nick. Only thing I'll be up for is
an uninterrupted cry."

He squeezed her shoulder. "I'll probably join you.
The main point is to do it together."

She reached up and patted the hand on her shoulder,
comforted. "Yeah. I think we're beginning to learn how.
And we'll have other times."

They were nearing Canal Street. He glanced down at
Sarah, slumbering in the carrier, then back at Maggie.
"Well. We've got a hell of a lot to tell the cops."

"And a hell of a lot not to tell them."

"You ready to face them?"

"They'll be pretty busy for a few minutes. And before
we go back I have to get rid of some stuff." She paused
by a mailbox, pulled a stamped envelope from her briefcase, scribbled her office address on it, and sent Steve's
ticket and passport on their way. Then she cocked an eyebrow at Nick. "Also, we've got other problems." She fumbled inside her trench coat and pulled out a plastic bag.

Nick whistled. It was stuffed with bundles of bills. "You hit the lottery!"

"Half a million, Rachel said."

He poked the bag curiously with one finger. "Do you think they're marked?"

She pursed her lips and shrugged. "Steve worked in finance. I'd bet it's clean."

He watched her slip it back into her coat. "What do we do with it? Obviously it's not Steve's."

"No. The police will probably want to give it back to old Busby."

"Who needs it like a third ball."

"Right. And at the moment I can't get real enthusiastic about his favorite cause," she said grimly.

Nick nodded. "Well, we could say Jaymie handed it to a tweedy Brit named Merrypebble. Then we could send it to Elaine. Or Muffin."

"Yeah. Except that it's not exactly theirs. And they don't need it either. And how could we slip it to them without Steve and Busby finding out?"

They turned into Canal Street, bright and bustling in the late afternoon sun. Nick said, "Us?"

A slow grin. "Best idea yet. We could buy up Fisher-Price for Sarah."

"And hire a cleaning service."

"And buy a bigger computer. And a Lear jet."

"And commission a musical about the life of Gladstone."

They walked on a few steps, awed at the possibilities, yet dissatisfied. Nick groped for something in his pocket and pulled it out. A grungy card.

"Actually," said Maggie, glancing at it and then running her finger thoughtfully along the drowsy Sarah's cheek, "I've got everything in the world that I need."

"Just what I was thinking. Maybe it's time to put people back together instead of blowing them apart."

She nodded, stopped at a tiny variety shop for a large manila mailer, printed the address on the back and "In memory of Ramona" across the flap, and sealed the money inside. Then they went into the Canal Street post office and mailed it.

"Think she'll be surprised?" asked Maggie.

"Not very," said Nick. "She knows God is weird."

They strolled back toward the waiting police, hands linked in the slanting sunlight.

# ABOUT THE AUTHOR

P. M. Carlson is the author of four previous Maggie Ryan mysteries: AUDITION FOR MURDER, MURDER IS ACADEMIC, MURDER IS PATHOLOGICAL, and MURDER UNRENOVATED. She has a Ph.D. in Psychology and is a former amateur stage manager and a theater fan who has seen plays in 19 different countries.